The Shell Collector

-A Story of the Seven Seas-

by Hugh Howey

The Shell Collector

A Story of the Seven Seas

Copyright © 2014 by Hugh Howey

ISBN-13: 978-150336-848-4
ISBN-10: 1-503-36848-3

Cover art by M.S. Corley
Edited by David Gatewood
Interior design by Hugh Howey
Interior Illustrations by Hugh Howey

www.hughhowey.com

Give feedback on the book at:
hughhowey@gmail.com

Twitter: @hughhowey

First Edition

Printed in the U.S.A

For Stewart Brand and Ryan Phelan
You make the world a better place

Prologue: The Beach

"The sea is emotion incarnate.
It loves, hates, and weeps.
It defies all attempts to capture it with words
and rejects all shackles."

— Christopher Paolini

-O-

My earliest memory of the beach is of it being a harsh place for a wheelchair. I remember the ruts the rubber tires made, how the sand grabbed and tugged. My mom would cuss and struggle and lean against the handles to get Grandma down to the sea foam and shells, close enough that she could hear the waves crashing. I would try to help, but I mostly got in the way. I remember the sweat dripping from my mother's nose and evaporating off the hot sand while Grandma sat wrapped in her blanket. She was always cold toward the end.

The shells were hard to find back then, but not impossible like today. Mom would tell us stories of what the beach was like in her time, and every now and then Grandma would tell us older stories still. Stories of bounty. Of seas teeming with fish, beaches crawling with crabs, skies dotted with birds.

She would whisper of shells with minor flaws that were left behind, of days when shellers picked over all that washed up and tumbled in the surf. I remember thinking Grandma had lost her wits the way Grandpa had before he died. I remember wandering down the beach, just six years old, hunting for shells rather than watch her waste away, rather than listen to stories of a world I did not believe in. A living world.

They say cancer runs in the family. In our family, it doesn't run so much as chase. It caught my mom the year I turned thirty.

I feel like I became her as I watched summer sweat drip from my own nose, her turn to shiver beneath a blanket, crooked ruts in the sand stretching behind us toward the boardwalk.

It didn't feel right, going through that a second time. It didn't feel right, being in my mom's skin, feeling what she'd felt those years before. It was the sudden realization that my dying granny, who had been distant and alien to me, was my mom's mom. The sudden realization that she had been *anyone's* mom or *anyone's* daughter. I never knew until I had to push my mother through that blasted sand and saw how more than half-buried wheels go in painful circles.

Sweat and tears and sunscreen. Stories about the shells we remembered.

My mother was from Antigua, a small island in the Caribbean. She used to say her greatest find was my father, this crazy white shell who washed up on the beach one day. She said if you put your ear up to him you could hear traffic and car horns and people from Boston talking funny. She said they were made for each other like the wind and the sea. Opposites, but unable to be apart.

Mom had this amazing way of describing the world, of seeing the interconnectedness of all things. She called her wheelchair the "stroller," said we'd come right back to where we'd started, her and me. But the part that tore me up about this cycle was the hole I could feel in the pit of my being. It was the missing child who was not scurrying about, not getting in the way, not there at all. Because Michael and I had lost her. And because of that, we'd lost whatever connection we had between us.

I knew it was over when he called me a shell. He said there was nothing alive inside me, that there couldn't be. He was drunk at the time, which maybe means he didn't believe what he was saying, or maybe means he finally spoke the truth. Either way, I couldn't forgive him. Because part of me agreed. It was the shameful part of me that thought I was broken, the part that grew up bombarded by insults because of my mixed race, the part that heard it often enough when I was young and impressionable that I couldn't let it go, no matter how hard I tried.

Because of our loss, there was no child to run along the beach with me and my mom as she wasted away in her wheelchair. There was no one there to hold. No one to have cling to my neck the day she passed away by the sea foam. There was no one to stay with her while I ran back to the car to fetch my phone. No one for me to comfort, to tell that it would be all right.

But that wasn't why I bawled that day. It wasn't why I screamed and shook my fist at the dead sea and the dead all around me and the dead space within me. It was for selfish reasons that I cried. There should always be another generation confused by the sadness, so new to life that dying is alien, tottering down the beach, looking for treasures among the swaths of broken shells.

I bawled that day because it hit me with the surety and finality of cancer: when my time comes, there won't be anyone to push ruts through the hot sand, no one to help me out of the car, no one to tuck in my blanket when I get a chill. I'll die beyond the boardwalk, alone, with not even the crashing sea to comfort me.

Part I:
We Don't Belong Here

- 1 -

The trees are a decadence. They line the gravel driveway on either side, staggered to look like they march on forever. Oaks, cherries, willows, and palms. They don't belong here, the palms. They were probably grown down in the Carolinas, or even farther south. I have no idea how they survive the Maine winters. Perhaps they don't. Perhaps these are million-dollar annuals whooshing by.

I consider the expense of transporting mature trees, one by one, and all the labor involved. Flatbeds rumbling up the interstate with "wide load" signs on the back. Or barges tugged up the coast and unloaded with giant cranes. All for trees that will succumb to the next ten-year storm or the next super freeze. Just to decorate the impossibly long driveway of a filthy rich man. Just to stand there as a giant screw-you to reality, a bold claim that seems to say: *Your world has gone to ruin, but not mine. I can afford to make any world I choose.*

It's excesses like these that brought me here to destroy a man.

It's the palm trees; it's the shells in my purse; it's all the things that don't belong here, including me.

The tires of my beat-up electric car crunch down the miles-long gravel road. I flinch with every pebble that kicks up against the underbody. I hate driving out of the city. The offer to be flown out on Wilde's helicopter seems less insane now, almost worth swallowing my pride for, almost worth the ridiculousness of it all. Other reporters have probably said, "Yes. Hell yes." And why wouldn't they? How many came out here *hoping* to get screwed rather than to do the screwing?

A rock hits beneath my seat, and my knuckles whiten on the steering wheel. Ahead, twin rows of crape myrtles dot the road. They're losing their flowers. Purple petals ring the trunks, fallen mementos of a past bloom like photos from college years. But unlike people, trees flower again in the spring; they age in great looping circles. We ride a roller coaster once around, shuddering up clacking tracks and then screaming our fool heads off all the way down.

You're only thirty-two, I remind myself.

I feel every day of it, I think back.

Another guard gate looms into view down the dusty road. It's the second gate I've had to go through, despite there being no way to access the road between the gates. If the first checkpoint was a testament to seclusion and privacy—with its tall, camera-studded walls marching off in either direction—this second blockade feels more like a padlock around a deeply paranoid mind. Why lock away even further what no one is allowed to see?

Ness Wilde used to live in the limelight. He seemed to bask in it for three solid decades, practically since the day he was born. But he hasn't been seen in public in four years. This from a man who once graced the cover of practically every gossip rag and shelling magazine, who was on every other TV channel, who must've been interviewed a thousand times.

And then, one day, he's gone. He refuses all interviews. Until this week, when the *Times* ran the first of four pieces I've written on him and his family. Now, suddenly, he wants to talk. And even if I don't care to oblige him, there are powerful people who insist that I do. People like my editor at the paper. Other people with badges and guns. The kinds of people you listen to if you want to stay employed and on the right side of the law.

I slow to a stop at the second gate, and a young guard steps out. He looks the part: broad shoulders, narrow waist, chiseled jaw, military buzz cut. He motions for me to roll down the window. I press the button, and the smell of honeysuckle and coconuts and the nearby sea fills the car.

"I checked in at the other gate," I tell the guard.

"Identification," he says.

"Seriously?"

I mutter this under my breath, and if the guard hears, he doesn't react. Rummaging in my bag on the passenger seat, I find my *Times* credentials and driver's license. I hand them to the guard and do little to conceal my annoyance.

"And the registration," he says, motioning with his hand.

"For the car?" I ask.

He waits. I curse him as I pop the glove box. This can't be normal. Some kind of punishment. I try not to be paranoid, try not to think that Ness knows who sent me here.

"So how often do marauders get past the first gate and make it this far?" I ask. I hand him my vehicle registration.

The guard ignores me and studies the ID. I watch his lips mouth my name: *Maya Walsh*. It's hard to tell if he's whispering for the benefit of the wire hanging out of his ear or if he's one of those people who can't read without sounding out the words. He glances up at me, checks something on a small tablet, and then holsters the tablet beside his gun. The IDs and registration are returned.

"Pull up in front of the main house," he says, pointing down the drive with the rigidity and precision of a crossing guard. "Do not drive any further."

The bright blue metal bar in front of my car's grille swings up. When I glance back to the guard to make sure I can go, I catch him staring down inside the car and at my chest. I cover myself with one hand and hit the gas and speed away. Once I have some distance between myself and the guard, I glance down at my blouse to make sure I'm decent. For a moment there, I'm terrified the wire the FBI made me wear is showing. But it's tucked safely away.

I take a deep breath, try to relax. While I'd love to curse my boss, or Special Agent Cooper, or Ness Wilde, or his creepy guard, the truth is I've got no one to blame for this assignment but myself. I got into this mess all on my own—and it's up to me to get out of it.

-2-

The Day Before

"What the hell is this?" I ask, slamming the morning edition onto my boss's desk.

Henry—the editor in chief of the *Times*—noisily sips his coffee. His mug has [REDACTED] printed on the side in blocky red letters. He glances at the paper and smooths his mustache.

"Where's my story?" I ask. "It was running when I left here last night."

Leaning to one side, Henry peers past me and out his office door. I don't need to turn and look. I can feel all the heads behind all those newsroom desks watching me. I heard the whispers during my murderous march down the aisle. Henry sets his mug down. He wouldn't be so calm if he knew how close I was to either quitting my job or jumping over that desk to rip his silly handlebar mustache off.

"I take it you haven't checked your email," he says.

"You mean since I left here at two in the morning?" I look at the clock above his desk. It's a little after eight. "No, some of us do actual work around here."

"Close the door and sit down," Henry tells me.

I cross my arms instead. Henry pinches one side of that ridiculous mustache, shrugs, and gives up, realizing he isn't going to win *the Battle of the Door and the Sitting of the Down.*

"Ness Wilde wants an interview," he says.

The temperature in the office soars. I can feel my pulse throbbing in my neck. "Are you serious?" I ask.

"Dead serious."

He seems relaxed—like what he's saying is a good thing, like I'm supposed to be pleased.

I rest both palms on Henry's desk and lean toward him. "So the first piece in my series runs yesterday, and you get a call from Wilde asking you to yank it, and you just fucking yank it? Just like that?"

I have to turn away. As I do, forty-three heads snap back to their computer screens so fast I think I can hear a whooshing sound out in the newsroom.

"He better not have paid you," I add, turning back to Henry. "Because I'll quit, and the *Post* would *love* to run that story."

"You're not going to quit," Henry says. And I consider that maybe, just possibly, over the last eight years, I've threatened to quit a hair too many times.

"When you gave me the arts and culture section, you said I could still do hard-hitting journalism—"

"And you can," Henry says.

"—that I wouldn't be running the birdcage and paint-splatter section of the paper—"

"You're not. Calm down for a second and listen to me."

"I'm goddamn calm!" I shout.

A few heartbeats pass. Henry smiles at me. I pray to god I'm not smiling back.

"Will you listen to me for just a second?" Henry asks. "You know, because I'm your boss?"

I cross my arms. "Fine. So how much did Ness Wilde pay to bring our august presses to a screeching halt? Pray tell. I can't wait to hear this."

"First of all, I didn't speak with him directly. I spoke with his assistant—"

"Figures," I say.

"—and his assistant said that if you want the full story on Ness's father and grandfather, that he'd like to fly you up to his estate to answer your questions in person. Three hours. Whatever you want to ask."

I laugh. "I've done two years of research for this story, and he wants to give me three hours? C'mon, Henry, don't you see what he's really doing here? When I got on the train this morning, people were still reading *yesterday's* paper. Not staring at their screens, but reading the goddamn *Times*. Because of *my* story. And now they're expecting the second piece I promised—"

"I know." Henry raises his hands. "Trust me, I know. Our editorial inbox is full of positive responses. And we've already seen a bump in new subscriptions. Which is why I told Ness's assistant to kindly go to hell."

"You did?" Now I'm confused.

"Of course. I slammed the phone down on her. With gusto. And then it rang again. Immediately."

"Mr. Wilde himself," I say. "So *now* he has the balls to call you."

"I wish it'd been Ness. I would've told him off in person. It was the FBI."

Before I can ask if I heard Henry properly, he leans forward and places a finger on a white business card sitting apart from the rest of the clutter on his desk. I can see the three letters in a large blocky font from where I'm standing. Looking closer, I see a round seal stuffed with an eagle, an American flag, a ring of gold stars, and probably a slice of apple pie in there somewhere. I pick up the card. It belongs to a Special Agent Stanley Cooper.

"I tried to save you a trip uptown," Henry says. "This guy wants to see you. I emailed you his contact info and left you a voice message—"

"I listen to my voice messages like once a month," I remind Henry. "You should've texted me."

"Whatever. Just go talk to this guy."

I check the address on the card: 26 Federal Plaza, down in the financial district. "What does the FBI want with me? And what's this got to do with you yanking my story?"

Henry takes a deep breath and nods at the card. "I'll let him explain. It's complicated. But listen, Maya, the important thing to know is that we're running the rest of your series. We're just going to run them weekly rather than daily. You've got my word on that. You know I want to nail this guy just as much as you do—"

"As much as I do? I spent seven years writing for the science section before you canned it. All those shelling reports I wrote, the sea level stories, the practical disappearance of Louisiana that I covered, the graft with the construction of the Manhattan levees, the day Times Square flooded? How about my editorials about the beaches that are washing away every single day—?"

"Those are my beaches too," Henry says, and I can see that his cheeks are red. He's angry. And maybe not entirely at me. "We're going to run the rest of the exposé. It's great work, Maya. You know that. If it were up to me, your second piece would be running right now. But it isn't up to me."

"Sure it is," I tell him. "Ever hear of this thing called freedom of the press?" I shake the business card and nearly call him a spineless ass, but the door behind me is open, and I haven't heard a single tap on a single keyboard since I walked into Henry's office. Even my insubordination has limits.

Henry grabs his coffee and takes a noisy sip. Whatever's on his face right then is [REDACTED] by the mug. He and I have a long history of throwing barbs at one another, but this is something else. This is serious. By the time he sets the mug back down, the tension is as thick as sidewalk crowds during lunch hour.

"The FBI isn't after you or me," Henry calmly explains, like this should've been obvious from the beginning. Like I should know that we at the paper are small fries. And the rest dawns on me before Henry can spell it out. I understand why he pulled the story. And why he wants me to go speak to this Agent Cooper.

"The Federal Bureau of Investigation is after Ness Wilde," I say.

Henry nods. "Bingo. And they want your help in bringing him down."

— 3 —

I hail a taxi and give the driver the address for the Federal Plaza downtown. Broadway is jammed. It's high tide, and of course a handful of pumps are on the fritz. A handful always are. Looking west down 39th, I can see a logjam of traffic backed up from the Lincoln Tunnel and a shimmer of standing water between the cars. People are sloshing through the traffic with galoshes on, despite it being summer and no rain in sight.

A friend of mine at the *Times* has lived in this city for over seventy years. He runs the obits, is semi-retired, says his job is to write farewell letters to old friends. He talks about the old days when New Yorkers didn't need to check the tide tables before their commute to work. He talks about days when you made sure your train was running, checked if you might need an umbrella or a scarf, not whether your levee had breached or if your neighborhood pumps were down. The man is a walking memory of less-flooded times.

But even in my lifetime, there's been a lot of change. I remember when I was young, thinking the sea was only capable of offering solace. She was only ever a calming force. I didn't see her angry side until I was in my teens.

Hurricane Julia. There was a mandatory evacuation. My sister and I helped Dad put the storm shutters over the windows while

Mom fretted over which irreplaceable things to pack in the car. We left not knowing what we would return to, if anything. The highway was a parking lot, so Dad took us down the coast before cutting in to the interstate. Driving along the beach, with the horizon a dark and foreboding gray, he pulled onto the shoulder so we could all marvel at the sky.

My sister and I begged to run up to the top of the beach access for a better view. A glance at Mother, our arbiter of risk, the slightest of worried nods. "Be quick," our father had said.

As loud as the wind was, the sea was louder. Like thunder in my bones. I heard the angry waves before we got up the slick wooden stairs. At the top of the walkway, I stood and gripped the rail and leaned into the wind and watched an ocean I thought I knew whip and thrash around like an enraged beast.

Mountains of white foam crashed down in avalanche after avalanche. The waves bashed the rocks and chewed up the sand. Our parents used to say that the shoreline was forever changing, that a storm might move an entire beach or that the rising seas would push inland and cover what used to be shoreline, but I was too young to notice these things, and I'd never seen a storm like this.

Watching the sea that day, I thought of the people on the local news who got interviewed about a neighbor who had done something heinous. "He was always so quiet," the neighbor would say. "He was the nicest person in the world."

That's how I felt then, seeing that something so familiar had become completely unrecognizable. A loved one had snapped, had become angry. The waves that normally drew us to her now caused our family to flee in terror.

I chose to blame the storm and the wind back then, rather than the sea. I made excuses for her.

As the traffic on Broadway inches south to a symphony of squeaky brake pads and prolonged horn blasts, I think back to the next time I saw the ocean angry. It was my freshman year in college. I went out on a boat with some friends and just assumed they knew what they were doing, that they'd checked the weather. We were five miles offshore when we saw the squall: a great cliff of clouds that stretched from the heavens down to the sea—white on top but a dark gray beneath, like a pristine wedding veil someone had dragged through the mud.

There was no going around it, so we tried to race back to the inlet, but the storm was moving too fast. Winds over fifty miles an hour. It hit us all at once like a heavenly fist, a mighty slam of stinging rain and raucous seas. The outboard came out of the water as a steep wave lifted us up, and the engine stalled. We huddled in the floor of the boat, gripping each other and the rails, quiet, shivering, drenched, the boat filling with water, all of us absolutely terrified. The sea rose around us in crashing pyramids. I thought she would swallow us, this thing from which I had only known love. I learned to fear her then, and to simultaneously hate myself for *feeling* that fear. Afterward, I made more excuses: I blamed it on the sky, on the weather, on the poor planning.

Abusive relationships often go like this: falling in love, not seeing the ugly side, coming up with rationalizations when you do. It's hard to get free, because you just want to recapture some lost feeling. You want to feel safe, respected, honored again. And you'll play games with your mind to make that happen. It's the alcohol's fault; it's the stress of their job; you may even make the great sin of blaming yourself.

By the time I was born, they'd already built the levees around Manhattan. Much was made of the project back when it was just an idea: how much it would cost, how unnecessary it was, debates about whether the sea would rise or not. Reading a historical account of the levee project today is strange, knowing what we now know. You marvel at the lack of impatience, at the bickering over details and budgets. Coastlines around the world were being redrawn while people argued whether anything was even occurring, much less whether it was our fault.

When the Hudson first breached the new levees, I was working as a young writer at the *Times*. It was a perigean spring tide, when the moon is at its closest to the Earth and it lines up perfectly with the sun. What used to merely flood the edges of Manhattan now marched across Broadway at midtown. The subways flooded. The city was brought to its knees by an extra six inches of water.

The Hudson River and the East River transformed overnight. No longer beautiful backdrops skirting the city, they became a coiled threat. A lingering drunk. Something to be wary of at all times. I can feel them right now, running down either side of Manhattan, their waters higher than these streets, held back only by great walls and elevated parks. Here I am trapped in the middle, creeping along in a trickle of traffic that flows slower than the tides. Those bodies of water could come together at any moment and drown us all. That's what they've become. And we let them.

Like a lot of people, I sold my car soon after the big levee breach and bought an old electric. Didn't care about the cost. I changed a lot of habits. And like a lot of people, I made excuses for the rising sea levels. I blamed the companies pumping oil and gas from the ground. I blamed the smiling CEOs at the helm, like Ness Wilde. I blamed the politicians who refused to do anything as they kept getting reelected. I blamed anyone other than the glorious sea of my remembered youth.

I blamed anyone other than myself.

=4=

The taxi lets me out on Worth Street, which is high and dry. Inside the Federal Plaza, I go through a security routine that has me patting my pockets for my boarding pass. I have to practically disrobe and send my bag, shoes, and coat through one machine while the rest of me stands inside another to get a thorough scanning. On the other side of the security station, I present Agent Cooper's card to a man behind an information desk. He picks up his phone and speaks to someone while I thread my belt back through my slacks.

"Fourth floor," he tells me, hanging up the phone. "Elevators are to the left. Someone will meet you up there."

I make my way toward the elevators, and now that I'm in this building, I wrack my brain for what Ness Wilde might have done to have gotten the FBI's attention. Tax evasion is the most obvious. Ocean Oil gets press every year for how little they pay in taxes compared to regular folk like me. Then again, people like me don't have entire divisions of tax experts on the payroll. And would that be the FBI's jurisdiction? I get all the three-letter agencies confused.

Whatever it is, I imagine I've got some rewrites ahead of me. Yesterday's piece was about Ness's great-grandfather. I broke the story up to cover each of the four generations of Wildes individually. If Henry plans to run them weekly, that gives me a few weeks before I have to turn in any revisions on Ness. Plenty of time to tack on whatever's happening here. A picture of Ness Wilde in handcuffs above the center fold flashes before me. I'm smiling as I step off the elevator.

"Maya Walsh?" a young man asks. He's dressed like a TV version of what an FBI agent looks like: black suit, scuffed black shoes, thin black tie.

"Agent Cooper?" I ask.

"I'll take you to him. This way."

I follow the young man through a maze of cubicles toward the far side of the building. We stop outside an office with Cooper's name on a brass plate. The young man knocks twice, then lets me inside. The office is dimly lit, the blinds drawn down over the windows. Cooper sits behind his desk, looking at an open folder. A single lamp illuminates the space. There's a scattering of seashells across the desk, lining the windowsill, and more on top of the filing cabinets. Cooper is obviously a serious collector, and I feel immediately more at ease.

"Ms. Walsh," he says. He closes the folder, stands up, extends his hand.

"Just Maya," I say. The young deputy backs out and closes the door, leaving us alone.

"Call me Stan." He smiles and holds my hand a little longer than necessary. Is he hitting on me? I can never tell. Either way, my mind does this weird New York thing where it imagines me dating every single person I meet, regardless of age, gender, or what part of town they live in. I understand that this is a municipal disorder and that I'm not the only sufferer. And while Agent Cooper is handsome and a collector, I don't see myself dating an FBI agent. I'm good at this: ruling people out with excuses as flimsy as they are fast.

"Please, make yourself comfortable." He waves at a chair, and I sit.

"So you're the reason my story didn't run in this morning's edition," I say.

"That's right. Your government needs you, Ms. Walsh."

He smiles to let me know he's being cheesy on purpose. And yeah, I am not dating a cop. I'm pretty sure the FBI are the cops. The CIA are the spooks, and the NSA monitors my online shopping habits. I feel like this is right. What I don't understand is the ATF.

"As you may know, Ness Wilde—"

"I have a quick question," I say.

"Shoot."

I lean forward. "What exactly do tobacco and firearms have to do with one another?"

Agent Cooper blinks. Twice. "I'm sorry, what?"

"The ATF. Why put those things together?"

"It's . . . uh . . . has to do with federal oversight of . . . state-level regulat—"

"Okay, so you don't know either." I settle back in my seat, reminding myself to Google this later.

Agent Cooper studies me for a prolonged moment, clears his throat, then seems to gather his wits. "Ms. Walsh—"

"Maya."

"Of course. Maya. Your editor informs us that you've been digging into Ness Wilde's past. You've got a series of pieces planned on him and his father, grandfather, et cetera."

"That's right. And I suppose I'm here because you've been doing some digging as well. Is this where we exchange notes?" I nod to the thick sheaf of papers Cooper was looking through when I entered. "Is that his folder?"

Agent Cooper laughs. He nods toward the row of filing cabinets that covers one wall of his office. "No. His folder is right there. This one is yours."

I lean forward and grab it, and Cooper flinches, but doesn't try to stop me. Inside I find a copy of an old résumé from a decade ago, one I think I uploaded to a public headhunting site. It's woefully out of date except for my degrees and a few internships. Behind this are printouts of various columns I wrote for the *Times*. They go back quite a ways, and I have a feeling all of this was printed out recently, like Cooper has been cramming rather than studying.

"If this is all you've got on me, I need to live it up a bit more."

Agent Cooper laughs. He opens a drawer in his desk and reaches inside. I half expect a different folder with some of my college exploits. Instead, he brings out a small plastic case, bright orange, about the size of a closed fist. "Three months ago, a man was found dead in his apartment in Portland, Maine—"

Cooper pauses as I gasp out loud and lean forward, eager to hear more. Worse, I think he can see my genuine excitement at the idea that Ness Wilde is guilty of actual direct murder rather than the indirect kind.

"The gentleman died of a heart attack," Cooper says. "He was seventy-two years old. No foul play suspected."

The reporter in me sags in her seat. The rest of me is happy for the deceased. I guess.

"Two weeks later, *this* goes up for auction alongside other items from the gentleman's estate."

Cooper slides the plastic case across the desk. It looks like one of those waterproof boxes snorkelers use to keep things dry while they're out in the surf. There's a complex latch with a slot for a key. It's unlocked, but the latch is stiff. A tight seal. When I lift the lid and see what's inside, the air seems to evacuate the room.

A lace murex, one of my favorite shells, is nestled inside. Medium-sized, just over an inch long. I move the box into the cone of light from the lamp and note the bright pink aperture and tight apex. The inner lip is so shiny, the shell must be wet. But touching it, I find it to be dry. It just hasn't lost its luster.

"It looks flawless," I whisper.

"It is," Cooper says. "I understand you know a thing or two about shells."

I think of all the articles he has in that folder, many of them from back when the *Times* had a science section where my shelling column used to run. "I studied to be a marine biologist," I say. "Being a reporter happened by accident." Which isn't quite right, but the truth is too complicated to get into.

"I'd like to hear your expert opinion on this piece." Cooper places a loupe on the desk, but I reach into my purse and retrieve my own. My palms are already a little clammy. It's not often that I get to handle shells this rare.

"Can we open those blinds and get some more light in here?" I ask.

He hesitates, then gets up and raises the blinds. The sunlight streaming into the office catches the ensuing shower of dust. "Thanks," I say. I bring the loupe to my eye and pull the shell close until it comes into focus.

The murex is distinct for the chaos of crenelations that adorn its edge. They jump off like crashing waves, like amoebas, or a pattern or paisley. The crenelations on this particular specimen are incredibly crisp. Untouched. And the sutures between the whorls are deep and pronounced. The lip of the aperture, where the slug would reside, hasn't been chipped. And there's no sign of sand-wear, no dulling of the periostracum from having been tumbled up a beach.

"Was it stolen from a museum?" I ask. For a moment, I wonder if maybe Ness Wilde isn't a suspect in a case at all, but that perhaps this shell was taken from his collection.

"At what price would you value that shell?" Cooper asks me. He waves his hand when he sees I'm about to complain or make excuses. "Ballpark," he says. "I've had others look at it. I just want your opinion."

"I wouldn't know where to begin," I admit. "It doesn't look like it rolled up on any beach." I look at the crenelations again. They rarely survive any kind of rough handling. "I shouldn't even be touching this without gloves, to be honest."

"Just throw out a number," Cooper says.

"Well, the market is a tad down right now, but a shell like this, I would guess the right buyer would pay between two and three million for it."

Just hearing myself say this, I have to put the shell back into the box. Gingerly. Cooper quietly laughs at something, and I have to assume it's my estimate, that their experts said something much different. So I start to defend it.

"You have to keep in mind that this species has been extinct for twenty or thirty years," I say. "And price is all about condition. I have a murex in my collection that I'd be lucky to get a thousand dollars for. It has dozens of chips, plus a hole clear through the—"

"Your number is solid," Cooper tells me. "Here's the problem: we dated that shell, and it's between two and three *years* old."

"That's impossible," I say.

Agent Cooper reaches into his drawer again and pulls something else out. He extends his fist to me. I hold my palm out to accept, and he deposits a second lace murex in my hand. While I'm gawking at it, he brings out a third.

"What do you think now?" he asks.

A glance tells me that these are in a similar condition to the first. And now I understand why the FBI is involved. I look over the second murex with my loupe. "These are the best fakes I've ever seen," I say. And I've seen my share. I don't keep reproductions in my own collection, but I have friends who are less scrupulous, or who just get taken advantage of. Across Manhattan, there are thousands of tourist traps with windows full of shells and camera lenses and electronics at prices too good to be true. And for a reason.

"You're in good company then," Cooper says. "They're the best fakes my department has ever seen. They're good enough to fool our testing equipment—"

"Wait," I say. I take in the collection of shells scattered around the room and see them in a new light. "I thought the Secret Service handled this sort of thing."

"You're thinking of currency," Cooper says.

"Oh, yeah."

"Like you, we assumed these were fake just from the condition. And the fact that someone was dumb enough to dump all three of them at once. So we took a sample and dated them, which was the nail in the coffin. At that point, we traced the shells back to the deceased."

"Who was he?" I ask.

"Dimitri Arlov. Former physicist, among other things. A polymath. When he died he was in the employ of Ocean Oil."

"The guy who owned these shells worked for Ness Wilde?"

"He worked for his company, yes. In exploration, we think."

"I don't get it. Ness is easily the foremost shell collector in the world—" But then I stop and think about what I'm doing in that office. I think about the fact that Henry hung up on Ness's assistant, and that the FBI called Henry right back. For some reason, I had assumed they were listening in on the *Times*.

I look up from the shell and study Agent Cooper. "You guys have been tapping Ness Wilde's phones."

"That's correct. We have a warrant, mind you. And I suppose now is as good time as any to tell you that all of this has to stay off the record. I'm sure you understand what it means to tamper with an ongoing investigation."

"All too well," I say. "So what do you want from me? Anyone could tell you that these shells are fakes."

"We want you to take Ness Wilde up on his offer for an interview."

"What? Why?"

"Because he wants to talk to you, and he hasn't been too eager to talk to us. We don't have enough here to bring him in. The connection is flimsy—"

"But you think these shells trace back to him."

"We think it's possible. We don't think this Arlov character would have access to anything like this. But his boss might have. There's also the chance that—" Agent Cooper seems to be searching for the right words. I think I know what he's about to say and help him out.

"You think there's a chance that there are more fakes like this out there," I say. "Maybe even in Wilde's collection." And my skin tingles with the idea that Ness Wilde, the great shell collector, might be a phony.

"Exactly," Cooper says.

"So, what, I go up there and interview him? You want me to wear a wire or something?"

"Precisely. And look, we're not asking you to do anything other than your job. Get what you can from him. Push him. Prod him. Our job is to sit back and listen."

"So he's the hornet's nest and I'm the stick."

"Something like that. Just hear what he has to say about these articles you're working on. Take him up on his offer. Get as close as you can or antagonize him as much as you want. It's up to you."

"What about these shells?" I ask.

"What about them?"

"Has he seen them? Have you confronted him with these?"

Agent Cooper shakes his head. "We're trying to be very delicate about the existence of these shells."

I dig into my purse and find a pack of tissues. Placing the first lace murex back into the plastic case, I pad the shell before adding the second, then wrap that one before adding the third.

"What are you doing?" Cooper asks, half-reaching for the box.

"If you want me to help, here's what I'm thinking." Cooper watches with a frown as the case disappears into my purse. "I'll go talk to Mr. Wilde and get what I need for my story. And then we'll hear what the great shell collector has to say when I show him these."

= 5 =

This is how I find myself in Maine, driving down a dusty road in my electric car, with an FBI wire tucked in my bra. I agreed to wear the wire even though I explained to Cooper's buddies that I plan on recording the entire interview with my cell phone. They said it made chain of custody easier on their end, and that often, what needs recording is said when the suspect doesn't know they're being recorded.

Whether or not I would take the assignment, of course, was never in question. I'm a reporter. Dropping these shells in my lap was like tossing a steak to a german shepherd. There was no way I wasn't going. I want to see Ness Wilde's face when I confront him with the shells.

What I did refuse was his offer to fly me up. I didn't want to give him the satisfaction or have him think I'm a pushover. A few hours in my car and two recharging stations later, I'm beginning to rethink that strategy. Just the guy's driveway goes on for miles.

Eventually—with the second gate behind me—the road takes a sharp bend to the left, and some innate sense tells me that I had been approaching the sea and am now heading north up along the coast. If so, the ocean is hidden by the ridiculous trees. The palms bend toward one another like fingers about to interlock. Their dangling coconuts hang like a threat. But they form a tunnel that seems to hold the damaged world beyond at bay. They bore toward a place where people can be wealthy enough to ignore what's happening around them.

That must be convenient for a man who played a large role in ushering our damaged world along. The irony is rich: Ness Wilde has made billions not just by drilling oil, but by collecting the shells made rare—and valuable—by the burning of fossil fuels. A double whammy.

Glancing down at my battery gauge, I imagine for a moment the horror of not having enough juice to get to my hotel tonight. When I look back up, a view of the house breaks through at the end of the road. As I get closer, I see that it looks a lot smaller than I imagined it would. On Google Maps, the house appeared audacious, a sprawl of additions and add-ons connected by breezeways and boardwalks.

But arriving from the front—because of the way the house is chopped up to stagger down the dunes toward the sea—the portion visible from the drive looks reasonable. Even adorable. Like a house rather than an estate. A small front porch with reproduction gaslight fixtures frames a pebble-bed walkway. The roof is pale pink tile. The siding is white clapboard with bright-blue trim. The house appears as though it belongs in the Caribbean, not on an isolated and prohibitively expensive patch of rocky Maine shoreline.

My car's tires crunch to a stop on the gravel circle. The drive continues and disappears around a high sandstone wall studded with conch shells. A six- or seven-car garage full of boy toys is probably just around the corner. As I get out of the car, trying to reconcile the incongruous modesty of the front of the house with all I know of Ness Wilde, I see that the drive isn't paved with gravel at all. It's made of tiny shells. Millions of them. Billions. Most are ground up into tiny bits from years of traffic, but some are recognizable. Some are even miraculously intact. Periwinkles, ceriths, ravenelis, and cockles.

The sight of so many shells spread out for so base a purpose causes my heart to sink. It's the sort of blow that stuns you so deep, the intelligent side of your brain can't signal to the emotional side that this effect might be on purpose. *Here*, the front of the house seems to say, *I am a normal person.* And then: *Here, you are parking on a fortune in shells.* And while reconciling these two: *Here, I'm opening the door so that you meet me in a weakened state—*

"Maya? From the *Times*?"

I turn from the audacious and miles-long carpet of shells to the foremost collector of them in the world. Ness Wilde stands on his small front porch, the door behind him open, and I realize that I'm half in and half out of my car, my hand resting numbly on the handle. Composing myself, I grab my bag from the passenger seat and shut the door. I force myself not to look down at my feet, but I can hear the tiny shells crunch beneath my shoes, little screams from hapless victims.

"It's Ms. Walsh," I correct him, ignoring what's going on beneath my feet. We shake hands, and Ness smiles as if he knows what I'm thinking, as if these are roles we are playing. It occurs to me that despite his recent seclusion, he's done hundreds of interviews over the years. Probably more than I have—and it's kinda what I do for a living. And then I wonder if he has the timing of coming to the door down to a science, watches on a video screen or peeks through the blinds, all to take the strength out of the knees of his guests as they see what they've been driving on for miles.

Suddenly, all the trash-talking I did in the newsroom yesterday afternoon comes back to haunt me. I assured Dawn that I wouldn't get flustered, that I'd eaten men like this for lunch. Hell, I've sat in the White House pressroom and tossed firebombs at the President of the United States. I reminded her of that, and Dawn had laughed. She had interviewed Ness Wilde before.

"Welcome to my home," Ness says. He half-bows and waves me inside. "Ladies first."

Despite what I feel about Ness, despite the suspicious shells in my purse, despite the fact that I've seen his face on a hundred magazine covers, in all the newspapers, and all over the news, his handsomeness in person still comes as a shock. It's his smile, however insincere it might be. It's his golden-bleached locks from years spent shelling. It's his physique from being wealthy enough to exercise just to pass the time.

I had guiltily hoped to find him broken and shattered, that this was why he was holed up. Forty pounds overweight, perhaps. Balding. Staggering drunk. Some obvious reason for his reclusiveness for the better part of the past four years. But he looks the same. Ness Wilde is one of those men who won't push forty so much as he'll shove Father Time aside. Only actors get away with remaining heartthrobs so late in life. Actors and master shell collectors.

"I've got a bottle of wine breathing and some snacks put together," he tells me. "Come downstairs. I'll show you the view."

It's like I didn't publish a story two days ago accusing his great-grandfather of flooding the world. It's like this is our third date. Considering how many times he's done this in the past, I imagine it's comfortable for him. Remembering what I'm there to do, I force myself to be even more comfortable. I *strain* to be comfortable.

Ness leads me inside and through a labyrinthine and multi-level layout that manages to chop up ten thousand square feet into small and cozy spaces. My heels clop-clop on sandstone tile. They sound ridiculously loud and formal with him walking ahead, barefoot. I wore one of my power suits: pinstripes and a lacy blouse that I thought went great with the FBI wire. Ness, meanwhile, has on white bottoms that look perfect either for sleeping in or practicing karate. For a top, he has on a pale blue button-up left untucked and only halfway fastened up in the front. Before he turned, I spotted a necklace dangling against his chest, a single shell or stone on a string. I wasn't brave enough to study it closely to ascertain the species—because this is probably just what he wants people to do: study and stare.

Much too quickly, I am led past priceless treasures. It's like being hauled through a museum after closing. A flawless junonia, probably six inches long. An array of ivory wentletraps, sitting out in the open. There's an entire wall of scallops and pectin raveneli with water trickling down them; a great fountain separating two adjoining rooms. I assume all are real. Otherwise, why have them on display?

"The competition," Ness says, waving at a wall of pictures. It's dozens of magazine covers, mostly gossip rags and weeklies, a lot of shots I recognize from my research and from years of riding the subway to work. Many of the cover shots feature Ness holding up some rare or impossible shell between his fingertips. He means the magazines, I realize, when he says "the competition." The competition we face at the paper. As if any of us are healthy enough to worry about the others.

Or maybe he means the reporters. I think back to the stacks of articles I've read over the years while writing my piece. How many were written by men? These Ness Wilde clones smile at me as I walk past, almost as if they know what I'm thinking. I'm thinking of how many of those reporters probably trailed dutifully down this hall, just like I am. I think of how many stayed the night. I know of a few, have spoken to them, but that story isn't set to run for another few weeks. This collection of framed trophies will have to feature in that story, I realize, and I make edits in my head. When I'm done with my own story, I have a strong suspicion that Ness will not frame what I write. Hell, there's a chance he'll be reading it behind bars.

"My publicist warned me that the newspaper wouldn't be as nice as the magazines," Ness says, almost like he can read my mind. We descend one last level to a bar and enclosed patio.

Cantilevered out beyond the sloping dunes, three walls of glass reveal a sweep of white sand and azure waters limned by a shoreline of foamy, crashing waves.

It's a legendary beach, privately owned and inaccessible, as so many of Wilde's properties are. The priceless shells decorating the house become background noise, a glittery hiss of pinks and purples that merely add to the aura of the vista before me. Here is the coup de grace of the perfectly arranged meeting. Here is the ploy to win a sheller's soul. I find myself fantasizing about sleeping over. Who wouldn't? Who could stroll across a carpet of crushed shells, through a hallway of amassed treasures, see that pristine sand picked over by no more than a few human beings in the last twenty years, and not dream, pine, hope for a morning spent here, a sunrise stroll, searching the low tide for the rare treasures dredged up by a recent storm—

Wilde clears his throat. It underscores the duration of my stunned gawking. A glass of red wine is being held out to me. I nod and accept it, then look for a place to set my bag. The shells inside are burning to get out, to expose him. But I have too many questions first.

"Do you always answer the door yourself?" I ask, fishing out my phone and my notepad.

Wilde pours himself a glass of wine and picks up a piece of cheese from a wooden cutting board in the shape of a whelk. "I live here by myself," he says. He bites into the cheese and takes a sip of wine. "The staff comes through and tidies up while I'm out."

"You mean out collecting?"

He smiles mischievously. "What else would I be doing?"

I taste the wine. It's excellent. Reaching for the bottle, I check the label and see that it's a local vineyard. I don't recognize the name. The year tells me why. The wine is older than I am.

"It was a beautiful place," Wilde tells me, watching me study the bottle. He stacks cheese and sliced meat on thin crackers, then tops each stack with half an olive.

"Was?" I ask. "They're no longer around?"

"Nothing grows on those hills anymore." He wipes his hands and studies his little creations. There's a white apron in a wrinkled hump on the granite countertop, as if he hurriedly removed it to answer the door. Everything feels like a prop, and I realize that I'm going into this interview jaded and tense. The jaded comes from years of pent-up animosity toward Ness Wilde. The tension comes from knowing the FBI will hear every word between us. Wilde watches me while I tap on my phone.

"You don't mind if I record this, do you?" I ask. And I have to suppress a laugh. I have to fight the urge not to look down my blouse to make sure the wire isn't showing.

Ness waves the knife he's using to slice the olives. "Of course not. I thought the interview had already begun, asking me about my help." He slides the plate of appetizers across the counter at me. "Unless you were just making sure we were alone."

I laugh and wave off the food. "Oh, I'd rather we weren't. I'd love to ask your staff a few questions."

And your ex, I add silently to myself. *And your daughter. And whoever else in your employ knows about these shells.* But those questions can come later. Starting there would spook him. Though he must know from my piece that this isn't another adoring housewife profile, another glossy bit of PR.

As the app begins to record, I take in my surroundings so I can describe them for the revised piece. Every shell in this room has been photographed from multiple angles. Every shell, especially Mr. Wilde's. My job is to crawl inside and shine a light on the shrinking torus deep within that pretty exterior. That's the story I aim to tell.

"Okay, fire away," Wilde says. He smiles and raises his glass in salute before taking another sip. And then, almost as if reading my mind, he adds: "Do your worst."

-6-

" **I** 'd like to start with your great-grandfather, if I may." I arrange myself on a sofa that probably cost as much as my car. Ness gets comfortable in an old leather reading chair, his bare feet propped up on a matching ottoman. "You must've read the piece I wrote on him—"

"I did."

"I presume you asked me here to set the record straight. So tell me what I got wrong. I'd love to hear your version of events."

Wilde swirls his wine glass, and I hold my notepad and pen patiently. The pen and pad are more than just props to remind him of our roles; they're for jotting down setting and non-verbal cues. It's often not what people say or how they say it, but how they visibly react to questions. The nervous tics and wide eyes that recorders miss.

"I didn't know my great-grandfather very well," Wilde says. "I've read books about him. I can tell you what his biographers thought."

"So what makes you think I was unfair with my piece?"

"I don't think you were unfair. But you were *about* to be."

"With my next piece?" I take a sip of my wine, partly because I want to hide my face. The way Wilde is staring at me, it's as though my thoughts are written across my cheeks.

"I suspect your next piece was going to be about my grandfather, judging by the little cliffhanger at the end—"

"That was a teaser," I say, setting down the wine. "A cliffhanger would've meant leaving the story about your great-grandfather in suspense."

"I see. Well, if you're going to write about my grandfather next, I'd rather you didn't."

I laugh. I didn't expect him to come straight out and grovel, but that seems to be his plan. "Is that so?"

"That's so. You'd only get everything wrong. Like everyone else has."

"And you'd like to set me straight? Okay. Tell me about your grandfather. What does everyone get wrong?"

He takes another sip of his wine—closes his eyes while he does so. I can't tell if he's composing his thoughts or savoring the vintage.

"They get everything wrong." He opens his eyes, and I find myself gazing down at my notes. The intensity of the man . . . it's like looking into the noonday sun.

"So tell me about him," I say, as I write something just to write something.

"I don't remember a whole lot. I was eight when he died. The men in my family have always waited too long before having kids—"

"Except you," I point out.

Ness flinches. It's the first time I've seen him react to something I've said. But then he smiles. "I'd much rather you write your next piece about me or my father. Just leave my grandfather out of whatever it is you think you're doing."

I've hit a nerve. I make a note about Ness's daughter. This is a button I can press. Dark truths are lured out by anger and sadness. And it's cheaper and swifter to cause the former.

"If you don't know much about your grandfather, why do you object to me writing about him?" I ask.

"I said I don't *remember* much about him, not that I don't *know* much about him."

"Fine. Tell me what you know. Make me believe he was a good man and not someone who got rich while this world went to shit."

Wilde turns away from this accusation, almost like I've slapped him. It feels like I've slapped him. Like I've said in a sentence what my series of pieces is all about. He stares for some time at the horizon, that gray line where the sea kisses the sky.

"After my grandmother died, my grandfather lived alone in a shack on a spit of beach. He wasn't anything like his father or my father. Or me, for that matter. I know what you're going to write, because it's the history everyone has written. With his vast wealth, my grandfather bought up near-coastal land, what he knew would become prime beachfront property once the sea levels crept up, and then he kept that land for himself. He blocked it off from the world—"

"And none of that is true?"

Wilde shakes his head. "It's . . . more complicated than that. My grandfather, he . . . wasn't a huge fan of people. Well, it's not that he didn't *like* people, I think he just enjoyed the quiet. Which is why I don't want to see your story, don't want people talking about him. He wouldn't approve. And you can do your series without involving him. I'll tell you whatever you want about me and you can run that instead."

I make a note here to dig even deeper into Ness's grandfather. Telling me not to look into something is the wrong play if that's what he really wants. Unless Ness knows this and is sending me down a blind alley.

"What about your father, then? He didn't seem to mind the limelight."

Wilde laughs, and I glance up from my notebook in time to see him with his head tilted back, white teeth flashing, wrinkles around his eyes. It's a dangerous laugh. I tell myself it's another prop, not to believe it.

"My father was the exact opposite," Ness says. "He hated people, but he loved taking their money. And he was good at it. I think it skips a generation, that drive. My old man took after his grandfather. As a kid, he climbed over oil rigs like they were his private jungle gyms. Didn't spend much time with his own father. The oil company was his life, his true family. And he took the company to another level, daring other industry leaders to catch up, taunting them, showing them where to drill, correcting their mistakes in public—"

"He wasn't scared of the competition?"

"No. My father knew he was the smartest man in any room."

"What about women?"

Wilde shrugs, seems confused. "My dad only had eyes for my mother."

"No, I mean . . . you said smartest *man* in any room. What about women?"

"I misspoke," Wilde says. "Sorry. It sounded sexist, didn't it?"

I don't answer, just let the accusation hang. "It sounds like resentment of absent fathers runs in the family. Boys raised by their grandfathers. Is that why you're protecting your grandfather? You say you don't remember much, but maybe he was there for you in those first years in a way your father wasn't. Showered you with gifts, or let you—"

"That's not it," Wilde says.

"So what is it, then?"

Wilde takes a deep breath. "My great-grandfather gave us the world," he says. "This was his gift to us. He made sure I would never have to work a day in my life, made sure my dad and his dad would have everything. He gave us the world."

"You say that like it's a bad thing. Like it makes you sad." I switch the pen to my other hand and wipe my palm on my skirt. There's an intensity in Wilde's eyes that I can't put my finger on, a glare at some distant past. That's what I want: whatever he's thinking right then. I wonder if I should push him for more; I wonder if I should show him the shells; but I worry even more that I might frighten some wary truth away.

Wilde sets his wine down and stands up. He is frozen in place for a moment, like he's locked in a fight-or-flight decision. He walks to a side table, opens a drawer, and pulls out a book. It looks like a Bible, and I wait for him to open it and quote scripture. I wonder if Ness has found God these past years, if that's why he has withdrawn from the world. Perhaps he is seeking forgiveness for what he and his family have done to the earth.

But as he brings me the book, I can see that it's a leather journal, worn soft. He hands it to me. The leather strap around the journal doesn't match the cover; the original probably wore through and fell apart. I slip the strap off and open the notebook. Pages of neat writing. It's almost calligraphic in its beauty, its timelessness. The pages feel on the verge of growing brittle.

"Part of the reason I asked you here was so you could read this," Ness says. "It was my grandfather's journal. His private thoughts. I don't think he ever meant for anyone else to read it."

My palms are sweating. Source material on the Wilde family is impossibly hard to find. It all comes secondhand or through interviews. As I flip the pages, a poem stands out for its short stanzas and the way it's centered on the page. I scan the first few lines:

> *The sea whispers and sighs*
> *her last breaths upon the beach.*
> *She is dying, and all I want*
> *is to end her suffering.*

"I need you to sign this before you read any more," Ness says.

I glance up. Ness has placed a thick stapled document and a pen on the coffee table.

"What is this?" I ask.

"A non-disclosure agreement. If you ever run a word of what's in that book, my lawyers assure me that I'll own not only you, but the *Times* as well."

"Is that so?"

He nods. "That's so. Of course, you can choose not to read it if you don't want to know the truth."

"If I can't write about what's in here, then why show it to me?"

Ness frowns. It's the most serious I've ever seen him, in person or otherwise. "Because if you read what my grandfather wrote," he says, "you won't write anything about him. Ever."

– 7 –

I have to admit that I'm intrigued. Intrigued enough to sign the document. This is not quite why I came here, but as a reporter I know not to turn down opportunities that arise unexpectedly. Besides, I like letting him know that my mind is open, that I'm only interested in the truth, before I grill him about the shells. And the journal is simply too good to pass up.

As I leaf through it, I begin to suspect that Ness didn't ask me here to interview him; he brought me here to commune with a dead man. He leaves me alone with the journal and the amazing view, as if this has been his plan all along. He tidies up in the kitchen, disappears for long stretches, passes through now and then like an intermittent wind. My wine seems to fill itself once or twice. The sky reddens then darkens. Occasional ships float by in the distance like stars on the move, while the actual stars hang like diamonds in the sky. And to the south, the horizon glows every ten seconds or so as a nearby lighthouse throws its beam in great orbits of the sky.

But all of this is backdrop to the notebook; they are the things I see when I glance up to digest what I've just read. I scan entries spaced months and even years apart. Angry screeds at the beginning—dating back eighty years—give way to confessions and measured doses of guilt later in life. One note in particular catches my eye. Halfway into the day's entry, written over sixty years ago:

How many children reject their parents' dreams, and how many are diametrically opposed? And of the latter, how many of those children forewent riches from questionable sources? How many cast off to live adrift, when the answer to reparations lay in their inheritances?

My father's allowance is the only power he has over me. To reject this is to reject him and to stand on my convictions. But my father's allowance is the only power I have over the world he harms. To cast myself adrift is to leave the world to drown. In this way, my convictions become the ultimate not in sacrifice but in selfishness.

Better to stomach all of this, to tear out and swallow these pages, these ruminations, and live as a dutiful son, conspiring in my own way, and amassing a war chest. Not to counter misdeeds with mere angry words to the hungry press, but to apply some salve to all the wounds my family has scratched upon this Earth.

I have to read it a second time. So Ness's grandfather rejected the legacy his own father made, but he did it in secret. To what effect?

There is more. Much more. There are more poems of nature worship and agony, and I find myself blinking tears away, however rough the prose. Here is a soul aging in reverse. Anger giving way to charity. Surety moving to curiosity. Judgment sliding into doubt. The last pages read like the youthful rebellion of the naive, the college spirit, the hopefulness that the world might change for the better. Early pages, meanwhile, read like the hardened cynicism of old age, like the generations of Wildes in my series of planned exposés. If this transformation was real, it transpired without anyone knowing.

I sip my wine. There is a small white light on the horizon following another light: the flash of a longline tug heading south.

My father taught me to read these nautical constellations on shelling expeditions that lasted into the night. I think of this journal in my lap as a tug of sorts, pulling me through dark waters. The compulsion to run a story based on what I'm reading is neutered by the document I've signed. But maybe it would be worth the worst that lawsuits might bring. A story of quiet redemption and private protest.

But what was the point of this protest? What was the outcome? His own son—Ness's father—picked up the mantle and carried on pumping oil, warming the air and the sea, ruining whatever plans this journal hints at. Even when Ness's father turned to green energy, it was a temporary stunt, and the pumping continued. He simply saw room for even greater profits by appealing to the masses. In my research, I found several quotes where Ness's father practically admits this. It's the crux of the third part of my story.

"Ness?" I call out. I have so many questions.

He appears moments later, and I am shocked back into awareness of where I am. The wine and the passing of these hours have made being here feel less surreal.

"Explain this," I say, indicating the journal. "What the hell is this?"

"That's a good man," Ness says. "Everything you wrote about my great-grandfather is true. Everything you'll say about my father and me will be true. But not him. You couldn't possibly write a true word about him."

"So the land he bought—what was the point?"

"To protect it. Practically every acre is now under federal protection—"

"But for tax reasons, right?"

Ness shrugs. "People don't see what they want to see. They see what they *expect* to see."

"I need to . . . I need to think about this." I hold up the journal.

"Can I take this with me?"

Ness laughs. "No way. But you can take as long as you like with it. You can come back tomorrow if you want. Anything to convince you to skip over him."

I check the time. It's not yet nine o'clock. The inn where I'm staying is only half an hour away, and fifteen minutes of that is just getting off Ness's property. I have so many questions. Even if the story can't be written, I need to know what Ness has pieced together about his grandfather. I need to spend some time going through the notebook more carefully. There's more here than anyone could decipher in a week. And I still haven't grilled him about himself or his father. I haven't asked him about the shells.

"Can I . . . do you mind if I get some air?"

"Of course. It's a short walk down to the beach." Ness takes my wine glass, opens one of the sliding glass doors, and shows me which boardwalk to take. It's a maze of steps that seems to float above the dunes and between the tall reeds and grasses. I leave my shoes on the deck. Ness offers me a flashlight, but the stairs are dimly lit on either side, and I don't want to shell. Impossibly, I don't want to shell.

As I head down, the sea calls from the black distance. I cannot see it and it cannot see me, but we seem to be aware of one another. I think of a poem from the notebook, the dying sighs and whispers, the last breaths, and just how long the final days of that great body of water have stretched out. Dying slowly, like my mother. When everyone thought the end would be swift, like it was for my dad.

Thinking of my father, I remember how we used to walk the shoreline near our house after Mom passed away. We carried bags, but not because we thought we'd find more than a stray shell here or there. The shells were rare enough that we only needed our pockets. The bags were for the trash. He and I watched the plastic index creep and climb from summer to summer, the measure of how much had dissolved into the sea. When I was nine, he and my mom took me on an eco-cruise to see the great raft of detritus caught in the swirling gyre of the Pacific. Each cruise scoops up as much as it can and brings home tons of trash to be recycled. Passengers buy tickets to pay for the fuel and the efforts. It's also a lottery of sorts, with winners catching glimpses of a lone whale, maybe just a spout or the tail fin before a deep dive. From fellow passengers, we heard stories of such sightings. At my age, this was like being near enough to unicorns, just touching the arm of an old couple who'd had such an encounter.

Then I saw the raft of trash for myself. You could walk across it in places, it was so thick and buoyant. The giant scoops from the deck crane barely made a dent. My mother explained where it all came from until I wept. After she passed away, my father and I kept her spirit alive by picking up trash on the beach. We tried to make the world a prettier place. At least until the next tide rolled in.

The sea has this effect on me, this helpless reminiscing. On Ness Wilde's private beach, I weep. I weep while the ocean whispers a death rattle of sublime beauty, of such grace. Such dying grace. Where I am standing would've been hillside generations ago. The old beach is out there somewhere, buried. Gone.

Straining, I can see the white foam of crashing waves lit by the half-moon. The lighthouse sends another ray around, providing me with glimpses of the shimmering sea. But this beach was bought with oil money. With plastic. Some other beach lies out there in the inky depths, drowned and forgotten. Flooded. And suddenly the cool sand is hot beneath the soles of my feet. And I turn my back on the graceful, dying waters and run toward the boardwalk, toward the stairs up and away, before the sea reaches out and takes me as well, before it keeps coming, absorbing all, washing me away.

= 8 =

"**Y**ou weren't gone long," Ness says as I slam the door behind me. My shoes are in my hand. I am shaking. I tell him I need to go, maybe come back tomorrow, and Ness asks if I'm okay to drive. I'm not. I tell him I need a minute. I hear myself say that I have too many questions. That it's too late in the day.

"Have a seat," Ness tells me. "I'll put on coffee."

I sit down and slip my shoes back on, the sand rough between my toes. I find my purse and dig out my key fob. It feels good to hold it, this means of escape. I feel drugged on more than just wine and sad remembrances. It's the blow of new knowledge. I remember feeling this at times in college, needing days to recover after seeing the world in a different light. If what I've glimpsed about his grandfather is true, then Ness was right, and I can't run my next piece. It doesn't stop the rest of my story, but it creates quite the hole. One I can't fill with the truth—for I have signed that right away.

"You understand this doesn't change what I write about your father. Or you."

"Of course. Do you take cream or sugar?"

"Black is fine," I say. Strands of my hair have come loose from my running, from the wind. I tuck these behind my ear and accept a cup of coffee. Ness sits. We are back where we started, except the stars are out and the view of the beach is gone. The lighthouse whirs in the distance.

"Four generations of oil men," I say. Ness nods. "Help me understand how . . . how you aren't all the same."

He laughs. "Because it's a better story and much easier to write if we're the same. But let me start from the beginning." He glances at the dive watch on his left wrist, possibly wondering how much time he has, what things to leave out.

"Please," I tell him. I'm sure I won't hear anything new, but I look forward to what things he chooses to leave out, where he decides to embellish. And I'm in no shape to drive. No shape to confront him with the shells. It might have to wait until tomorrow. I'm going to have to take him up on the offer to come back.

"My great-grandfather William built Ocean Oil from scratch," Ness says. "He worked on deep sea rigs while he was in his teens. Dropped out of high school after ninth grade, ran away from home, and became a roughneck on a Shell Oil platform. By the time he was twenty, he was a shift foreman. At twenty-two, he had his own rig. This was ten years younger than anyone in company history."

"Because of your great-grandmother, right?"

"No. Because he produced barrels like no other, and that was all anyone cared about. He met Shelly, my great-grandmother, after his promotion. I know . . . that name, right? It was the most common name for both boys and girls at the time. A curse. She was eighteen, and accompanied her father on a rig inspection."

"And her father was CEO of Shell Oil at the time—"

"Shelly's father wasn't CEO yet, just VP of Engineering. One of my dad's biographers got that wrong, and he got the timing wrong as well. Everyone keeps repeating the same wrong source until it's gospel."

I make a note of this.

"By the time William—I only ever knew him as Paps—and Shelly started dating, Paps had his own rig. It wasn't some kind of favor to him. He earned everything he ever got. If anything, the rig got him that first date, not the other way around. The story is that Shelly fell in love with him at first sight. Saw this young man ordering around people twice his age. He was covered in grime, refused to wear a hardhat but cussed out anyone who neglected theirs, used to say God made his head plenty hard enough."

"That's the kind of detail I wish I'd had a week ago," I say. "I reached out to your publicist several times—"

"And if she ignored your inquiries, she earned every penny of what I pay her," Ness says.

Until I ran the story you didn't like, I think to myself. But then I have to remind myself that the story I ran isn't the one he's worried about. It's the next one.

"So your great-grandfather was climbing the ranks pretty fast. He had his own rig, was dating a VP's daughter. But then he leaves the company."

"A few years later, yeah."

"Seems abrupt. He was twenty-five at the time?"

"A few years can be a long time," Ness says.

I think of the years Ness has been a recluse and wonder if he's speaking from experience. I wonder exactly what he's been doing with his time. Surely not sitting idle. Maybe he spent that time perfecting the shells in my bag.

"A lot happened during those years," Ness says. "Look—" he glances at his wristwatch again. I touch the screen of my phone to wake it up, make sure it's still recording. "My great-grandfather saw the future of drilling at a young age. He was ambitious. Driven. He had good ideas for getting at oil that no one thought we'd ever reach. He could've worked his way up the company. He was young and smart and determined, probably would've been CEO of Shell before he was forty. Instead, he quit his job, filed a few patents, and started begging for capital to start his own company."

"Which didn't go so well."

"No. It didn't."

"And your great-grandmother Shelly, how did she take this?"

"The two of them were married on an oil platform by a roughneck who'd been an army chaplain. Shelly's father was CEO by then, and he said never come home again, and Shelly didn't. Paps managed to borrow enough to buy an old platform that wasn't producing. He spent five years refitting it and drilling where people thought he was crazy to drill. The story goes that the tugs sent to repossess the rig were throwing lines to haul the thing away when he struck a gusher. Five miles down. Nothing like it had ever been done before. Of course, he would have a dozen platforms running within a year of that day. And he made it a point to buy every one of the tugs sent to repossess his rig."

Wilde sips his coffee. The sky throbs with the light from the lighthouse. I don't know how he lives within range of a metronome like that.

"Paps gave us the world, you see. From his son to my father to me. He gave us the world, but he broke it before he handed it over. That's his legacy. He gave me and my dad the world in a million little flooded pieces. If I remember anything else about him that's not in the history books, I'd rather not say."

"To protect him? Like your grandfather?"

Wilde laughs. "Yes, because whatever I say wouldn't be kind."

"Tell me about your grandfather, then." I make a show of turning the recording app off, show him my phone, thinking all the while of the FBI wire. "Off the record. I swear." Off *my* record. I swear.

"I'll take your signature over your swear any day of the week," Ness says.

"You have both."

Wilde stares into his coffee. I take a sip of mine.

"What was he like? From your reading, if not your memory."

"My grandfather was a complicated man. I like to say that he walked in his father's shadow, but with a flashlight."

"To dispel those shadows?"

"To erase him in a way, yes. By the time my father inherited Ocean Oil, my granddad was already blaming *his* father for destroying the world. It wasn't just Ocean Oil, of course, but you couldn't tell my granddad that. Sea temps were up five degrees and sea levels eight inches from when my great-grandfather was born."

"Everything I've read said the company bypassed your grandfather because of his age. Because of lack of interest."

"And I showed you the real reason." Ness indicates the leather journal sitting on the coffee table. "My grandfather wanted to dismantle Ocean Oil—"

"And that was why your father inherited the company instead?"

Ness nods.

I make a mental note of this. This is not the history anyone else knows. The popular accounts are of an unchanging and evil empire, handed from father to son, each of them perfectly like the other. A convenient tale, because it's easy to understand. We can transfer our ire from one generation to the next, no forgiveness required, no need to get to know a man. Just judge him by his father's sins.

Studying Ness, I allow myself to consider for a moment that I'm wrong about him as well, that he has nothing to do with the fake shells. Maybe the person I think I know is just a caricature of the real man. I've sensed this before with other celebrities and political figures I've gotten close to, that they're just people saddled with unachievable expectations. We make of them what we need them to be, good or ill.

"So your father was supposed to keep the company safe," I say. "But then *he* was the one who nearly tore it apart."

"For different reasons. Selfish reasons. He saw the laws making their way through Congress. He knew the end of big oil was coming, saw the peak of production. Hell, this was before Manhattan flooded for the first time and the levee project got underway. My dad refused to waste the company's money lobbying against the inevitable—not because he cared about the environment, but because he hated to see lawyers get rich when they couldn't win. The board of directors disagreed. They worked in the background to have Dad removed as incompetent."

"I didn't know your dad lost control of the company," I say, making a mental note of this as well. Henry was going to fall out when he got my edits, and I hadn't even gotten to Ness yet. But Ness was doing the impossible: convincing me to shelve one story while revising another.

"The board didn't take the company away from him for long. My dad had been working on his TideGen program for almost a decade by that point, all in secret. It was a personal project. He paid for it out of his own pocket—"

"I'd heard that part."

"Yeah, it became part of his legend, that he privately financed the oil company's first green initiative. As everyone knows by now, the whole thing was bullshit. When he couldn't get the program to work, he turned it into a PR move. Used it for deflection. What's interesting is when he gave the speech that turned the stock around, he technically wasn't CEO of anything at that point. The board was waiting until close of markets on Friday to announce, just so they could handle the spin. They were scrambling that same week to name a replacement. Meanwhile, my father was about to shock the world and rescue the company."

Ness leans forward and places his hands on his knees. He looks at me for a long pause, a half-smile on his lips. The most distracting thing about this man isn't his handsomeness, but his confidence. It isn't fair for any human to visibly worry so little.

"Can I show you the video?" he asks.

"I've seen it," I tell him.

"I want to show you something interesting."

"Is there any way I can verify this?" I ask. "That your father wasn't CEO at the time of the speech?"

"Let me show you the video," Ness insists. "You like personal details. I want to show you how my parents met."

He gets up and disappears down the hall. I take a sip of coffee and count the time between sweeps of light. Twelve seconds, not ten. If I had a chart of the Maine coast, I could find the lighthouse based on its period. I'm thinking of my father and all he taught me when Ness returns with a tablet.

He sits down on the sofa beside me. I try to slide over, but the armrest has me pinned. His knee presses against mine. Maybe he isn't aware of this. He calmly starts the video, and I feel a flush of heat from too much wine or the coffee or from him sitting too close. On the tablet, his father is giving a press conference on the deck of an oil platform, and all I can think is that this man—who I have been chasing down for two years—is now far too close. I've been trying to pin him down, and now he has me pinned. I'm overreacting, I tell myself. I feel like standing up and running away from here, but some tiny voice says this is irrational, to calm the fuck down.

"Listen," Ness says, turning up the volume. He has fast-forwarded past the start of his father's speech. I've seen this before. I try to concentrate on what's happening on that screen, not in the room. The speech occurred a few years before I was born, but every journalist has seen it. Nathaniel Wilde is standing on that symbol of ecological disaster, that oil platform, announcing that it was one of fourteen that drew its own power not by burning the oil it pumped but by the swell of the sea. And now was the time to announce Ocean Oil's plan to wean itself off oil altogether and that the future of tomorrow's energy needs would be a mix of geothermal and the incessant wave energy of the ocean tides.

"Here," Ness says, pointing at the video. The camera has turned to a group of reporters sitting on folding chairs arranged across the deck of the rig. A woman is holding a pen up in the air, rises to ask a question. "Tara Brighton, *UK Daily*," she says. "You don't really expect us to believe that Ocean Oil is going *green,* do you?"

The camera cuts back to Ness's father. But Ness rewinds the video again. When the camera shifts to the reporter, he pauses the screen. I glance over at him, waiting for him to explain what I'm supposed to be seeing, when I notice the sweep of the lighthouse flash in his wet eyes.

Tara Brighton—the name comes back to me.

"That's your mom," I say.

Ness nods. The tablet must be getting heavy, for I note his hand is trembling, falling.

"Is this how they met?" I ask.

"Right there," Ness says, his voice quiet. He fiddles with the shell dangling from his necklace. "What's wild is that they met in front of so many people, but no one has ever commented on it. No one sees her, I guess. It happens so fast, and everyone is concentrating on my dad. But I think this is . . . important in understanding who he was. What motivated him."

I look back to the screen, to the woman holding the pen and asking the handsome man behind the podium a question. And when I glance up, it's the wall of magazine covers down the hall— that grid of trophies—that catches my eye. And some grave truth seems to scream out, some fucked-up psychological disorder, and I can't tell if this is the moment when Ness will attack me and add me to that wall, or if my sentiment is supposed to get the better of me and this is where he expects me to pull him against me. All I can think of is the dozen other women who sat on this sofa and watched this video and saw him tear up, just moments from doing something they would regret. And I wonder if he's used his grandfather's notebook countless times, if he has a stack of signed NDAs, if that's why the leather band wore out, if this is all a trick, some play here on this stage with this room of props, some game of sniffing out foes and vanquishing them. I reach for Ness's trembling wrist as his hand and tablet fall toward my lap—

"I have to go," I say, pushing his arm and the tablet away from me. I stand up too fast, and the room adjusts itself around me. Wine and coffee compete for my senses. I reach for my phone, for my bag with its damning evidence. A new story forms in my mind, a story about a serial manipulator and a fucked-up family four generations deep, chasing along in their fathers' shadows not with flashlights but with burning torches.

"Right now?" Ness asks. "But I haven't shown you my collection—"

"I've *seen* your collection," I say. I shove my pad and pen inside my bag, then point at the wall of framed magazine covers. "I'd rather not be added to it."

I turn and head up the stairs to get out of that place.

"Wait," Ness tells me. He follows me toward the door. "Just one more minute, please—"

"It's not going to work on me," I tell him over my shoulder. "Whatever you're going to say, however you're going to try and manipulate me, it won't work." I reach for the front door, half expecting to find it locked, myself trapped. But the knob turns easily. I open the door to feel that the air outside has chilled in the last half hour. Or maybe it's me.

Ness catches the door as it swings shut, and I can feel him standing on the stoop as I crunch around the car to the driver's side.

"What do you mean, *manipulate* you?" he asks.

I glance at him over the roof of the car, catch the bewildered look on his face from the flickering porch light. Damn, he's good.

"I think you're a sociopath," I say bluntly. "You tell people what they want to hear, make them vulnerable, make yourself appear vulnerable, and then you take your prey to bed and revel in the gushing stories they print that never tell anyone a goddamn thing. You hang us on your wall, collecting bylines like frat boys collect panties."

I open the door and get into the car.

"You wanted to know my story," Ness says. "You wanted the truth, and I'm trying to give it to you."

He looks bewildered through the passenger window. Or upset. I realize now that I won't be coming back tomorrow. Or ever. Agent Cooper can unravel this on his own. I'm going to run my stories and expose this man for what he is.

I press the start button and place the car in gear, attempt to spin out, but the car doesn't move. The low battery light is blinking at me. I glance over at the glove box, which is hanging open, the dimmest of glows leaking from inside. Fuck me.

I look to the porch, but Ness has disappeared back into his house. I slap my steering wheel in frustration. I could've sworn I'd closed the glove box when I put my registration away.

=9=

The light on the porch is still on. I stare at my phone and consider calling the inn or a taxi or a tow, but I don't know how to get any of those people past Ness's double guard gates. With no other choice, I get out of the car again and approach the house. My shouted accusations hang in the air, are still ringing in my ears. Ness answers the door holding his glass of wine, has switched back from coffee. The barest of swallows is left in the bottom of his glass.

"I need to borrow some juice," I tell him. "My battery's flat."

Ness studies me for a moment. A painful moment.

"I would like an apology," he says.

Through clenched teeth, I say, "I'm sorry." My anger has been cooled by my embarrassment at needing his help to get out of here.

"I have a battery booster in the garage. You can wait here if you like."

I decide to follow him, and he doesn't stop me. Ness heads around the low stucco wall studded with conchs and around toward the garage. Lights above the garage doors flick on automatically and the courtyard blooms bright. Bugs begin to gather around the floodlights. There are three bays. Ness punches a six-digit code into the pad on the wall, and the center bay slides open.

The light inside the garage comes on, and Ness squeezes between a covered car and a rack of shelves. I step inside and lift the cover on the bumper of the car, see the candy-apple red beneath. I also note the exhaust pipe. A gas burner.

"I don't have a thing for reporters," Ness tells me as he digs noisily through shelves of tools. "Half of what they've written about me over the years is complete fiction. Not that I care. You can write whatever you want. Tell people I came on to you."

"Didn't you?" I ask.

"Does it matter?" Ness lugs the orange battery pack my way. I drape the car cover back over the gas-guzzler and step out of the garage. "I asked my dad once how he and my mom met, and he made up a story. He'd make up a different story every time, depending on who was asking. My mom would do it too. I figured it out on my own. Thought you'd like to hear about it."

"So you want credit for figuring that out?" I follow him back toward my car. The lights wink off behind us. "Well done. Great investigative reporting."

"I confronted him about it," Ness says. "This was after my mom died. I asked why he never told me the truth. And it was the first time I ever saw him cry. I mean, bawl like a child."

Some distant and professional part of me cries out that this might be important, worth writing about, but the rest of me is too riled up to care or even make mental notes. I follow Ness around to my car and watch as he pops the hood and attaches the booster to the battery posts. He checks to make sure the pack is switched on. "Should give you an hour or so of juice. We'll have to leave it plugged in for half an hour."

"Convenient," I tell him. "I'm trapped here."

"Unless you want to stomp down the driveway in a huff, you are." He smiles, seems to be joking.

I nearly ask Ness if he opened the glove box while I was reading the journal, but I realize how paranoid I'm being, how crazy that will sound. I'm already feeling the slightest twinge of guilt for blowing up on him.

"Why do you think he kept it a secret?" I ask. "Did he say?"

"He did. And I would have shared that with you, but now I'm not so sure." He studies me in the dim glow from the porch light. "Maybe it was a mistake to ask you out here. I should've just let you run the story however you liked. What difference does it make?"

"I'll skip to your father with the next piece," I tell him. "You've shown me enough to doubt the veracity of some of my research. But not enough to replace it with anything more forgiving."

Ness seems to relax. His shoulders drop an inch, like he's been carrying something heavy there and suddenly it's gone, suddenly he doesn't have to tense up against the weight of it all.

"I hoped you'd say that," he says. He smooths his hair back with his hand. Lets out a held breath. "This isn't how I imagined tonight going."

"What did you imagine?" I ask, not sure I really want to know.

"I thought we would talk shells. I remember your old column. I was a fan. I thought I'd show you my collection, let you see what my life has been about. Because it hasn't been about drilling for oil. All that goes on without me."

"But you profit from it."

"I do. And so did my grandfather. And he put that money to good use."

I recall what Ness said about some things skipping a generation. Or was that me who'd said that?

"You do know you have a reputation," I say. "Journalism isn't a large field. Reporters hang out in the same circles."

"And you believe everything you read in the papers?"

I don't have a quick response to that.

"Why don't we go inside while this is charging?" he asks.

"Why can't you just admit what's going on? Have you spent any time examining this? Your father fell in love with a reporter, and you seem to be fascinated by that. And now you're older than he was then, and look at this pattern you've formed—"

"I don't just date reporters."

"Congratulations."

"I don't. It's just . . . that's who I meet. Who else do I socialize with? Have I dated more people than you have? Have I dated more *reporters* than you have?"

"Yes," I say with confidence. I eye the battery booster; I could probably get to the end of that long-ass driveway on five minutes of charge, then call a cab or have the inn send someone. Ness glances at his watch.

"It's ten," he says. "Come inside so you don't freeze. We don't have to sit in the same room if you don't want—"

"Tell me about Dimitri Arlov," I blurt out.

Ness stares at me across the open hood of my car. Bugs swirl about, meandering toward the beacon that is the front porch light.

"Where did you hear that name?" he asks.

"Did he work for you?" I hug myself, shivering. I can't tell if it's from the cold or the adrenaline rush of confronting him about this.

"Dimitri is dead," Ness says. "Come inside."

I clutch my bag. "If I come inside, it's just so I can show you something," I warn him. "And I don't think you're going to like it."

-10-

I leave my car charging and follow Ness back up to the porch. Again he gives me the overly polite *Ladies first* while waving me into the house. I feel clammy as I go over and over how best to show him the shells. I finally decide that Agent Cooper's method was most dramatic. So I pull out a stool at his kitchen counter and sit down, my bag on the granite between us.

Ness pours himself another glass of wine. I wave him off before he can offer me any. "I need to drive," I remind him.

"And I need to calm my nerves," he says.

It's almost as if he knows what's coming. But he must be referring to our confrontation from earlier.

"What did Dimitri do for the company?" I ask.

"A lot of things. Dimitri was a bright man. I'm assuming you know that he passed away this year."

"Yes. Were you close to him?"

"Very close."

I open my bag and dig out the box. "I'm sorry for your loss, then."

"The whole world lost something when Dimitri passed. They don't make them like that anymore." Ness raises his glass toward the ceiling and takes a large gulp. As I set the small case on the counter, I hear him nearly choke and fight to swallow. He eyes the plastic case like it's a lump of radioactive material. I almost don't need to open the thing to know what I needed to know.

"Tell me what you think of this," I say. I open the box so that only I can see inside, and I pull out one of the lace murexes. I pass it to Ness. He barely looks at the shell as he takes it, is still eyeing the box.

"A murex," he finally says. "In good condition."

"In flawless condition," I say. "Museum quality. One of a kind, wouldn't you say?"

Ness nods. "Sure."

"So explain this."

I place the other two shells on the counter. I can't believe I'm doing this. And maybe since I just had one battery fail me, I worry about the amount of charge the FBI recorder has. I should have turned on my phone recorder as well. I try not to worry about that and just concentrate on Ness's reaction as he studies the three shells.

"They're nice," he says. But he sounds distant. Far away.

"Any idea where they might have come from?" I ask.

Ness shrugs.

"I think you know," I tell him.

He reaches for the bottle of wine, but I grab his wrist and stop him. I slide the bottle of wine toward me and out of his reach. Ness looks at me with a film of tears across his eyes. Worry at being busted? Nerves?

"I think . . ." Ness hesitates. "I don't know why he would have taken them. It doesn't make any sense. He could have just asked."

"So these are yours?" I can't believe this. Ness looks staggered. Numb. He would probably tell me anything in this moment.

"Yes, they look . . . familiar. They were probably mine."

"Where did you find them?" I ask, knowing they didn't wash up on any beach.

"I . . . they came into my possession a while back. A few years ago."

"They're only a few years old," I tell him. "They're fakes. But you must know that. Any collector worth his salt would. These have been extinct for twenty years—"

"Thirty years," Ness says.

"So explain them to me."

"I can't."

"How much of your collection is fake?" I ask. I feel bolder the more beat down Ness appears. His confidence is gone and mine surges. Like a seesaw. I forget why I was even nervous. Why I hesitated to do this. There's a Pulitzer in this. Henry will go ballistic. Hell, I could probably get the science section rolling again, I'll have so much leverage.

"They aren't fake," Ness says, but his voice is a whisper. He doesn't even believe himself.

I laugh.

Ness looks up at me. His eyes widen at some thought. "I can prove it. Hold on."

He goes to the kitchen and rummages through several of the cabinets, comes back with a heavy mortar and pestle, the kind used to grind up spices. Ness takes one of the lace murexes and places it in the mortar. Before I can stop him, he cracks the shell with the pestle. I feel the destruction in my chest, like those are my bones snapping.

He fishes out a piece of the broken shell. All I can think is that even a fake of such quality could pay my rent for the year. Even with the buyer *knowing* it was fake!

"Look," Ness says. "Wait. I'll get a loupe." He turns away from the counter, and I hear myself say that I have one. I fumble in my bag. Ness is animated again, excited. "Look at the shell wall," he says. "You'll see a pattern where the slug's foot scraped back and forth."

I look through the loupe. I know exactly what he's talking about; I feel like reminding him that I studied to be a marine biologist. Instead, I say, "This could easily be part of the mold."

I hear another crunch. The mortar is emptied onto the granite again, forming a second pile of debris. And as I pull the loupe away, there's a third crunch as the last shell is cracked open.

"Look at these," he says. "They should be different."

I'm too busy taking in the fragments and the powder everywhere. It's as thoughtless as the driveway. Senseless waste.

"Look," he insists.

And so I do. And sure enough, the patterns are different. The shells are distinct. So, not from a single mold.

I pull the loupe away. Despite what I'm seeing, another thought occurs to me. Ness is a collector. And no collector in his right mind, whatever their collection is like, could destroy three lace murexes without batting an eye. Without flinching. Much less seem to recover their spirits while doing so. His confession came by destroying the shells. All I can think of now is getting to the inn and calling Agent Cooper to let him know what happened here.

"You believe me, don't you?" Ness asks. Almost with desperation.

"Sure," I say. I check the time on my phone. "I think I should go."

-11-

My car is beeping at me as I coast into the inn. I leave it with the valet, grab my overnight bag out of the trunk, and remind the young man a second time to make sure he plugs the car in. The registration desk is empty. There's laughter from the bar, but the rest of the facility is winding down for the night. A man emerges from the back. I hand over my business card, ask for any available upgrade, and get a room key to a suite. I figure Henry owes me for yanking my story.

I find the suite and spend a few minutes unpacking. I catch a flash of myself in the mirror and decide that I look like a wreck. The first person I call is Agent Cooper. I try his cell and brace for the grumble of the half-asleep. Instead, he picks up on the first ring. Sounds chipper as he says "Hello."

"Do you ever sleep?" I ask.

"Who is this?"

"Maya. Maya Walsh. From the *Times*."

"Of course. Sorry. Been one of those days. So how did it go?"

I imagined him waiting around breathlessly for my call. Instead, it sounds like I'm just one of many things on his mind. "It went great," I tell him. "The shells definitely link back to Ness . . . Mr. Wilde, I mean. And the case you had the shells in, did it belong to Mr. Arlov by any chance?"

"Yeah, why?"

"Because he recognized it. And when I asked him if he knew Mr. Arlov, he said they were very close. I think those were his exact words. And then get this—he wondered why Dimitri would have taken the shells from him. They were definitely Ness's."

"And you recorded all this?"

"It should all be on your device. Hold on a sec." I unbutton my blouse, work one arm free, move the phone to my other hand, and wiggle out of my top. Unsnapping the back of my bra, I let it fall away and unclip the recorder from the underwire. "Yeah, the little light is still on. So I should've gotten it."

"Anything else?"

"Yeah, he tried to convince me the shells were real. Was adamant about it."

"I bet."

"He even had me look inside the torus at how all the wear marks were different. But I was thinking maybe the molds are a one-off, you know? A different mold for each shell."

"Wait. He did what?"

"He showed me the foot rubbings for the slugs. Each one was unique. But I figure he just—"

"How did he show you the inside of the torus?"

I took a deep breath. My heart was racing from the long day and the coffee and the confrontation. "He cracked them open," I said. "Which he never would've done if they were real, right? I mean, forget the value of the things. He's a collector. If those were real—"

"Maya, you still have the shells, right? Tell me you have the shells."

I rest a hand on the bathroom counter. My hair is mostly loose from my clip, is hanging around my face. "I told you, he . . . the shells. He had me look inside—"

I hear Cooper take a deep breath and let it out. I imagine him still at his desk, working all night in the pale glow of that solitary lamp, and now he's probably pushed back from his desk, is running his hand up through his hair.

"So he destroyed our best evidence right in front of you," Cooper says.

I don't say anything. I just study myself in the mirror. The room spins around me.

"Look, it's okay," he says. "Just come to my office when you get back in town. Bring the wire. That might be enough to get a search warrant. And you may have spooked him into doing something dumb. We'll keep an eye on him."

"I'm sorry," I say.

"It's okay. He's a crafty guy. If he wasn't, we'd have nailed him by now. Get some sleep. We'll regroup when you get home."

"Okay," I say. I appreciate him trying to make me feel better, but it doesn't dent how idiotic I feel. "See you soon."

"G'night, Maya."

The phone clicks.

I check the time and debate calling my sister, who loves hearing about my fuck-ups and is great at making me feel better about them. I decide it's too late. I run a bath instead, letting the water run hot enough to throw up steam. I'm about to step in when my phone rings. I answer immediately, expecting Agent Cooper or possibly even Henry.

"Hello, Maya?"

Ness. It's crazy that I recognize his voice. "How did you get this number?" I ask.

"The internet. You're listed, you know."

I wiggle out of my pants and underwear and test the water. Scalding hot. I get in anyway.

"What do you want?" I ask. "It's late."

"I was calling to see if you were coming back tomorrow. To look at that journal some more. I need to let the outer gate know."

"I don't think so," I say. "I think I got what I need."

"Okay."

There's a long silence. Like he wants to say something else but doesn't know how. I don't allow myself to care or be curious.

I just slip down until my shoulders are submerged, only my head and the hand holding the phone out of the water. I can feel the tension melt out of my muscles and joints in the hot water.

"I was thinking," Ness says.

I wait.

"You used to do those shelling columns. And you've obviously got a story you're working on about me. And you're curious about those shells you brought over—"

"The ones you destroyed," I say.

"So I was thinking maybe I could show you where they came from. Give you a shelling angle to your story. I think . . . I think I might be ready to share some of my secrets. My shelling secrets."

I start to ask if by "secrets" he means how he forged the shells, but something even worse pops out of my mouth. "Did you kill Dimitri Arlov?" I ask.

"What—? No. Are you serious? Absolutely not. He was . . . a very good friend. Absolutely not."

"Did you know that he stole from you?"

"No. I didn't. And . . . you wouldn't understand."

"Try me," I say.

"Okay," Ness says. "But you'll have to trust me. Come spend a week with me, and I'll take you shelling. I'll show you . . . where they came from. I think I *want* people to know."

"You'll show me where those lace murexes came from?" I ask, making sure I understand.

Ness hesitates. I wonder what he means by letting people know, what he means about sharing his secrets. Does he know the feds are closing in on him? Does he think he can save himself with a confession or by appealing to the press or to the public? Is he that desperate?

"Yes," he finally says. "I'll show you where the laces came from. Give me a week of your time, and I'll give you the story of a lifetime. I promise."

Part II:
Drowning

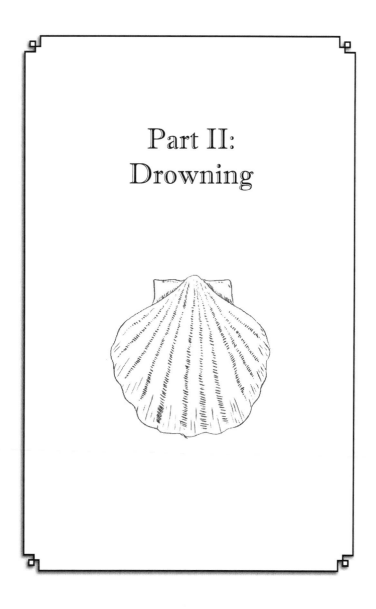

-12-

"**Y**ou're doing *what?*" Henry asks me.

"I'm going back up there," I tell him. "For one week. And you're sitting on my cable."

Henry gets off my desk, and I unplug the charger for my laptop, wrap it up, and shove it in my bag.

"What do you mean, you're going back up there? We've got to get your second piece out next week. We're running part one again on Sunday. Everyone wants to know when you're getting to Ness."

"Sounds like she already got to him," Dawn says from her desk.

I flip her the bird.

"This is bigger than that piece," I tell Henry. I lower my voice to a whisper. Everyone in the newsroom is watching us. "This is front page. Real news. I'm telling you. Have I ever been wrong about these things?"

"You really want me to answer that?"

I check my email one last time. Nothing that can't wait. I shut down my computer.

"If you leave here without telling me what in the hell's going on, you won't have a job when you come back."

"I won't *need* this job when I come back." I turn and walk past Margo's desk toward the elevator. Margo smiles and wishes me luck. I don't ask her what she means.

Henry hurries after me. We both know the other is bluffing: he won't fire me and I won't quit.

"Do you hear yourself right now?" he asks. "You're the one who didn't want to go in the first place. Is this the feds? What're they investigating? You're not fucking him, are you?"

I whirl around at Henry and point a finger at him. He nearly crashes into me. "I'm not fucking him," I say. "Ness Wilde is *exactly* who I thought he was. His family stands for everything wrong in this world, and he sits on his private estate where everything is fake, nothing is real, and he sits in the middle of these . . . these shells within shells, and he is working on something awful. I've seen a glimpse of it. I mean—Henry, he has these trees that don't belong there. Palm trees. Thousands of them. He's totally messed up. His driveway is a freaking fortune in crushed shells."

"That's why we have to run these stories, Maya. The one on his grandfather is brilliant. It sounds just like him. Living alone, buying up land that he knows will be beachfront one day—"

I shake my head. "No. I told you, you can't run that piece. Promise me. We skip to his father."

Henry crosses his arms. I place a hand on his shoulder. "I'm going to bring you the piece of our lifetimes, Henry. I swear. I can feel it. You're the one always saying that real journalism is dead. Dead as the seven seas. Well, this is the kind of story that will bring it back to *life*."

"I need more than that, Maya. C'mon. Give me something. A hint. A headline."

I hesitate. If I had the shells, I would show him those. And then I remember I have something a fraction as good. I dig my phone out of my bag and bring up the image gallery, sort through the recent pics. I find the one of the three lace murexes sitting on my kitchen counter. It's the pic I sent to my sister as a gag.

When I show Henry the picture, his eyes widen. "So he bought you," he whispers, his voice dripping with disappointment.

"They're fake," I tell him.

Henry pinches the picture to zoom in. Studies the image closely. "Are you sure?" he asks.

"I'm sure." I lower my voice. "Henry, he cracked these open in front of me and tried to convince me they're real. The feds are investigating where they came from. I'm telling you, they're fakes, but they're *good* fakes. They could crash the shelling market. Or send it skyrocketing. Hell, I don't know."

"So why are you going back up there?" Henry asks.

"Because I think he wants to come clean. He said he wants to show me his secrets. The guy is losing it, Henry. The feds say he never leaves his property. I think he trusts me, and he wants to let me in on something. I think he wants to confess. But Henry, you have to promise to keep this between us. He insisted on no leaks for a week. No stories. He made me promise."

Henry nods. Slowly. I have to pull the phone away from him. I slip it into my bag.

"I'll call you when I've got something," I say.

I leave Henry rooted in place and hit the elevator call button. Dawn is standing a few paces away, getting a cup of water from the cooler. She smiles at me. As I step inside the elevator and ride down to the lobby, I wonder how long she'd been standing there. I wonder how much she heard.

-13-

The drive up to Ness's estate is different this time. At first, it's hard to say why. I stop at the same service station in Massachusetts to quick-charge the car. I see the same scenery as before. The trip takes the same five hours on the expressway. But then I realize that no journey is ever truly the same the second time around. What felt interminable the first time now passes with a quickness borne of familiarity. It makes me wonder if life seems to accelerate as we get older simply because our days and our experiences become routine. The things we recognize flash right by, where once they held our attention. Only the new bears careful contemplation, and the new gets harder and harder to come by.

As I cross into Maine, I remember to call my sister. I haven't told her about this trip, partly because life has been hectic the past few days, partly because I know she'll worry about me. Which is a bad sign that I'm making some kind of mistake.

She picks up after three rings. Her greeting is a half-whisper, like I've caught her in a meeting. "Hey," she says. "Everything okay?"

"Yeah. Sorry if it's a bad time. Just wanted to let you know I'll be out of town for a week in case you don't hear from me."

"Assignment?"

My sister works for an investment bank and lives vicariously through what she calls my "abnormal life." Of course, my life feels perfectly normal to me. I did have to admit to her the day before that the Ness interview was a little out there, which she called a colossal understatement. I brace now for what she'll make of this.

"It's kind of an assignment. I'm in Maine again."

"Shut up," my sister hisses. I can hear movement on the other side, like she's trying to get some place where she can scream. "I thought you weren't going back."

"I changed my mind."

"What's gotten into you? I thought you loathed this guy."

I flash back to a couple years' worth of phone conversations while I was hip-deep in research for my piece. I may have cursed the Wilde family name a time or two.

"I'm not up here to *date* him," I say. "It's for the piece I've been working on about him."

"Good, because you know how you hate men with better shell collections than yours."

"I do not."

My sister laughs. "You totally do. But I'm single. Put in a word, okay? Is he still gorgeous?"

"Sarah, stop."

"He is, isn't he? Oh, God, are you falling for him? Tell me you aren't falling for him."

"No—of course not. He's got issues, Sarah."

"So why are you up there?"

"Because . . . it's complicated. Let's just say the FBI is involved."

"Oh, shut up."

"Seriously."

"Your life is bizarro. I'm undergoing death by PowerPoint over here and you're . . . I don't even understand what you're doing."

I laugh. "I just called to tell you I love you and not to worry if I don't get in touch for a few days. Talk to you next week if not sooner."

"So jealous," Sarah says. "Love you, you lucky ass."

She hangs up, and I have one more person to call before I reach the estate. I find Agent Cooper's number in my call log and dial it. I met with him yesterday and handed over the wire. What I didn't tell him was that I'd already decided to take Ness up on his offer. As far as I'm concerned, my story and his investigation are two separate things. He promised me the scoop if they turn up anything, and I promised to sit on what I already know.

"Hello?" he says.

"Agent Cooper. It's Maya Walsh."

"Stan," he reminds me. As if I could ever call him that.

"Just wanted to let you know that . . . I took Ness up on his offer. If I learn anything that might help you, I'll fill you in."

"Where are you now?" he asks.

"I'm in Maine. About half an hour away."

"You should have told me. This is a bad idea, Maya."

"Maybe. But it'll be good for my piece. And he promised to show me where the shells came from, so if I learn anything, I'll pass it along."

"I appreciate that. But please be careful." I hear him take a deep breath. "I wish you'd told me. I would've talked you out of it."

"Seriously? You talked me into coming the last time." The truth is, I knew he would've objected. Probably why I didn't say anything. "Look, I'll check in when I get back into town—"

"Oh, Maya?"

"Yeah?"

"I was thinking about the marks last night. Inside the shells. One way they could do that is to move a non-extinct species in after they cast the shell. We're thinking here that it would be cheaper than unique molds."

"Yeah, I thought of the same thing."

"Okay. Good sign that we aren't crazy. So be safe."

"I will. Thanks for everything."

We hang up, and I stay lost in thought until I reach Ness's estate. I allow myself to daydream about the shelling ahead, the access I may have to raw beaches, the fact that Ness told me to bring a wetsuit and my snorkel gear.

What I try not to do is allow myself to think of Ness as a regular guy, as a man my age. Being taken on a tour of—whatever he has planned for this week—excites the sheller in me far more than the journalist. I remind myself that this person has an ugly history, that he's the face of one of the companies I blame for the encroaching sea. I also remind myself of the exquisite fake shells and whatever it is they portend. And as I reach the edge of his estate, I let his misplaced palm trees remind me that all with Mr. Wilde is not as it seems. That his outer shell is not to be trusted.

The guard at the first gate smiles at me in recognition. He tips his hat and "ma'ams" me as I hand him my ID. After jotting something on his tablet, he leans out of his booth, peers down the driveway toward the estate, and whispers something into his radio. He nods at some inaudible reply. "Just one second," he tells me.

This is different. I wonder if maybe someone is coming out to meet me.

I tap my fingers on the steering wheel and wait.

I lower the visor and check myself in the mirror.

I pull out my phone to see if there's anything urgent in my inbox.

"Okay," the guard eventually says. He hands me my driver's license and press pass, and the tall iron gate swings open in greased silence.

I enjoy the long driveway this time, because it holds no surprises. I leave the windows down and take in the smell of moss and mulch, search the air for that sea breeze, watch out for any stray coconuts. The car chews up the road, and I try not to think of what the gravel is made of. Racing along, the back end of the car sliding with each small adjustment of the steering wheel, I enjoy this feeling of being on edge. This dangerous place. Here is where time slows down, where we can take it all in, where life becomes digestible, each moment new and therefore able to be savored.

Trees that don't belong whiz by. The bent trunks of palms. *Whoosh, whoosh, whoosh.* Bright birds flit across the road, searching for bugs and worms. And then I notice that the air is dusty, that I'm entering a fog, but it's just a plume kicked up by a vehicle ahead. I roll the windows up to keep the dust out. As it thickens, I ease off the accelerator in case the other car is going slow. I watch for taillights, wonder if I'm overtaking one of the guards who works the inner gate. It's a little after five. Might be when they change shifts.

And then I break through the dust cloud and back into clear air. Checking the rearview mirror for a car on the shoulder, I see nothing. I almost let the mystery pass—almost think nothing of it—but I find myself braking to a dead stop. The dust kicked up by my car trails after and swirls around me. I hesitate for a moment before deciding to throw the car into reverse to go back and investigate.

The road is still choked with the thick plume my car stirred. I stop where I think I broke into clear air. There isn't room on the shoulder to park, so I hit the hazards and leave the car in the center of the narrow drive. I let the dust settle before stepping out.

There is a breeze, the scent of pine and salt air. Leaves whisper against one another, and I think I can hear the distant crash of the sea, but it could just be wind chasing wind through the branches, or the rustling together of palm fronds.

"Hello?" I call out.

The silence that answers makes me feel silly, makes me want to scurry back to my car and keep driving. I walk along the road instead, and my eyes are drawn to the gravel, to the crushed shells. I'm reminded of the meandering swath of shells that used to lie along the tideline at the beach where I grew up. I remember crawling along that path, even years after I could walk, searching for the rare intact jewel that everyone else had overlooked. Hard not to do that here—like the impulse to search a field of clover for that one mutant with four leaves—

My fixation on the road is the only reason I spot it: a place where the shells spill onto the shoulder. Bits of white and pink mix with the mulch and the sparse grass. The dust has cleared from the air. I search up and down the long drive, but it's just me, my car, the trees, and the soft wind.

The grass is flattened in places. Tire treads. They head into the woods, though there is no drive marked here. Just mulch, a gap in the undergrowth, and enough space between two trees for a car to squeeze through. Peering deeper into the woods, I see a black gate. There's a keypad beside it, glittering in the wan light filtering through the canopy above. I start into the woods, want to explore further, when the cry of a bird jolts my senses, and the darkening hour reminds me that I am expected elsewhere.

Torn and reluctant—duty overpowers my curiosity, and I hurry back to the car. Its red hazard lights throb a mild warning to no one. As I pull away, the double guard gates finally make sense. Whoever comes through the outer gate has access to this hidden drive but not to the house. For all the sense of mystery, I'm certain I've just discovered the rear entrance for the estate's help, which grounds like these invariably have. An access road for the gardeners, the arborists, the housekeepers. I decide to ask the next guard if this is the case. It's a dumb detail, but I'll feel proud for having deduced it all on my own, just from a disappearing trail of dust and little more.

The young guard from my previous visit is manning the inner gate. He steps out of his small booth and holds out a flat palm, signaling me to stop. As if I would bash through his bright blue steel bar if he weren't there to warn me. I have my info ready, including my registration, but he doesn't ask for these. Just asks if I'm okay.

"Uh . . . yeah," I say. "I guess."

The guard frowns at me. "No car troubles?" he asks.

"No." I shake my head.

"It's just that—" He rests his forearms on the roof of my car, leans his head down close. "You checked through the outer gate quite some time ago, is all."

I can smell the coffee on his breath. "Oh, that," I say, and the plan to ask him about the hidden drive vanishes in a puff of paranoid self-preservation. "I saw a cardinal. Haven't seen one in ages. So I got out to take a picture."

He glances toward my bag, which is sitting on the passenger seat. "Get any good shots?" he asks.

"No," I tell him, in case he asks to see. "Never saw it again. Beautiful time of day though. You're lucky that you get to work in an office like this. You should see the view from my desk." I laugh. I realize I'm babbling. It's what I do when I'm nervous.

The guard just smirks. He pats the roof of my car in a way that's mildly possessive, mildly offensive. Like I've said something cute. Like I'm adorable. Like he might pat a waitress on the ass as she passes a booth full of him and his friends.

"Go on in," he says, stepping away from my car. He tips his cap, the bar lifts up, and I hit the gas before he can ask any more questions, or before my mouth can get me in trouble.

-14-

I don't know what I'm expecting when I get to the house. Ness said we would spend the day shelling, so I imagine something extravagant, like a helicopter with its blades slowly spinning, a pilot flipping switches above his head, and word that a private island somewhere is staging for our arrival. Or maybe a large yacht docked behind his estate, a giant crane on its upper deck that scoops sand from the depths and sifts it through complicated onboard troughs to unveil ancient, fragile treasures. Anything other than Ness sitting on the front porch, waiting for me, in a t-shirt and a loud pair of bermuda shorts.

"You're late," he says, glancing at his watch as I get out of the car. The bridge of his nose is white with zinc oxide. As he gets off the bench, he dons an oversized hat with a full brim. All he needs is a bulky camera dangling around his neck to complete the tourist outfit. He looks like he belongs in Times Square, gawking at the electric billboards or getting his picture taken with Spider-Man.

"I got a late start," I tell him. I pop the trunk and grab my two bags, one full of clothes, the other with my snorkel gear, wetsuit, and toiletries. Ness takes both bags from me and leads me into the house.

"First rule of shelling," he says. "Don't be late. Every single thing you do with the ocean depends on the tides, depends on the cycle of the moon." He glances over his shoulder. "It's a lot like relationships."

I think he means to amuse me, but I'm startled instead. I nearly launch into my theory about how shelling is exactly like relationships in hundreds of little ways, but Ness's manic energy has me struggling just to keep up with him. I follow him down a flight of stairs and through a hallway. He has to set one of the bags down to get the door, and then we're out through the back of the house and on a rear deck, facing the Atlantic.

The sun glints off the sea, a field of jewels on a blue tapestry. Waves chase each other in jagged white lines toward the beach. Two peninsulas of rock jut out into the ocean. One is natural; the other was made to look natural, but it curves out and then runs parallel to the beach to shelter a small bay to the north. An empty dock and a boathouse sit in the bay. The boathouse would be a fine main residence anywhere else. Boardwalks and a labyrinth of stairs lead down to the bay as well as to the beach directly below the house—which is where I descended after dark on my last visit. I try to take it all in, but I have to hurry to keep up with Ness.

"I'm putting you in the widow's watch," he tells me. His voice is nearly lost in the hiss of the distant waves and the wind. We descend several flights of wooden stairs, follow a boardwalk that runs parallel to the steep dunes, and head to a house separate from the main estate. An in-law suite. But Ness called it something else. To me, it looks like a dollhouse swelled up to accommodate grown people. A little bigger than my New York apartment, it juts out from the dunes on thick beams. And there appears to be an even smaller house nestled on the roof. Ness lets me in and follows with the bags.

Somehow, the spectacular view outside is even better when framed by the floor-to-ceiling windows along the east side of the house. There's a bed in the middle of the room, facing the view. White linen curtains are pulled back. I imagine the sunrise that will greet me in the morning. The house seems to levitate over the beach, and the windows compress the view to just the sparkling sea. It's a dream. This will be like sleeping out on the clouds.

"Gorgeous," I whisper.

Ness places the bags on the bed, then turns and studies the view for a moment, like he's forgotten what it looks like. I try not to feel dismayed by the possibility that this room hasn't been stepped in by anyone other than the housekeeper for years, that it just sits here empty and unappreciated.

"The better view is up top," he says. "I figured you'd be more comfortable if we weren't under the same roof. Considering my . . . reputation." He smiles at me. Wags his eyebrows. I can't decide if he's being crass or if his sense of humor is just that unseemly. It's like he's forgotten my accusations the other night, or just wants that spat behind us. "Since you write for a living," he says, "I also thought you'd enjoy the reading nook." He leads me to a spiral staircase just off the small kitchen. The metal treads ring as he hurries up. I tear myself away from the view and follow him.

"I built this place for Holly, before she was born," Ness calls down the stairs.

I laugh at the thought. "Most people paint the bedroom they've been using as an office, install a crib, change the outlet covers. You build this."

"It didn't seem like much. My dad bought a chain of islands when I was born and named them after me. *That* seemed excessive."

I swallow any rude response. Several come to me with little bidding. At the top of the stairs, I find myself in the small room nestled on the roof. Four walls of glass, with a cushioned bench running along three of them. Two shelves of books ring the room beneath the bench, and more books are lined up along the deep sills. Ness cranks one of the windows open—they're the kind with a spinning lever at their base. I turn and work the window opposite him. The sea breeze courses through the small space, whistling its way inside, between us, and then back out again. I glance up at the exposed beams overhead where a wind chime made of seashells softly rattles.

"Holly never really took to the place. It was my fault for making her sleep out here by herself when she was little. She got scared, tried to find her way back to the house in the middle of the night, and got lost." Ness opens the door on the front of the small room and steps out onto the deck. He invites me to join him, then points down at the boardwalk leading toward the enclosed bay. "She fell asleep behind the rocks down there, out of the wind. I found her the next morning. It was the first really big fight Vicky and I ever had. I don't think Holly has been in this house since. I just use it for guests now. Replaced all the children's books with classics." He waves his hand at the collection behind us. "I don't think any of them have even been cracked."

"Must've hurt, finding her out there." I peer down at the rocks and think about what it must've been like for his daughter, running around in the pitch black, the crashing sea deafening and the wind chapping her face with her tears.

"I think I've overcorrected since then. Never really put pressure on her to be adventurous, to try new things. I have more regrets over all the stuff I *didn't* do later in life than I do over that night."

If this were a normal person, a normal conversation, I would ask how old his daughter is. But it's Ness Wilde, so I know she's twelve. If this were a normal person, a normal conversation, I might reach out and place a hand on his arm, let him know he's not alone, that we all have regrets, that I feel his sadness, and that I'm sorry for him. But it's not a normal conversation. In fact, I feel a sudden out-of-body sensation, the same surreal and disjointed feeling I felt in the White House, shaking the President's hand. Like the Earth is tilting beneath me.

As my sister would say, my life is already strange enough day to day, with devoted readers recognizing my name as I make a reservation or hand them my credit card to buy groceries, that it takes the truly absurd before I realize how dumb lucky I am, how bizarre my life is. I'm standing above this commanding view with one of the most infamous and now most inaccessible men on the planet. Moments like this come with my job, but some still fill me with vertigo.

"I'm sorry, what did you call this place?" I ask Ness, trying to reel myself back down to reality. "Some kind of a watch?"

"A widow's watch," he says, perking up. He seems just as glad for the change in topic. The breeze tries to steal away his hat, but he grabs it in time and tucks it under his arm. He points toward the horizon. "A lot of the houses up and down the coast here had these before the sea swallowed them. They don't build them as much anymore. Back in the day, women whose men went to sea would sit up here and watch for the sails that told them their husbands were returning. Often, they would come up and watch the empty horizon long after there was any hope. I have to admit, it's a morbid name, when you think about the literal meaning."

"I think it's sweet," I say. I stop myself from saying "romantic." But that's what I mean. The idea of such powerful longing, of hoping for a return, a reunion, is incredibly desirable. Most of the relationships I've been in lately, one or the other party was just looking for a way out, not a way back.

"Well, we've already missed the tide, and now it's more my fault than yours, but if you want to get changed, we'll hit the beach. I've got a very precise sequence of days laid out to show you where those shells came from."

Ness shields his eyes and studies the shore below. Then he peers down the coast, and I turn and notice the lighthouse for the first time. The widow's watch is just high enough, and the guest house juts out of the dunes just far enough, to see the tall pillar of mortar and stone sitting on the high bluff south of the estate.

"You brought sandals, right?" Ness asks. "The boardwalk will be warm. You can kick them off once we get to the beach."

"We're shelling right *here?*" I try not to sound disappointed. It would be anyone else's dream. "It's just . . . I would've thought those shells you showed me came from someplace far away from here, someplace exotic. I mean, no one's seen a lace murex in years. And the quality—"

"They didn't come from all that far away, in fact." Ness turns and heads back inside. I follow him, close the door behind me, and we take the stairs. "Besides, we're not going to look for the murexes right now. I've got to show you what led me to them. It was years in the making, but I think I can tell the story in a week."

"Why not just show me the molds?" I say, unable to stop myself from coming right out and doubting their veracity. "I was thinking maybe you move other slugs in, like a different species, after the shells are cast."

Ness laughs. "You're jumping ahead."

"Of course I am. I'm a reporter. As much as I look forward to the shelling, I want to know where the murexes came from. I want to see this mythical beach you seem to believe in where extinct shells just roll up with nary a mark on them."

Ness stops at the bottom of the stairs. Turns to me. "Let's say you wrote a piece in four parts," he says. "Each part is thousands of words long. And your readers decide to skip all the way to the last paragraph of the last part and read only that. What would you think?"

"I think that would suck," I say.

"Exactly," Ness says. "So don't suck. Let me show you the whole story. No skipping ahead. Promise?"

I hesitate. Ness gives me that intense look of his, that unwavering gaze. "I promise," I finally say. And then, perhaps because of the morbid nature of the guest house, I add: "Hope to die."

"That's the spirit. And don't worry, I'm going to show you where the shells came from, but I want you to understand a little history first. See what led me to them. Which means you're going to have to tolerate my little cliffhangers."

"I think you probably mean teasers this time," I tell him. "And I feel like you're just delaying this because whatever you're doing with those shells isn't legal."

"Oh, it's not legal," Ness admits. "It's highly illegal. But you promised not to jump ahead."

-15-

I'm not sure how I can jump ahead when it's difficult enough just to keep up. I'm a fast walker. You can't live in New York City without also being on the cusp of qualifying for the speedwalk event at any given Olympics. And yet I find myself trotting across the boardwalks and taking stairs at an unsafe clip, while Ness seems to casually stroll ahead of me.

"There used to be homes all along here," he says.

I descend the last set of stairs and find myself back on the beach I visited a few nights ago. I kick off my sandals. Ness and I both have our shelling bags, our hats pulled down tight against the breeze, the smell of sunscreen in the air. Scanning the beach, I see why the bay is so loud. The two jetties of rock—the natural one and the manmade one—funnel the sea up the beach. They also corral the noise, so you get the crash of the ocean as well as the echoes of those crashes. Sound waves pile up like sea waves, overlapping and amplifying. In an east swell, I imagine the break here is amazing. It makes me wish I'd brought my board.

"So did the sea take the homes that used to lie along here, or did you?" I ask Ness. It's an honest question, but it sounds harsh now that it's out in the air. As if I mean to say that, either way, his family had a part in clearing out whatever beach communities used to lie here, either by purchase or by environmental ruin.

"The sea took them," Ness says. "We like to build on the edge, don't we? Right on the edge of disaster. Because if we don't, it leaves room for someone *else* to build between us and whatever it is we desire. We're all like Icarus in that way." Ness points toward the natural jetty to the south. "Let's walk the shell line this way."

"Icarus flew too close to the sun," I point out. "That story is about ambition."

"The story is about understanding nature's limits," Ness claims. "It's about craving more than we can possess. It's about ego. And don't forget, it was the sea that killed him. Not the sun. Icarus drowned."

A periwinkle catches my eye. I stoop to pick it up and add it to my bag.

"There's a better one just over there," Ness tells me. He points an impossible distance away. I can't tell if he sees the shell or if he knows it's there from being down on the beach earlier that day. I inspect my specimen. It's the finest shell I've picked off a beach in years. The lip is cracked, the crown chipped, a hole straight through the apex, and the interior is dull from too much time in the sun. But it's gorgeous. Rare. I slip it into the bag.

"A week from now, you'll step right over that shell," Ness tells me.

"I hope you're wrong," I say. "I don't want to ever get like that."

He shrugs. I see a nutmeg and an auger. Both worn. I wonder how long they've been bouncing along on this beach, no one here to pick them up, to rescue them.

"Are you old enough to remember when everyone had shelling stories?" Ness asks.

"I'm not much younger than you," I say. "But thanks for asking."

He turns and smiles at me. I have to remind myself that his family made their fortune by ruining the world. And while the rest of us agonized over the floods and the erosion and news of every sea life extinction, Ness was at a fancy college, rowing boats, getting into trouble, always smiling, always having a good time, not a care in the world. I am constantly reminding myself of this around him. My story is not going to change. I'm just here to write a second story, the story of the lace murexes.

"So, I have a theory on why we don't hear shelling stories like we used to," he says. "Why those stories suddenly stopped a few decades ago."

"You mean because shells have become vanishingly rare? Because sea life is going extinct?" I stop myself from spelling out the ecological disaster that led to this. Or pointing out that most people don't have gas-burning cars in their garages any more.

"Good shells have been hard to find for a long time, but when the fad hit, and the magazines for collectors came out, and the stupid shows hit cable TV—the *Shell Hunters, Diving for Sand Dollars*, all that nonsense—there was a flurry of boasts, but then everyone clammed up. No pun intended."

"Lightning whelk," I say, retrieving a half-buried shell and seeing that only the lip is chipped. A stunning specimen. I put it in the higher pocket of my shelling bag so it doesn't rub against any of the others.

"Nice find," Ness says. He seems sincere. I note he has yet to pick up a shell. The wind catches the end of his empty bag and twists it and flaps it around. "And then *News Journal* did their big piece about the value of shells, and within weeks, they all seemed to disappear." Ness snaps his fingers. "Which isn't possible. What really happened, I think, is that everyone shut up about their finds. Not just *where* they found them, but that they'd found anything at all. It was about this time that people started calling what you and I do the latest Dutch Tulip Craze."

I notice that he lumps us together, me and him, as if our shelling is anything alike.

"People were getting up at four in the morning, three in the morning, two in the morning, and grabbing every shell they could scoop up. Shells kept rolling in, but someone would be there immediately to take them. Nobody trusted anyone else not to follow them to their favorite spot. You remember when just a handful of cars by a remote beach would cause rumors and then traffic jams?"

"I remember," I say. "My dad used to wake us up in the middle of the night, say he got a tip from a friend, or just had a feeling, or that some storm had just hit the beach, and we'd get dressed, grab our bags and flashlights, and jump in the car. It was the only time he let me eat fast food. That's what I remember the most, when I was young. Breakfast biscuits in the middle of the night."

The memory is so clear: my mom and dad in the front seat, me and my sister leaning up between them, my mom telling us to buckle up. I pretend to study the sand, lowering myself to one knee, and wipe my eyes.

"It was twenty years before the shells really thinned out," Ness says. "I mean, they were dying off before. The reefs were dying long before that. Have you ever been to the Great Barrier Reef?"

"No," I say.

"You should go. Everyone should, as soon as they can. I went when the reefs were at ten percent of their former glory, and I remember thinking before I flew down there, 'Why bother?' But you should have seen the reefs then. And if you wait another ten years, you'll kick yourself for not seeing them now." Ness points toward something a dozen paces away. "Imperial venus. Still intact. But you're more of a gastropod girl than a bivalve, aren't you?"

I find the shell he's referring to. The two halves are still joined by a sturdy hinge. Shades of pink slide into ivory white. I slide the gorgeous shell into the padded bivalve pouch along the lip of my bag. "I like both," I say. "I've always loved shells. And I can see your point. My dad got real secretive about our favorite shelling spots. And I remember him and my mom arguing about whether it made more sense to stay up until one in the morning or go to sleep early and set alarms for two. It got crazy there for a few years."

"Exactly. But even my grandfather had memories like that. Back in the eighties, people still got up early on vacation to beat their neighbors down to the beach. Shellers watched the tides. And my dad used to tell me about snorkelers beyond the breakers when he was a kid, swimmers trailing bags of finds behind them—"

"And now people use subs and cranes," I say. "They mine for them like minerals. They use abandoned oil platforms. Takes the romance out of it, don't you think?"

Ness inspects a shell on the beach, then places it back where he found it. "I think it can," he admits. "But not always. One of the most romantic places I've ever seen was a gem mine. The way the walls sparkled in our flashlights. Water dripping everywhere. It was industrial, sure, but it was intensely beautiful."

All I can imagine is it being intense. Overbearing. Then again, the sea is throwing up walls of foam right beside me, roaring like a great, incessant engine, churning up the waters and depositing small finds upon the beach. To me, nothing gets more romantic, more hauntingly lovely, than this setting right here, and yet the surf can be a dangerous and deadly place.

"I don't want to skip ahead," I say, "but I'm guessing the murexes didn't wash up here."

"This is the first stage of shelling," Ness says. "Walking the tideline. Picking through whatever is deposited here. The history of what we've done to the sea can be told in where we do our shelling. It started on the beach, where a distant abundance of life allowed shells to leak out at the edges. There used to be so much life that it appeared where it was never meant to. You need to see this to understand how my journey started. Because it started with an idea."

"What idea is that?" I ask.

Ness stops and turns to me. The wind toys with the brim of his hat. He holds up a shell for a moment before tossing it back to the beach. "You and me," he says. "We collect dead things."

-16-

I used to tell Michael until his ears bled all the ways that shelling is the greatest metaphor for relationships. I told him this a thousand times, back when we were married. He got sick of hearing it, but I have hundreds of examples, and now here's one more: Be careful of the bounty you pine for.

This came to me after my first day of shelling with Ness, which was both the best day of shelling that I've ever had and also the most disappointing. Maybe disappointing is the wrong word. How about *unsatisfying*.

Just as with relationships, you think you know what you want, but once you have it, the hole you thought it would fill is that much bigger. The *want* is what exists, not the thing we lust after.

I feel very Buddhist, thinking this. I've arranged myself in the reading nook at the top of the guest house, my spoils for the day arranged on the bench around me. I washed the sand off them in the sink and dabbed each shell dry with one of the terrycloth towels from the bathroom. None of the specimens are flawless. None are museum-quality. But there are at least four shells here that are in better condition and of rarer variety than any shell I own. And I scooped them all off a single beach in a single afternoon in *daylight*. The shells in my apartment back home represent two decades of striving. What I collected today was just too easy, and so the victory feels a tad hollow. A little depressing.

The lighthouse to the south swings its beam through the reading nook, and I think back to Jacob Sullivan, my first boyfriend in high school. It's not our first kiss that I remember, it's the sudden ownership of a boy that I could kiss at will. The night we made out for the first time—after we had taken a break because of him fumbling for my belt and freaking me out—I remember leaning forward and kissing him on the lips just because I could. Any time I wanted. The forbidden and impossible were now at my beck and call.

So many shells arranged around me. And there's the knowledge that I could go for more. There's a beach beyond my door that I won't have access to forever. There's a flashlight. My bag. Half a moon. I am dying to lean out for another kiss, to pour goodness into emptiness faster than it can leak out.

But part of me is worried that I can't take these shells home. Not that I don't have permission—Ness told me whatever I pick up this week is mine to do with as I please—but that it will break something inside me to add this bounty to what I have labored to collect over the past twenty-odd years. It would be like bringing a harem home to join an otherwise monogamous relationship. The sudden infusion of so much threatens to cheapen the intense enjoyment of so little.

I convince myself that it's okay, that I can consider this later, even as I decide to go out for more. I grab the flashlight and a light jacket, leave my pajama bottoms on, and work my way down the boardwalk and the flights of stairs. For a moment, I imagine what Ness's daughter must've felt out here that night, alone, as a young child. Ness says the lamps were added to the boardwalk after the event, that he hates the light pollution, but that his ex-wife insisted. And now he just leaves them on.

I wonder if there isn't some deeper reason that he leaves the lamps burning. The lighthouse throbs against the high clouds, and I think of the signals we put out without knowing, the invitations, the warnings. I think of the way I left my social media status as "married" until a year after the divorce was final. Some part of me wanted Michael to know that it was okay to come back, to watch that reef, that rocky shoreline, that it can be dangerous around here, but look: a clear path to safe harbor. If you choose.

I don't know what I'm looking for on the beach. Nothing, maybe. In a literal sense. What I hope to see is a blank expanse of sand, exactly what I'm used to, for the world to make sense again. When Michael left, after we lost our child, the suitors were endless. Men I had thought were friends. Coworkers I didn't know I had. From life in high school and college where dates were nearly impossible to find, to this . . . scared me. Something was wrong. There were shells everywhere I looked. I assumed they were fake. Lies.

Not much has changed. Abundance frightens me. Or maybe I believe that I only deserve joy when it's hard to come by.

I'm only a hundred meters down the beach when I see someone heading my way. The bob and weave of a flashlight. Ness and I didn't talk much over dinner. I was too stunned from the shelling, and he seemed content to leave me to my thoughts. But something changed between us, a sheathing of my sword and a lowering of his shield. An unspoken promise, perhaps, to not play roles this week. To just be.

It was a dangerous sensation. I was reminded over dinner that what I've mocked from afar, what I've learned to loathe, is only a caricature of Ness. The actual man is just that—a man. However flawed. And it's hard not to feel something being alone with him. It has nothing to do with what he represents, only that we're nearly the same age, apparently single, and spending hours alone together along this spectacular beach.

I watch the flashlight approach. All around me are shells scattered in the sand; they flash wet and shine in the beam of my flashlight. I would rather they be pared down to one. A sensible number. The absence of choice. Take these thousand lies and give me one thing that's real. Something I can cling to, believe in, and trust.

Ness is coming down the walkway for me. He has sought me out while I have gone looking for answers of my own. And I'm in a weakened state, thinking of Michael, of all the opportunities missed, of the sad existence of that lighthouse to the south, spinning its warning, unable to break from its foundations and join the little lights out at sea. Stuck. Dire.

If Ness comes to me and stands too close, I might throw my arms around him. I might cling to him and sob, like a near-drowned sailor who has found a rock. Not because I want him, but because I feel horribly alone here, with the sea crashing at my back, my mind swimming with wine and with recollections, my heart pounding and empty, my emotions strung out like a piano wire.

If he leans into me, I may not resist. I hate myself for this. I loathe myself in that moment, and I know I'll hate myself even more tomorrow, but I feel in that split second the need to be needed, and I see myself down where the sand is packed and cool, an arm beneath my neck, lips pressed against mine, the lingering scent of coconut and sunscreen and the Merlot we had with dinner, and the mad, selfish, insane desire to be kissed by someone, even him, and told that everything will be all right—

"Ms. Walsh?"

The beam lances me in the face. I recoil and throw my arm up to defend myself.

"Sorry, ma'am." And the light drops to my feet. "Saw the alarm go off. Thought we were being raided again."

I catch the glint of a gun before it's holstered. I see the uniform, the bright buckle, the shield on the chest. It's the young guard from the second gate. He must work the late shift.

"You should be careful out here," he tells me. "We get people coming in by boat now and then to take shells. Infrared cameras usually spot them, but all the same it's not safe to be out here alone."

I hadn't thought of this. I'm walking around in the middle of a jewelry store, my flashlight not a beacon of warning but an invitation. "Sorry," I say.

"I can join you if you like. You lookin' for anything in particular?"

I don't know if it's because of my state or something in the way he says this, something in the way he takes another step toward me, closer than would be comfortable, but this offer sounds like a proposition. He's either being helpful or coming on to me, and as it tends to work with men, I have no idea which.

"I'm fine," I say. I no longer feel like shelling. I no longer feel like company. If this man were to touch me, I would scream. His gun makes me feel *less* safe, not more so. "I was just restless. I think I should go to bed. We're getting an early start tomorrow."

I glance up at the main house, where nothing moves.

"You sure?" the guard asks.

"Yeah," I say. I take a step back toward the boardwalk that leads up to the guest house. "I appreciate it, though."

"Because Mr. Wilde lets me shell here any time I want. I don't mind joining you."

"No, that's all right. I appreciate it."

I turn to go. A small beam of light follows me, and another one, larger, arcs across the sky. I am in a dangerous place. I am in a wild place. I wish I could say that reefs were all around me, but the threats I feel all lie within.

-17-

The following morning, I am awoken by a glowing horizon, by a blooming dawn. No alarm bleeping at six, no traffic noise, no blaring horns or car alarms, no urban cave with curtains closed tight, no headache or grogginess— just the trickling awareness that it is a new day, a slow slide to consciousness, rolling around in fine sheets while the sound of a crashing sea permeates the walls.

It isn't even six yet, and I'm wide awake and rested. A breeze swirls down from upstairs, where I must've left a window open. In the small kitchen, there's one of those capsule coffee makers. I choose a dark roast and find a mug in the third cabinet I try. Peeking inside the fridge, I find basic staples: milk, eggs, butter, sliced deli meat, cheese. None of it is opened. I'm dying to meet Ness's housekeeper. Things are seemingly done by magic around here.

While the coffee is brewing, I decide to take a quick shower. The walls of the shower stall are made of transparent bricks the colors of sea glass. I watch the sunrise through them as I soap up and rinse off. It occurs to me that someone on the boardwalk could see my silhouette inside the shower, which makes me feel suddenly exposed. I decide not to care.

I chalk the lack of concern up to my general good mood. And I chalk up the good mood to the great day of shelling the day before. It's human, I think, to be buoyed by a sudden increase in resources. This is how I try to be clinical about my rising spirits, rather than trust or embrace them. It helps me forget the moment of abject weakness the night before and what might've happened if Ness had been the one to find me on the beach.

I towel off and put on a clean bathing suit, a sundress over top. The coffee waits beneath the brewer. I take a sip and find it passable for instant brew. The worrier in me is troubled by how absolutely perfect the first half hour of my day has gone. I expect trouble ahead to balance it all out.

Watching the sunrise from the deck, I cup my mug in both hands and enjoy its warmth. Several gulls cry and chase along the beach, and I try to remember the last time I saw more than one or two sea birds together in the wild. I spot at least four here, a sign of some feeble life in this corner of the sea. I remember being a kid and seeing dozens of birds at a time: high-flying Vs of seagulls and low-gliding pelicans whose wingtips seemed to graze the water. I remember tossing french fries from the aft deck of a ferry once, and not a single fry reaching the ship's wake; they were gobbled up mid-air by a hovering flock of birds. Years later, on the same ferry, you could toss bread over the rail and nothing would come to claim it. The bread would disappear in the water. Michael told me to stop wasting it.

One of the crying gulls over Ness's beach tucks in its wings and plummets into the sea, sending up a small geyser. I'm too far away to see whether or not there's a fish in its beak as it reemerges, but the two birds that immediately give chase let me know breakfast is on. I feel like a child again, witnessing a glimpse of the secret goings-on of Mother Nature. And just as quickly, I'm saddened that such a banal scene has become a rarity to treasure.

There's a tremble in the wood rail. I turn toward the house to see Ness descending my way. Probably been watching for any sign that I was up. He has two large duffel bags, one on each shoulder, the straps crisscrossed over his chest. They look heavy, just judging by the way they're pinned to his hips and not swaying. But Ness moves down the steps like they weigh nothing at all.

"Good morning," he says.

I lift my mug in salute. Ness drops the bags, lifting the straps over his head, and they thud and clank to the deck. "You brought your fins and mask?"

I nod. "Are we going snorkeling today?"

"I had planned to. But something may come up this week that I'll have to attend to. Just in case, I thought we'd skip ahead to diving."

"I don't dive," I tell him. "Never have."

"Well, today you start. Have you had breakfast?"

I shake my head.

"Eggs? I'll make some eggs and toast. You take cheese in your eggs?"

"Sure," I say.

Ness lets himself inside. I stay on the porch and enjoy the feel of the first rays of sunlight slicing through the morning chill. The air feels dry, the day promising to be warm. I glance down at the duffel bags, butterflies in my stomach. Michael tried to get me certified during our honeymoon in the Caymans. I was too scared to go through with it, chickened out on the side of the pool, said I wanted to spend our honeymoon not feeling any pressure. What I felt the rest of the week was the burn of his disappointment.

Funny how that disappointment made me never want to get certified, even after Michael left, and even though most of my friends dive. So much baggage. Heavier than those duffels with their tanks and all that gear. I watch Ness busy himself in the kitchen, whisking eggs, and consider the decision I need to make. Refuse to get in the water once again? Or, for the sake of the story, soldier through?

For the story, I tell myself. Because I'm a professional. Not because I want to. Not because of any pressure or fear of disappointment. I can't let this be about that. I can't be thirty-two, making more of this day—any unimportant day—than I made of my honeymoon nine years ago. But I can't make the same mistakes, either. I can't let every opportunity pass me by.

-18-

After a quick breakfast on the deck, we carry the duffels down to the manmade breakwater and the enclosed bay with the docks and boathouse. I insist on carrying one of the bags. It must weigh fifty pounds once I add my fins, mask, and wetsuit. I let Ness walk ahead of me and thank my Pilates instructor that I'm able to haul the bag without complaint. In fact, I feel strong. Maybe it's the coffee or the good night of sleep, or the day on the beach, but I feel a power in my limbs. I feel courage and conviction. I'm going to learn to breathe underwater.

Ness leads me across the beach and to the boathouse. At the end of the dock, a metal ramp leads down to a floating platform. The ramp is hinged on both sides so it can move with the tides. There are cleats here for smaller boats to dock up. We set the bags down, and Ness flips a smaller ramp into the water. It's a beach entry for launching kayaks and the like. I imagine we'll be walking down this ramp and into the bay.

"A few safety rules," Ness says. He starts unpacking his bag, and I follow along and do the same with the gear in my bag. "You don't dive deeper than sixty feet, and you don't stay that deep for more than ten minutes."

"How will I know?"

He shows me a fat wristwatch with a black rubber band. "You've got one of these in your bag. It shows your depth, how much air you have left, and how long you've been diving. I'll teach you how to use it. Don't worry, it's simple."

"Sixty feet. Ten minutes," I repeat. I really don't want to die. I don't want this story to turn into an obituary. My heart is racing, and it occurs to me that I'm placing my life in the hands of a man I barely trust.

"The most important thing is not to be nervous," he says, like he can read my mind. "If you're nervous, you'll breathe heavy, and you'll go through your tank in no time. Stay calm and breathe deep, nice and slow, and you'll be able to enjoy the dive longer."

I nod. This feels a lot like a piece I wrote years ago, which got me into surfing. I was terrified at first, but I eventually found my footing. The root of a good interview is to throw yourself into someone else's world with wild abandon. Seek new and scary things. It occurs to me that I could've been a better spouse if I'd approached my marriage the way I tackle my work.

Inside the dive bag, I find a black steel tank. The one in Ness's bag is bright pink. I like that he doesn't ask to switch, just begins showing me how to hook up what he calls the first stage of the regulator to the tank. He then teaches me how to check the small rubber ring on the tank, make sure there's no sand or debris there, how to crack the main valve and listen to the hiss of air, and how to blow out any water that might be in the valve. We then begin to hook up the tangle of hoses to the tanks.

"Mine feels loose," I say. Everything is a worry. A possible danger.

"That's good. You want it a little loose. It'll tighten when you open the tank. The air will blow that rubber gasket out."

That doesn't sound like a good thing, but I crack the valve, and sure enough, the regulator stiffens where it's attached to the top of the tank. Ness shows me how to test the air flow from what he calls the "second stage" or "regulator." I press the button, and the mouthpiece hisses. Ness puts his in his mouth and takes a deep breath. I do the same, not knowing what to expect the air to taste like. It doesn't. Maybe a little metallic from the tank, or a little plasticky from the hose, but that could be my imagination.

"Okay, second safety rule. When you ascend, you're always exhaling, okay?"

"Ascending is going up," I say, knowing this is right but seeking confirmation just in case. My temples are throbbing and it's hard to think. I really don't want to die because I assumed something or because I didn't want to look stupid in front of someone I barely know.

"Correct. When you go down, the pressure of the water around you will compress the air in your lungs and make it take up less volume. But you'll be filling your lungs with new air. So when you come up, that air is going to expand. As long as you're breathing out the entire time, that expanding air can't hurt you."

I start to say something, but Ness continues. "Don't worry, we won't be going deep enough or stay down long enough to get the bends."

That answers my next question.

"There are a few things that can freak you out when you're diving, and that's the regulator coming out of your mouth, your mask filling with water, and losing your sense of which way is up. We're going to put our tanks on, walk down this ramp, and I'm going to show you how to deal with all three. Twenty minutes of instruction, and you're going to be a pro."

Ness smiles, and I believe he's being sincere, that he knows what he's doing, that I'm going to live through this day, which started out a bit too perfectly and would be nicely balanced by a gruesome death. In fact, this would be one quick way to put an end to my questions about the shells. I flash to an image of a police boat there at the dock, blue lights flashing, my inert body being hauled up from the break wall, Ness saying he doesn't know what went wrong. I think back to how calmly he crushed shells that should've been worth a fortune. Getting rid of me would be like getting rid of more damning evidence.

"Don't be scared," Ness says. I refocus to find that he's watching me, a look of genuine concern on his face. What I assume is genuine concern.

"I'm fine," I say. "Just spaced out. What's next?"

Ness shows me how to attach the tank to something called a BC, then shows me my weight belt, which explains, besides the tank, why the duffel bag was so heavy. I take off my sundress, thinking as I do that at least my sister and Agent Cooper know where I am. Henry, too. No matter what happens, Ness won't get away with it. And anyway, I'm being paranoid. Unreasonable. Whatever Ness is, he isn't a killer.

I drill this into my head as I squeeze into my wetsuit, which is an act as awkward and oddly intimate as getting re-dressed past airport security. But Ness is donning his own suit, and he doesn't glance my way once. He's either uninterested or a gentleman. And there's a vast gulf between the two.

"I would've thought you'd hire a dive master to be here, doing all this for you," I tell him.

"I *am* a dive master," Ness says.

"No, of course, I assumed you would be, what with your shelling experience. I just mean—"

"You mean hiring someone else to do half-ass what I can do for myself." He smiles at me.

"I guess. Yeah." What I really meant was: *If you're trying to murder me, it's smart not to have witnesses, and I'm on to you, buddy.*

"If it makes you feel better, I have Monique packing us a picnic lunch. And Vincent, who takes care of my cars, is going to get the boat ready for us. I don't do everything around here."

"Monique?" I ask.

"My housekeeper. You've got your valve on? Air flowing?"

I press the button on my regulator, and there's a loud blast of air. Ness lifts the BC—which is like an uninflated vest that the tank straps to—and helps me get my arms through. There's a hose that runs from the top of the tank to the vest. Ness shows me what to press to inflate the vest and how to let the air out. With this and the right amount of weight around my waist, he says I can stay level at any depth. And if I need to get to the surface, I can just inflate the vest and enjoy the ride. "Just breathe out the entire time," he reminds me.

I wonder if I should tell him that when I panic, I tend to either not breathe or hyperventilate. Instead, I tell myself, over and over, to always breathe. To exhale. *And to stay fucking calm, Maya, you're not going to die.*

"It's not deep at the bottom of the ramp, so remember that you can always stand up if you're uncomfortable for any reason. And I'll be right there beside you."

"Okay," I mumble around my mouthpiece. I get my mask situated. Ness has me leave my fins off for now. Walking carefully—all that weight on my back threatening to topple me over—I follow Ness down the ramp. I don't understand how people enjoy a sport that involves so much heavy and bulky gear. I feel exhausted already, and I haven't even started doing the actual diving.

I'm so nervous shuffling down the ramp—the water creeping up my ankles and then my knees—that I don't notice Ness is holding my hand or that I'm holding his. Or that he's steadying me, another hand on my shoulder. All I feel is the coolness of the morning sea rising up, the initial shock before my wetsuit fills with water. It takes a moment until the water is trapped and warmed by my body, and then it's no longer so bracingly cold. I also notice how the weight of all the gear disappears now that I'm in the water. It's only awkward on dry land, like a fish staggering along on its poor fins.

"When you're ready, just lower your head beneath the surface and take easy breaths," Ness says. "It's just like snorkeling."

This is not like snorkeling, I want to say. But I can't scream over my pounding pulse, can't talk with the regulator in my mouth. Snorkeling is breathing through a plastic tube sticking up in the air. No physics involved. No warnings needed. A child can sort out how that works. This is me strapped to a contraption, a deflated vest on, tubes hanging everywhere, a bulky watch on my wrist blinking with all kinds of numbers. This is not snorkeling.

I descend until my feet leave the ramp and find the sand. The water is up to my chest. Ness is watching me. My visor has already fogged from the nervous heat of my cheeks. I take the mask off, dunk it into the water, consider spitting inside it to keep it from fogging, would normally do this, but not in front of Ness. I put the mask back on. It's now or never.

"I'm right here," Ness says softly. "You'll be fine."

I nod, gather my courage, and remind myself that people do this all the time. I'm already breathing through the contraption, aren't I? I realize that I'm breathing a lot. Huffing and puffing. I hear the hiss of my exhalations. I remember what Ness said about being calm, about breathing easy, and I try. I really try.

"Here goes," I mumble incomprehensibly.

I bend my knees, lower my body, and the water comes up to my neck, and then my chin, and then over my mouth, up my visor, the weights around my waist helping me sink under, until I'm seeing the sand and the rocks and the ramp through my mask. A silver fish flits past, chasing after some unseen breakfast. And I hear a hiss as I breathe in, see bubbles as I exhale, and I'm doing it. I'm breathing underwater. Tears blur my vision. I blink them away. There are clams or some kind of bivalve growing over the rocks that make up the breakwater. Small fish peck at the algae along the rocks, signs of life clinging where it can. An entire world of feeble life surviving here.

And I'm among them. Floating. Face-down. Under the water. Ness's hands are on my stomach and on my shoulder, steadying me, and I'm breathing. I scoop the water ahead of me, swim forward, allowing myself to drift a little deeper, and even though I'm slowly sinking, it feels like I'm flying.

-19-

It takes me half an hour to get comfortable removing my mask underwater, putting it back on, and then "clearing it." This last part requires breathing out through my nose while I pin the top of my mask to my forehead with both hands. The water around my eyes is gradually replaced with exhaled air from the tank. Opening my eyes without being able to reach inside my mask to wipe them feels strange and burns a little, but I survive the ordeal. Ness makes me do it two more times.

He also teaches me how to put the regulator back in my mouth underwater, press the purge button, and start breathing air instead of the Atlantic. It feels weird, the forced blast of air filling my mouth and puffing my cheeks, but I decide I can survive this as well. I feel like an astronaut undergoing emergency NASA training. I'm no longer terrified to get to the beach and do some diving. I'm almost excited. Ness helps me out of the water and up the ramp, when I hear him mention something about getting the boat ready.

"Where are we diving, exactly?" I ask. "Just off the beach, right?"

"No, we're going a little ways offshore. There's a great wreck I want you to see and some good shelling spots. Don't worry, it's not deep."

"Sixty feet ten minutes," I say, partly to myself. I gather my soaked hair into a bun and squeeze the water out. Ness is laughing at my worried mumbling, but he seems tickled by it rather than mocking.

"There's Vincent," he says.

I turn and see a man in tan coveralls standing in front of the boathouse. Olive skin, thick mustache, dark hair. He has a real cigarette between his lips, not one of those vapes. He rubs his hands with a white rag. The pointy white bow of a center console is visible inside the open doors of the boathouse, which Vincent must've been working on while I was learning how to not drown.

"Boat's ready, boss," he calls out, seeing us looking his way.

The entire spectacle of Vincent—with the cigarette and mustache and coveralls—is just too cliché. As is this calling Ness "boss." The most annoying part of my job as a journalist is when I have to *leave out* details to make a story more believable. Life has a way of being both more surreal and more predictable than readers can tolerate.

Ness, of course, is oblivious to this. He just waves his thanks.

Beyond the boathouse, a slender woman in a white mid-thigh dress descends the steps from the boardwalk. She has a basket in one hand, a small cooler in the other. "Vincent will get that," Ness tells me, as I bend to collect our dive gear. "I want you to meet Monique."

We walk to the boathouse in our dripping wetsuits. I suddenly feel aware of the tight-fitting neoprene. It's the two people who *aren't* wearing dive suits who make me self-conscious. I shake Vincent's hand as we meet on the boardwalk, and then he heads over to retrieve our duffel bags, tanks, BCs, and the rest of our gear.

"Hey Monique, this is the reporter from the *Times* I told you about."

I shake Monique's hand, noting that Ness has mentioned me before and that I'm "the reporter."

"Pleased to meet you," she says. A hint of a French accent. Another detail I would choose to leave out, but I've already decided to edit Monique out of the story altogether. I tell myself it's for the sake of believability.

"Your favorite sandwiches," she says to Ness. "Fruit. A salad. I put a selection of drinks in the cooler, wasn't sure what your friend would want." She smiles at me.

I try to smile back. The annoyance I feel is hard to place— might just be the infernal cattiness I sometimes sink into around women when we first meet, which usually dissipates once we get to know each other. I worry for a moment that my attempt at a smile looks more like a sneer. I'm trying, I swear.

"Sounds delicious," Ness says, studying the supplies. "You know how famished I get after a dive."

"Of course," Monique says. And to me: "Nice to meet you. Good shelling."

I'd forgotten we were going after shells. The diving and the boat and the introductions have me scattered. I try to remember that this is going to be a perfect day. *Not* a day for dying. Or being murdered.

Vincent arrives with the gear, and I jump in the boat to take the tanks from him. The smell of the gas engine, the vinyl seats, the rot on the low-tide pilings, the gurgle of the idling outboards, all remind me of days out on the water with my dad. He kept our boat on the grass beside the driveway, and the salt water from the bilge kept a patch of the yard brown and lifeless.

Surprisingly, Ness's boat isn't much nicer than the one we grew up with. There's a small cuddy cabin up front. A bait well in the floor. Dad kept our bait well full of closed cell foam for nestling the shells in. When the shelling was bad, we'd cast nets for bait and come home with fish instead. We weren't allowed to come home empty-handed. It sometimes meant staying out after dark, which was when he taught me to recognize the lights of the boats on the water. Green over white for trawling. Red over white for fishing. All those twinkling, colorful constellations meant something to my father. The amount of time a buoy flashed— long, short, short—and he knew right where he was.

I miss him powerfully in that moment, standing aboard Ness's boat, packing away the gear, all these things I did when I was eight that I do now at thirty-two. So much like Dad's boat that I almost expect to turn and see him there, standing behind the wheel, telling me to cast off the lines, but it's Ness saying it. He's as old as my father was when he used to take me out. So young in retrospect, but Dad seemed impossibly ancient to me at the time. I thought I'd never be as old as he was, and yet here I am. And here he isn't.

"You're all clear," I tell Ness, taking the last of the dock lines from Vincent. The mechanic pulls the dangling cigarette from his lips, smiles, and waves bon voyage. Pilings and the walls of the boathouse slide by, and then the low sun hits us again, and we are in the bay, pulling away. Monique and Vincent watch us with shielded eyes before they turn to tidy up.

"Sunscreen," Ness reminds me. He hands me a bottle, and I start applying it to my face and neck. The wind picks up, and I lean with Ness against the wide bench seat behind the console. I watch him navigate the breakers, and I enjoy the thrum of the deck and the rise and fall of the bow as the sea reaches around the rocks and we race out to meet her head-on.

"That sandbar makes a nice break," I say, raising my voice over the blat of the outboards and the hiss of the hull against the waves. I gesture toward the beach as we round the seawall; the backs of curling breakers can be seen as they topple and race toward the shore.

"You surf?" he asks.

I nod. "I took it up about ten years ago. It changed the way I shell."

"Totally," Ness says. "I've always said surfers make the best shellers. No one watches the sea and gets to know her rhythms like surfers do. When you study the breaks, you get to know what the world is like beneath all that water—"

"You can see where the pockets are," I say, finishing his thought. "You can picture what the reef looks like. Where the crags are and how the shells tumble in and get caught up. If it were me, I'd snorkel right out behind that point—" I gesture toward the natural jetty to the south.

"It's a good spot," Ness says. "If we weren't skipping snorkeling, I would've taken you there." He leans back, steering with just two fingers on the wheel, the lightest of touches. "This is the progression of my journey, really. As shells get harder and harder to find, we have to chase them back to the source. We can't rely on them to wash up the beach. This is the path that led me to your shells—"

"The murex?" I ask. "Is that where we're going today?"

"No," Ness says. "Today is about showing you a phase of my journey. Trust me. You want to write your piece in installments, allow me to do the same."

I feel like he's punishing me, drawing it out like this. Getting back at me for my series of planned articles about his family.

"Diving is different than snorkeling, anyway. It's too deep to read the swell. So we rely on instruments." He indicates the depth meter and fish finder. The latter reveals the depths in a jagged line that must mean more to him than it does to me. "Knowing where to dive is the hard part," he says. "In a lot of places, the sand *moves* under there. It's different every day. And each year, we have to go deeper and deeper to get the good shells before someone else does. We have to fight over what few shells remain."

"Soon we'll be finding the loves of our lives in grade school," I say.

Ness turns and studies me, his brow wrinkled in confusion, and I realize that I spoke out loud.

"Do what?" he asks.

"It's . . . I have this thing about shelling and relationships," I say. I imagine Michael up at the bow, looking back at me and rolling his eyes. But the analogy is too good to leave be. "What you just said, about getting to the shells early, it made me think of another way that shelling is like love. Shelling along the beach, grabbing the remnants, that's like dating people our age, you know? People in their thirties and forties. They're all roughed up. Late catches."

Ness laughs. *Really* laughs. He slaps the steering wheel. "So snorkeling would be like dating in college," he says.

"Or maybe at work," I offer. "Diving would be like dating in college. If you don't find someone early, all the good ones are gone. Just like with shells."

Ness nods. I make a mental note of this metaphor. Michael would absolutely loathe it. I'll have to email it to him.

"Shelling is like relationships," Ness says. He turns away from me and scans the beach, makes an adjustment with the wheel. "I can see that." He nods to himself. "Yeah, I can totally see that."

-20-

I watch the shore recede until it becomes a thin, dark line. Only the lighthouse remains distinct, a finger of black jutting up from an outcrop not far from Ness's estate. There is a gentle undulation to the sea, a rhythmic swell. The outboards roar. We pass patches of drifting seagrass. In the distance, a handful of birds trace lazy circles against the sky, signs of sporadic life in this watery wilderness.

Finally, Ness throttles back and the bow dips. The boat slows. We are in a patch of sea that looks like any other on the surface, but I see Ness studying the GPS, which shows our boat as a small triangle on top of a classic symbol for a shipwreck: a curved hull with what might be a sail-less mast but looks more like a cemetery cross.

"I thought you said it was just offshore," I say. Ness reverses the throttle briefly to kill our speed, then looks back toward land.

"Seven miles," he says. "Practically on the beach."

He goes forward to toss out the anchor. I slide over into his spot and study the GPS. The large screen shows the depth of the water in feet. Right by our position, the numbers range from 70 to 120. There's a steep ridge here. The water is much deeper toward land before rising back up again. If all the oceans were stripped away, these would be rolling hills overlooking a majestic valley. Instead, it's a world invisible, the contours seen only in a scattering of numbers and covered over by fathoms of blue dirt.

"You said earlier that I shouldn't dive deeper than sixty feet," I point out. Maybe it's the shipwreck symbol or my bout of paranoia earlier, but I have a bad feeling about this plot of sea. Like something awful will happen here.

Ness throws out the anchor and watches as coil after coil of rope zips over the rail. When the line begins to slide away lazily, he cinches it off on a cleat. I remember helping my father do that. It was my job on the boat. Here, I'm an anxious spectator.

"It's a little over eighty to the bottom," he says. "You don't have to go that far. The wreck sits up off the sea floor, so it's less than sixty down to the conning tower. Besides, there's not much good shelling this shallow unless you get pretty remote. It's all been picked over. But you can see the wreck, and if you're comfortable hanging out for a few minutes at depth, I can show you where I used to make my finds."

"I thought you'd be with me the whole time."

"I will. If you don't feel comfortable, we can come right back up. Just give me this sign." Ness points straight up. "Do it with both hands, if possible. If you don't feel like you're getting air for any reason, do this." He makes a choking gesture.

"Comforting," I say.

"And if everything is okay, give the okay sign. If you give me a thumbs-up, I won't know if you're doing great or you want to go up to the boat."

"Sixty feet, ten minutes," I tell him.

"It's a guideline," Ness says. "Don't worry if you go a little below that or stay down fifteen minutes. It gives you a lot of leeway. We won't be long, and we'll come up nice and slow, maybe even make a couple safety stops just to make my dearly departed dive master happy."

"Whatever's the safest, that's what I want to do."

"Don't worry. We'll be perfectly safe. Trust me."

I try to. He and I drag our duffels to the stern of the boat and begin setting out the gear. There's a small door on one side of the outboards and a narrow dive platform. I figure out how to work the door, and I kick the stainless steel ladder hinged to the platform into the water. Somehow, effecting my doom lessens the worry. Nerves are like carsickness: I get less nauseated if it's *my* hands on the wheel.

Ness starts prepping his tank, and I do the same with mine, repeating the steps I learned just an hour or so ago. I appreciate that he lets me do it myself, but I make sure he's keeping an eye on me. I assume he'll tell me if I do anything wrong. When I crack the valve on the tank, there's a brief sputter of air, and then the rubber gasket catches tight.

"Let's get your weight belt on," Ness says, "and then your tank. You can sit on the platform to do your fins and mask."

I look at the platform. It's only wide enough for one person at a time.

"I'm not going in first," I say. This is a statement of fact. Not a complaint. Or question. Or suggestion. To my editor, I would say that this has been properly vetted. It is a *true thing.* I am not getting in this water, nearly out of sight of land, all alone.

"You'll be fine. Ladies first, right? I'll be in right after y—"

"No, not 'ladies first,' Ness Wilde. Not ladies first. I am not getting in this ocean before you do. Do you hear me? I'm dead serious."

Ness studies me for a moment, and I can't tell how this is going to go down, if we'll have to take the boat back to the dock, if I'll have to sit here while he dives alone, if I'll end up snorkeling, which would be damn fine with me. But then he smiles, and it feels like the most genuine smile I've seen from him. The happiest I've seen him. Me telling him he's dead wrong about this me-getting-in-the-water-first business that he's suggesting.

"Okay. We'll get you situated on the dive platform, and I'll go over the side. We'll make it work. I'll be in the water waiting for you."

I barely hear what he's saying. It takes a moment to process. But my pulse eventually stops pounding in my ears, and the sun doesn't beat down quite so hard. I realize I'm sweating inside my wetsuit, which is soaking up the summer morning heat. I finally nod and agree to his plan. He helps me cinch the heavy weight belt around my waist, then lifts my BC, and I get my arms through, do the buckles myself. Ness has me sit on the edge of the swim platform, my legs dangling in the water, and I put my fins on one at a time. I dip my mask in the water, and not wanting to take chances with it fogging, I say *screw it* and spit on the inside of the lens and rub it around, just like my mom taught me. I dunk the mask again to rinse it and put it on my forehead, then turn to see how Ness is going to get in around me.

He already has his BC on. Balancing on one leg at a time, Ness kicks on each of his fins standing up, the boat rocking gently beneath us. He grabs his mask, tests his air, and then sits on the side of the boat, his back to the water.

"See you in heaven," he says. And then he rocks back, tipping dangerously, his tank and the back of his head flying toward the water, and I can't see around the edge of the boat, but there's a mighty splash, and I'm wondering what in the world he meant and if I can figure out how to crank the boat and get back to the dock by myself, when Ness bobs up by my feet, pulls his regulator out of his mouth, and flashes that famous smile.

"That seemed violent," I say.

He holds the platform beside my thigh to steady himself. "Don't try to go in slow," he says. "You'll hit your tank on the platform, or you'll hit your head on the outboard. You want to fall forward. Tuck a little bit and hold your mask to your face with both hands so it doesn't fall off. Look to the side if that makes you feel better."

This feels dumb. Like the worst way to get in the water ever. I start to ask if I can't just turn around and descend the ladder, but I've spent enough of my life in fins to understand how poorly that would work. I trust him. Maybe not with anything else, not with the fate of the world, or with the truth, but I trust him in this moment not to get me killed. I fully appreciate the insanity of this paradox, but I accept it anyway. And letting go of the boat, and a decade of fear, and all the thoughts and worries that plague me, and my concern for my mortal coil, and any connection I have with the world above the sea or with the cosmos that sustains me, I tip forward and crash into the Atlantic Ocean, and she wraps me in her soft embrace.

-21-

All I see are bubbles—both from the turbulence of my entry and my panicked exhalations. The regulator is half out of my mouth. I wrestle it back in. And then the buoyancy of my suit and my frantic kicking and remembering what Ness taught me by the dock about bubbles going *up*—and I break the surface, sputtering and cursing and spitting out my regulator to take in huge gulps of air.

"Not bad," Ness says. His hands are under my arms. I almost feel lifted out of the water by his steady kicking beneath the surface. But from the waist up, he is still and calm. I cling to his neck for a moment, then force myself to tread water with my arms. As a defense mechanism, I remind myself that he's done this with a hundred reporters over the years. This is new and dangerous for me but not for him.

"How the hell are we supposed to get back in the boat?" I ask. The white fiberglass hull bobbing in the sea beside us looks like the snowy face of Everest. I am already imagining us dying here, that we forgot some crucial step. Like a crane, or a handful of stout deckhands.

"We shed the tanks in the water," Ness says, still holding me with one hand. "Don't worry. I promise, everything's gonna be okay. Now, do you want to swim around a bit? Breathe through your regulator?"

I spit and sputter as one of the small swells rocks the boat and spray kicks up in my face. My mask is fogging. Repeating in my head are the words: *I told you so I told you so I told you so. Bad idea, Maya. Dumb idea.*

"Swim toward the bow with me," Ness says. "I want to check the anchor." He fishes my regulator out of the water, hits the button to expunge some air, and presses it into my hand. I bite down on the mouthpiece and take hissing lungfuls of air. As another swell lifts me up—and my head begins to sink down below the surface—I emit a half-swallowed scream. I've snorkeled a thousand times in my life without ever feeling panicked. It's the heavy weights around my waist. The wetsuit, which I hate wearing anyway. The tank and the tangle of hoses. All are conspiring to drown me—

"Right here," Ness says. "Look at me."

He holds my head, a palm on either side of my face, steadying me but also forcing me to look at him, mask to mask.

"You can breathe," he tells me. "Up here, down there, on the moon, anywhere. Just breathe."

I try. My hands are around his wrists. He is not a person, not the subject of a story, not a mentor nor a guide. He is a small island. I cling to him.

"Ready?" he asks.

I nod as much as his hands will allow. I blink back tears of worry.

"Here we go."

Ness stops supporting me, and I don't fight the sinking. A part of me is resigned to my fate. I know in this instant that I will die here, and some truncated and indiscernible version of my life flashes before my eyes, just like they say it does. I see my parents, and then my sister. I see a beach that is somehow the sum of all the beaches I've ever visited. A memory of driving with the windows down, music blaring, hair whipping in my face. I see a newspaper with my byline. And then the water covers the regulator in my mouth, covers my mask, closes over my head, and a miracle happens. The impossible. The turbulence and noise and rocking boat and beating sun are replaced with a near-silence. A near-weightlessness. A floating of mind and body. I breathe in and out, just like by the dock, and air fills my lungs. Bubbles flow. I make another odd sound, a muffled squeal of delight, a noise like I've heard dolphins make, because I'm doing it. I'm diving. Floating in the great and wild open sea.

Ness holds my hand, and for a moment, I think he's going to guide me around like this, but he's pointing at my wrist, showing me the face of my dive watch. The depth gauge reads ten feet. I glance up, and the surface of the sea is a shimmering wall of quicksilver overhead. White foam spits around the hull of the boat as it rocks in place. The outboards jut down with bright props like old-timey circulating fans. Ness points toward the bow of the boat. The mooring line is there, angling through the water, and I can see the anchor lying on the sand far below. He kicks toward the line and motions for me to follow. I do. I also fumble for the air fill controls on the BC and experiment with adding air and releasing it again, getting a feel for how it controls my depth. I keep a nervous eye on the readout, both to see how deep I am and also how much air I have left. Between my lessons earlier and getting off the boat just now, I've already used a third of my tank.

When we reach the anchor line, I grab hold of it, eager to have something solid to cling to, some way of knowing I'm not sinking nor bobbing toward the surface. Ness flashes the okay sign as a question, and I flash it back in response. He motions for me to stay there. *Okay*, I signal. He turns and kicks to descend down the line, and I notice the wreck for the first time, this great and unnatural manmade form resting on the seafloor. It looks like a container ship, lying almost on its side. A giant steel reef, portholes unblinking like the eyes of the drowned.

No . . . not a container ship, I see. The deck where the metal boxes would go is laced with thick pipes and large round hatches. It's a tanker. I know this wreck. The name is on the tip of my tongue. And then I see that the name is also there on the side of the ship, faded but still legible: *The Oasis*.

This tanker went down before I was born, was en route to the Saint Lawrence Seaway when it broke up in heavy seas. It's part of a long list of oil tanker disasters in US waters: *Argo Merchant, Bouchard, Valdez, Mega Borg, Westchester, Eagle Otome, Oasis, Shinyu, Aponia*. I can only remember the names if I recite them in order, sing-song, like we learned in grade school eco class. And here it is below me, an ignoble piece of history. But it looks so calm. The water is crystal clear, the destruction a memory. Fish swirl around the ship, an explosion of life, like bugs swarming a rotting corpse.

Ness checks the anchor and swims back up to me. *Okay?* he asks. *Okay*, I signal. He points at the wreck. *Okay,* I signal again. This is the extent of my underwater vocabulary. In truth, I'm far better than okay. I'm dizzy with excitement. I don't know that I would have the words even if I were able to write them. We have entered an inhospitable and alien world, and I can survive here.

I kick after Ness, and we float down over a large school of what look like amberjack. The fish undulate as one—the most fish I've seen in a single school in the wild. Only in aquariums do fish like this exist. As we pierce the school, they seem to divide and meld around us. We continue down, my wrist telling me thirty, forty, fifty. We're now level with the jutting tower of the *Oasis*. The deck is much farther below, but I won't be going any deeper. I swim toward the tower, which is at a lean. Several of the windows are busted out. There are fish inside, and barnacles along the hull. There's more reef here than I've seen practically anywhere since I was a child. More sea life than I've ever seen in one place. Ness signals for me not to go any deeper, and I see that I've drifted down to sixty-five feet. I put some air in my BC and check my tank supply. I also check the time. We've been in the water for twelve minutes. I could stay forever. I could live here.

Ness descends further. He slides down the sheer cliff of steel to the sand floor, where a scattering of rocks and kelp-like plants break up the desert sameness. I watch him search along the base of the wreck. Only a few minutes left to enjoy this. I kick toward the tower until I can reach out and touch the barnacle-rough rail. A monster fish swims past one of the windows, and I grunt a veil of bubbles. A reef shark. The black mark on the tip of its fin tells me what kind. *They feed at night*, I hear my father say, consoling me.

The black-tip reef shark disappears into the tower, and I decide to back off. Only a quarter of my tank left. A few more minutes down here, that's all I have. I search below for Ness and see him rising up to join me, trailing a veil of bubbles. Together, we kick toward the surface, this thing I've avoided all my life taken away from me far too abruptly. I remember to exhale as we ascend. I exhale the entire way up, letting out this swelling breath that I've held for years and years.

-22-

"That was amazing," I say as soon as we reach the surface. "Unbelievable. Like being a fish."

Ness treads water beside me. He has me inflate my BC and then helps me unbuckle the clasps and shrug off all the dive gear. The tank and all the hoses float on the surface of the water. I see how it works now, and also why you don't get in without putting the gear on first. Sorting it out in the swell would be a pain in the butt.

He holds my tank for me while I kick off my fins and sling them into the boat. Now it's just like snorkeling, and I'm a pro. I haul myself up the swim ladder, hold the boat with one hand, and take my tank and BC from Ness. When he gets his off, I take that as well. I feel like an equal partner in the dive now. I'm ready to go again. I want to know when I can go again. And deeper next time. Stay down longer. I have a fever for this. It's more immediately addictive even than surfing.

Ness throws his fins into the boat, has his mask up on his forehead, and climbs up to join me. "How was it?" he asks.

"Over too quick," I say. "I want to do it again."

"You should get certified."

"I will." And I plan to. I'll even let Michael know. Maybe see if he'd want to go on a dive sometime. As friends. I'd like that.

Ness hits a switch on the console and pulls up one of the hatches to the livewells. Water is gushing inside, filling the area where the bait is kept. I watch as he lowers a canister into the pool of water and releases something. A shell. A fly-specked cerith. Tiny. I have to stoop to see it. And then I see the pink foot of the slug inside.

"It's alive," I say.

"Oh, yeah," Ness says, watching the creature. "Ceriths have done well around here. There's a professor at Stanford who spends a few weeks every summer on this wreck. She says the spill set these puppies up for success in the ocean we have today. They adapted to a toxic environment that's becoming more and more the norm. In a weird and tragic way, the wreck and the spill were good things. She's had a hard time getting her papers published, of course. Nobody wants to hear about the life around the ship." Ness closes the hatch.

"This isn't the sort of shelling I thought we'd be doing," I say.

"I'll show you another spot on the way in," Ness promises. "We can switch tanks and I'll just free dive. There's a fissure a mile off the beach where the good shells get trapped. Still some museum pieces along there. Nobody else has found the spot yet. Of course, I'll have to blindfold you if you want to go."

"Absolutely," I say. And I'm pretty sure he's kidding about the blindfold.

"Are you hungry?" he asks.

It's not yet eleven, but I'm starving. Boats and sun and swimming do that to me. "Famished," I say. I watch as Ness unzips his wetsuit and peels it down to his waist, allowing the empty arms to dangle. It's impossible not to admire his physique. Ness has a swimmer's body: powerful arms, shoulders that taper to a narrow waist. Tan and lean like a surfer. The boat sways beneath us.

"Tahitian black pearl," he tells me.

"I'm sorry?" I shake my head and meet his gaze.

Ness touches the small object around his neck, held there by a leather cord. It's the necklace I caught a brief glimpse of the other day. "It's a black pearl," he says. "From Tahiti. You looked like you were unsure."

"No, that's what I thought it was," I say, pretending that was indeed what I had been looking at. I step closer. The pearl is oblong and puckered on one end. Imperfect. A hole has been drilled through it, the cord knotted on either side.

"Probably not worth five dollars," he says. "But I found it on a dive with my mom. It was one of our last days together."

I don't have to ask. I know the story. His mother died in a boating accident in the Pacific. It's the first time I think about what we have in common, that he might have been just as scared to go on without her as I was to live a day without my mom. Ness turns away from me and pulls the cooler and the basket out from one of the storage benches.

"Let's eat," he says.

I grab my sunglasses, squeeze the water out of my hair, unzip my wetsuit, and cinch the sleeves around my waist. I make sure my bikini top is in place. The small boat bobs up and down on the gathering swell, and birds circle nearby, showing us where the wreck is. *The Oasis*. A ship mocked for its name back when it was full, but now living up to that moniker in the form of an empty shell.

Part III:
The Monster

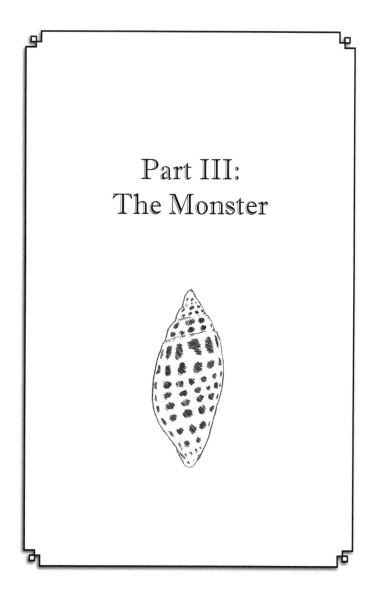

-23-

I have underwater dreams that night. Dreams of reefs and caves and swirling sharks. But they are peaceful dreams. I am not drowning. I am flying, and the ocean is the sky. Beyond the ocean, the old sky is some inhospitable realm, some outer space. Only the flying fish and the dolphin dare leap so high. For the rest of us below the sea, that shimmering plane is our ceiling. We catch wavering glimpses of people peering down at us from the other side. We pay them no mind.

When I wake, I realize I've slept later than I did the day before. Partly out of exhaustion, I think. Partly because I don't want to leave these dreams. And partly because of the hypnotic beat of the rain on the metal roof above.

The sun is already up, but the sky is a dark and heavy gray. This is the antithesis of what I saw the morning before. Yesterday began with perfection and ended with dinner on the dune deck, a moonlit night, another incredible bottle of wine from Ness's cellar. Is this storm an omen of what today might bring?

Rain patters the roof and hisses against the windows in gusty sheets. A trickle of a breeze descends from the widow's watch, and I remember that I cracked a window up there the night before. Throwing the sheets off, I rush up in my underwear and crank the window shut. The floor is wet. I move some of the books around, see a copy of *Treasure Island*, and set that aside to look at later. Grabbing a towel from downstairs to mop up the rain, I imagine that this is when Ness will appear, with me dashing around a glass house in a pair of full-bottomed cotton panties and no bra. I dry the floor and hurry back down to get a robe on. Glancing up the boardwalk toward the house, I see no movement, no sign of Ness. The rain is torrential. Maybe we're waiting it out.

I asked over dinner the night before what the plan was for today, if it involved more diving. "In a way," Ness had cryptically answered. He refused to tell me details of our plans and reminded me of my promise not to skip ahead. All he would say, again, was that we were following a natural progression in his discovery of the lace murex shells. I told him I needed to know if that journey ended with us breaking the law, that I didn't want to be any part of that. Ness had grown quiet. Dour. He said I could leave any time I wanted, that he would make no such promises.

After dinner, I considered calling Agent Cooper to check in, to let him know that Ness seemed sure of himself, that he seemed to be leading me somewhere, and that he had twice now somewhat admitted that what he was doing was illegal. Instead, I wrote some notes in my laptop up in the widow's watch, jotting down memories for my piece before they faded with time. But the writing session turned into journaling. It turned into an admission of my wavering certainty.

The shells were obvious fakes, but the motive doesn't make any sense. Ness has more money than God, more status than most politicians, and more notoriety than any film star—and he seems to care little for any of it. What he has in spades is a passion for the sea—a passion I'm very familiar with. Perhaps the shells are a way of sharing that passion? Educational tools? But that's even more ridiculous. It's too much trouble, and it doesn't explain the shock I saw on his face when I pulled out that box, or the hurt he felt at his friend having taken the shells from him.

The ornate and intricate way he's going about giving me the answer—this retracing of some journey that led him to the shells—is a hint. He's putting off the inevitable. Delaying. And yet his enthusiasm seems genuine. So Ness either has some master plan, or the man has no grip on reality. I came here wanting to believe the latter, but last night I confided to my journal that the former was at least some dim possibility.

No matter what, I can already feel sadness at having to leave this place, this beach, this small home on the dunes. I was hesitant and wary of coming here, but now the estate has its claws in me.

I start coffee and take a quick shower, the sea-glass bricks muted this time by the dark clouds outside. The handful of ingredients in the fridge force me to cook eggs-in-a-hole, a staple of my youth. With a tall glass, I punch out a perfect circle in two slices of bread, butter up both sides, then throw them in a pan and crack an egg in each hole. The removed discs of bread get toasted with a lot of butter. There's no jam in the fridge, but I find honey in a cabinet. Fending for myself makes this place feel a little *mine*. I dream of spending a month here to work on that novel I keep saying I'll finish. I wonder if every journalist who has ever stayed the night has thought the exact same thing.

Still no sign of Ness. I eat at the small table by the window, propping open *Treasure Island* by tucking one side of the book under the edge of my plate and laying a knife across the other. The rain is violent. I can easily imagine the sea storm described in the book. The house becomes a rocking ship, and it's hard to say if the sounds of the crashing waves are out beyond my door or in my imagination. I glance down at the beach, and that's when I see the note.

It's inside a plastic bag, which has been wedged between the doors. I never locked up the night before—the note must've been wedged there while I slept. I retrieve it, pat the bag dry on my robe, and sit on the edge of the bed to read. I glance at the signature first to make sure it's from Ness. It is.

Maya,

Sorry to do this, but that something I mentioned yesterday that might come up - it came up. We've still got plenty of time to show you everything you need. Should be back after lunch. Make yourself at home up at the house. Lots of movies in the TV room. Sorry there's no cable. Numbers for Monique and Vincent below. Dial 9, and you'll get Security. Maybe enjoy the day off and write nasty things about me!

-Ness

Phone numbers for Monique and Vincent are jotted below his name. I feel a roller coaster of emotions. First comes the disappointment that whatever he had planned for the day has been called off. But then I taste the excitement of open potential, of a day with absolutely nothing to do. I haven't had one in ages. I could sit on the bench upstairs and read a novel all day. I could write. I could say *damn the rain* and put on my wetsuit and go for a snorkel to add to my collection of shells. The boundless opportunities have me seeing this as a blessing in disguise. A vacation within a vacation. I could easily not leave this little house perched on the dunes until the sun goes down. I can subsist on toast and eggs.

But a glance up at the main house crushes any such fantasy of me taking a day off. There's a reason I haven't taken one in ages. My mind won't stop spinning, assembling my next story, and while the healthy thing to do would be to stay in and rest, to not set foot in that house, it would be unprofessional of me *not* to go up there. A dereliction of my duty as a reporter and a missed chance to make up to Agent Cooper for losing the shells. Ness has formally invited me to make myself at home, to rummage through his movie collection—and who knows what else.

I check the time. Not even seven yet. The note says he'll be back after lunch. I could go snoop for two hours without any chance of seeing him. And even if I do, he has *invited me in*. This is as big a mistake with journalists as it is with vampires.

Hanging my robe up to dry, I pull on shorts and a t-shirt, stuff I don't mind getting wet. I'll find a towel up at the house. The side door is more out of the wind, and I'm just steeling myself for the dash across the boardwalk when I consider the chances Monique will show up to tidy the main house and catch me poking around. I turn and grab Ness's note. My hall pass.

I feel invincible. The journalist in me can't believe my good fortune. Carte blanche in the inner sanctum of the subject of my exposé, and the prime suspect in an FBI investigation into shell forgery. I can hear Henry and Cooper both urging me along, rooting for me, grins on their faces.

I wait for the next gust of wind to pass. Sheets of rain roll in like an ocean swell. A hiss moves down the side of the house, and I slip through the door and run, bare feet slapping through puddles, wind and rain pushing at my back, feeling a temptation to squeal from the cold and from how quickly I'm absolutely drenched.

Mindful of slipping, I keep a hand on the rail. Up one flight of steps, across another boardwalk, and then the three steep flights to the covered deck—past the landing with the lounge chairs and fire pit, past the al fresco dining table—until I'm in the would-be shelter of the house's generous overhang. But the sideways reach of the heavy wind whips the rain across my back even here.

I don't have time to contemplate, to knock, to peek inside. I test the door, find it unlocked, and hurry through. Fighting the shoving of a fierce gust, I manage to get the door closed behind me.

Dripping wet and shivering, I call for Ness and then Monique. No answer. My shirt is soaked, and I see that the dark bra was a poor choice. My legs are covered in goose bumps. The AC and my wet clothes threaten to turn me into a giant ice cube as a puddle begins to form at my feet.

I hurry to the guest bath and find just a sink and a toilet. There's a small and useless hand towel threaded through a ring— the decorative kind you can never tell if you should actually use. The kind that barely absorbs water anyway.

I look elsewhere. The house is a maze. I've only seen parts of it: the overhang room, the main hall, the foyer, the kitchen. A breezeway leads off to another wing. The windows are all closed, turning the breezeway into a sheltered glass hall. I follow it, leaving wet footprints behind me, hoping to find guest quarters with proper bathrooms and proper towels. This is already going badly. But it'll be a long time before Ness returns. I hope.

At the end of the hall, I pass through a reading room. Bay windows jut out toward the sea. There are shells everywhere: on the walls, in glass cabinets, decorating every surface. Shelling books are scattered on a table. There's an open sketchbook with a detailed drawing of some torus. I can look later. My teeth are chattering. I need to find a thermostat and turn off the AC.

Past the reading room, I enter a bedroom twice the size of my entire apartment. It has its own sitting area with a fireplace, a breakfast nook, a desk in a far corner, matching Tahitian-style furniture, and flowing white drapes that frame a view of the beach. I can see why the house is arranged as a scattering of joined rooms along the dunes. Every room has a sweeping view of the sea.

Through a door on the far side of the room, I pass through a walk-in closet and, finally, a bathroom. Towels. Hallelujah. I grab one and pat myself dry, squeezing my hair in the folds, and realize my clothes are not going to dry for a while. There's a robe hanging on the back of the door. I close the door, strip naked, and don the robe. Wringing out my shorts in the sink, I remember the note and fish it out. The piece of paper is soaked through, the blue ink turned to blotches. It's barely readable. But Ness is the only person who could get angry about my being here, and he knows he wrote it. I lay the note out to dry, wring out my shirt and underwear, and drape everything over the shower door.

Rather than snoop around in Ness's robe, I decide to borrow clothes from the closet. Wrapping my hair up in a fresh towel, I step back into the wardrobe. I find a shirt and a pair of shorts. Both will be too big, but they'll keep me decent. I'm pulling on the shorts when a small voice tells me I'm making a mistake, that I need to slow down, that the rain and my wet clothes are a blessing.

No one can blame me for coming up to the main house. I'm a guest. Our plans got rained out, and my clothes were soaked through. Of course I would want to find a change of dry clothes. Who wouldn't?

I put the shorts and shirt back and pretend I never saw them. If I'm caught rummaging around, I can say I'm looking for something dry to put on. I can't use that excuse if I'm already wearing something. It's perfect. Agent Cooper would be proud.

Back in the bedroom, I go through the nightstand first. Two books with dog-eared pages, one on Tahitian wayfinding, the other on rogue waves. Both are from university presses. Expensive and dull. There's a pen and a notepad, but nothing written on the first page, and the indentations are too faint to make out what was written before. A tangle of wires and two electrical chargers, nothing interesting.

I try the desk on the other side of the bed, passing by a display case full of rare shells. The problem with looking for excellent fakes in this house is that there are museum-quality pieces everywhere. Even if I had my loupe, the last specimens overcame close scrutiny by both me and the FBI. What I need are notes, passwords to his email accounts, letters from accomplices, something like that.

The small desk mostly turns up pictures of Ness's daughter. They're everywhere—in frames arranged across the desk and loose in the drawers. They start with her as a toddler and progress to a gap-toothed smile and then to a gangly young woman on the verge of puberty.

The rain outside is a steady roar. The metal roof rattles from the downpour, and overflowing gutters create a veil of water so thick that it's impossible to see the beach, hard to even see the end of the deck. It's also impossible to hear anyone in the house.

"Uh, hello?" a voice calls. "Ness?"

My heart drops. I close the desk drawers in a panic and hurry toward the bathroom. I'm halfway there when someone steps through the bedroom door. A woman. I'm so startled, it takes a moment before I recognize her. Victoria Wilde. Though she goes by Carter now, I think.

"Who are *you?*" she asks.

I freeze in place. Ness's ex-wife hasn't changed at all from the last tabloid pictures I saw of her, years ago. She has on a black dress, heels, a white pearl necklace. She appears to be dressed up for some event, maybe a funeral. I start to answer her, to explain what I'm doing there, when she raises a hand.

"Never mind. I don't want to know. Where is Ness?"

"I—I don't know," I stammer.

"Woke up to an empty bed, huh?" She crosses the room toward the desk I just left. "Let me tell you, that's the good Ness. Try living with him for eight years. It's when you're falling *asleep* in an empty bed that you've got trouble."

"I'm not sleeping with him," I say. I feel young all of a sudden. Guilty. Full of excuses. It all comes from having been caught, but the bad thing I was doing wasn't the bad thing I'm suspected of doing. The desire for truth won't let me just shut up. "I'm a reporter," I say.

"Of course you are, darling." Victoria rummages through the same desk that *I* was just rummaging through, and while neither of us belongs there, she makes it look okay. I hear another voice somewhere in the house. Victoria is writing a note, presumably for Ness.

"No really," I say. "I'm with the *Times*. I'm doing a piece on Mr. Wilde—"

Victoria turns and looks me up and down for the first time. I touch the towel on my head, then close the robe tighter across my chest and see that Ness's initials are embroidered there. This looks bad.

"Research, I suppose." She waves a pen up and down at me, then points it at the bed and raises an eyebrow. Part of me wants to blurt out that yeah, we're having epic sex, and he wants me to move in with him. But it's a vindictive part of me that I'm immediately ashamed of. I just want to hurt her because her presence is making me feel like a bad person.

"Holly's riding lessons are rained out." Victoria jabs the pen at the window. "Obviously," she adds. "And I can't watch her. I'm already going to be late for my luncheon. Make sure Ness gets this note. And don't worry, she can take care of herself until he gets back."

"His daughter?" I ask.

"*My* daughter," Victoria says. She slams the pen down on top of the note, leans on the desk for a moment, then laughs at something and shakes her head. She turns toward the door. I want to say something, to ask her to stay for a coffee, to talk to her, get to know something about her, when she turns, takes in the room one more time and my presence in it, and says, "Don't rearrange the furniture."

"What?" I'm still clutching the robe tightly around me.

She waves her hand at the room, at the whole house. "Just leave it like this. You'll want to make it your own, but he won't give a shit about you in a week and he'll just have his staff put it all back where it was. All the little dents in the carpet will vacuum out in a few days. So save yourself the time."

"I—"

"And another thing: Don't let his smile fool you. It's a shell. Ness is not a happy man. He never will be. You'll drive yourself crazy thinking you can change that."

"Look—" I say.

"Oh, you'll think I'm a bitch for a month or so. You'll hate me because I got the closest to him. But in another month or two, you'll remember this conversation, realize I was right, realize I was being nice to you, trying to save you, and you'll thank me. You might even write me a nice note." She smiles. "I have quite a few of those."

And then she turns and walks away before I can tell her that she's wrong. Before I can thank her right then. Before I can tell her that she's confirming everything I already think about the man, giving me the power to resist my baser urges while reminding me why I'm here. That if I knew where to send it, I'd write her that note right now. And I am newly resolved to reach out to her for an interview before I publish my final piece. I now have my in: I can tell her she was right, that I want to thank her in person, and that I want to know more about Ness's unhappiness, where it comes from, and why he keeps it so cleverly hidden.

I'm running all this through my head when someone says, "I'm hungry."

I refocus and see the gangly girl from Ness's pictures standing in the doorway. Holly. His daughter.

"You're the new one, huh?" she asks. And before I can answer: "What can you make me for breakfast?"

-24-

" **I** 'm Maya," I say. I reach out my hand, and Holly studies it a moment before accepting.

"Riding practice got canceled," she says.

"So I heard."

"Mom says I'm not old enough to stay at our house by myself, but she leaves me alone here all the time. I think if I get hurt, she wants it to be on his property."

"Or maybe if you break something, she wants it to be his," I suggest. I smile and hope she knows it's a joke.

Holly smiles back. And then I feel a pang of sadness at how this seems normal to her, talking to a strange woman in her father's bedroom, a woman who is wearing her father's robe, and asking that woman to fix her something to eat. Thankfully, she turns and leads me toward the kitchen, and I'm able to use the robe's lapel to dab at my eye.

"Let's cook something outrageous," Holly calls out above the noisy rain. "How about a peanut butter omelet? With a cranberry chocolate milkshake. We'll get flour everywhere."

"I don't think any of those things take flour," I say. I re-knot Ness's robe around me as I follow her to the kitchen. No use changing into his clothes now, no use explaining. Everyone has already made up their minds.

"The flour won't go in anything we *make*," Holly explains. "It's just *because*. And if we ask Monique nicely, she won't clean up after us. Dad'll have to do it."

Holly cracks the fridge and pulls out eggs and a carton of chocolate milk. Even with the note suggesting I make myself at home, it feels strange to rummage around Ness's kitchen. Especially in his robe and with his daughter.

"You don't think your dad will mind me raiding his fridge, do you?" I ask.

Holly turns and looks at me with stern seriousness. "Dad says when he's dead and gone, all of this will be mine." She waves her arms at his house and the estate beyond. This proclamation seems to come out of nowhere. I'm trying to make sense of it when she continues: "So how do we know he isn't already dead?"

Two heartbeats pass before she smiles at me. She turns and brings out a handful of items that no sane person would combine: pickles, blueberries, cheese, a stick of butter.

"Are you pregnant?" I ask, catching on to her sense of humor.

"Twins," Holly says, not missing a beat. "So triple portions for me."

"Have you ever had an egg-in-a-hole?" I ask.

She scrunches up her face. "That sounds disgusting. Make me one."

"Okay. Why don't you put on some music. I couldn't figure out how the radio works earlier."

I don't even know that there *is* a radio. But Holly shouts "Righto!" and trots to a wall panel. Like magic, there's music in the room, the lilting up and down of reggae. That distracted her for all of five seconds. I arrange her ingredients by the stove and study them the way a chemist might. I can make this work, I tell myself.

"Do you want to sit at the counter and keep me company while I cook?" I ask.

"Yes I do," Holly says. She pulls out one of the stools and arranges herself in it, props her elbows on the counter and rests her chin in her hands. "I hate the rain," she says. "There's nothing fun to do in the rain."

"Naps are good in the rain," I offer. I open a few cabinets, looking for a pan.

"To the right," Holly says. "And naps are boring. Unless you get a good dream, and that's like winning the lottery. Too much luck involved."

"What about reading?" I ask.

"Booooring," she says, but I suspect that's going to be her reply no matter what I say. So I try a different tactic.

"You got me, then. I now hate the rain as well." Grabbing a spatula, I turn and offer my hand to her a second time. "We shall form the I-Hate-Rain Society," I announce. "Lovers of rain need not apply."

"Righto!" Holly says. With a grand gesture—elbow crooked up in the air—she takes my hand and gives it an exaggerated pump.

"We would spit on our palms to seal this pact," I say, "but that's too much like getting rained on."

Holly laughs. I get the pan hot and show her how to cut the holes out of the bread slices. She does the second piece herself. I feel like my mother all of a sudden. I see myself in this squirmy, fidgety, ornery, bright, funny little girl.

Butter goes in the pan. I wait for it to melt, then add the bread. The eggs are cracked into the holes we cut out of the middle. After I flip them, the cheese goes on top. When I plate the concoction, I add two slices of pickle. It actually looks like a fine addition to the family recipe. Holly pours herself a chocolate milk and takes a bite. She murmurs her approval, and I cook the middles on one side of the pan and mash blueberries on the other side, add a little more butter, and put this on the toasted rounds. It's a real improvement, I think.

"Almost as good as peanut butter omelets," Holly mutters around another bite.

I wonder if that's a real thing. And then I imagine another reporter standing right where I am, holding this spatula. A string of women, in fact, none of whom know how to cook. An endless parade of people sharing moments like this with Ness's daughter, whipping up whatever they can, and her sitting there smiling, wiping her mouth with her sleeve, full of omnivorous delight and thinking this is the most normal thing in the world.

"These are great," she says, taking a bite of one of the blueberry centers. I start rinsing the pan and the utensils. More of my story writes itself in my head. And even the happy bits have a way of making themselves sad.

"After breakfast, maybe you can show me where the laundry room is," I suggest. "My clothes got soaked in the rain, which is why I had to borrow your dad's robe. Be nice to get them dry."

"M'kay," she says, then slurps on her milk.

"And then maybe we can watch a movie? That's a good thing to do in the—" I stop myself, remembering the society we just formed. "Or we can do whatever."

"Is the cable on?" Holly asks.

"I don't think so," I say, remembering Ness's note.

"We can call the company and have them turn it on. I added myself to his account. I have his passcode. They call me Mrs. Wilde when I call. I lower my voice like this."

"I'm surprised they don't call you *Mister* Wilde, talking like that."

"Okay, not quite that low. But we'll go from zero to five hundred channels just like that." She snaps her fingers.

"You can watch TV if you want," I say, trying to make it sound like she has my permission but that it's the least cool thing one could possibly do. "*I'm* going to figure out how to get down to the other house and retrieve my book. Ever hear of *Treasure Island?*"

"My dad owns islands," Holly says. "I think one of them is called Treasure Cay."

"This is different," I say. "It's a book about untold riches and action and survival. I read it when I was about your age. That's what I'm going to do with my day. Because I hate the rain."

Holly squints her eyes and studies me. Her head tilts to one side, and I feel like she's about to blow my cover and accuse me of manipulating her. I remember being that age and being whip-smart. As adults, we tend to forget how clever we were when we were younger, and so we underestimate youth just like we hated being underestimated when *we* were that age.

"You're gonna get soaked if you go out there," Holly eventually says. "I got wet just getting out of the car, and I had an umbrella."

"I will armor myself against the rain," I tell her. "Not a drop will touch me. That's a rule in the I-Hate-Rain Society. You wanna come?"

Holly shrugs and looks away. I can tell I just lost her. "Nah, I don't like that place. I'm gonna watch TV."

I remember what Ness said about the first night he made her sleep down there alone, and that she has rarely been back. I shouldn't push her; there's no point in making her do something she doesn't want to do. But I'm weak, and I like her, and I want her not just to like me back, but for the two of us to do something she's never done with any of the other women who stay over. Because I'm not having sex with her father, and I need her to know I'm not the same as them.

"Well, I guess I won't be able to read my book then," I say, making myself sound sad. "I'm pretty sure it would take the entire Society to get down there in this heavy rain. Maybe I'll just go take a nap instead. If I get lucky, I'll have a good dream."

I leave the dishes and head toward the breezeway that leads off toward Ness's room. I have no idea what I'll do in there if she lets me go. Sit in a chair and look at an empty fireplace or gaze out at the rain.

But she doesn't let me go. The ultimate threat for Holly is that she'll be left alone, that I won't beg her to play with me, which is what I suspect she's used to.

"Wait," she says. And I turn back to her.

"We can beat the rain," she tells me in a conspiratorial whisper. "But it won't be easy. And we'll have to work together."

-25-

"I'm starting to think the saran wrap isn't a good idea," I say. "Turn around one more time." Holly has me spinning in the kitchen as she holds a spool of plastic wrap sideways. I still have the robe on, and the clear cocoon forming around me is causing me to sweat inside it.

"I can't move my arms," I say. "And how exactly am I going to breathe if you wrap my head up?"

"Good point. Reverse." Holly makes a spinny gesture with her finger. I twirl the other way, and she gathers all the plastic in a ball. I don't dare tell her that I'm not really interested in getting to a book I read years ago, or that I would be fine running out there in that crazy storm and just getting drenched again—because now it's a mission for us to get from A to B without getting a single drop of water on us.

"I've got an idea," Holly says. "Better than this one." She gives me a serious look when I raise an eyebrow at her. "My ideas just get better with time. I think you should know this about me."

I laugh and follow her down the north breezeway. We pass the utility room, where my clothes and the two towels are drying, and go past the guest bedrooms and Holly's room, which she showed me after we got the clothes going. At the far end of the house, we go up a flight of stairs and through a door into the garage.

Holly hits the lights. "Yes!" she says. She dances through the empty space where Ness's red gas-guzzler had been the other day and scoops up the bundled car cover from the ground. "It's rain-proof. Because normal people don't use these in their garages."

I almost point out that the cover keeps the dust off as well, but I agree with her: it's a bit much for a car kept in a garage. My car sits in the New York sun and the New York snow and the New York floods and mostly gets driven only to move it from street to street so the sweepers can get through.

"Grab the edge," Holly says. "Meet me in the middle."

We lift the car cover over us and paw at the ceiling as we work our way into the middle. Neither of us can see a thing. I think about the lazy summer days when my sister and I would make forts out of furniture, sheets, and sofa cushions. Holly is giggling. I can feel her breathing on my arm. We jostle and spin and laugh in the darkness together.

"We'll stay dry," I say, my words swallowed by the fabric and the deep shadows. "But we'll never see how to *get* there."

"We'll feel along the rails. But through the tarp."

"Won't we get lost?" I ask.

"Don't worry," she says. "I can get around that boardwalk with my eyes closed."

I remember Ness's story. But his daughter sounds so much braver than he made her out to be. I wonder how many years ago that was. Five? Six? Probably feels like ages to her.

"What about our feet?" I ask. "Won't they get wet?"

"I've got just the thing."

Holly extricates herself from the folds, leaving me in there alone. I work myself free as well. She has disappeared back into the house, returns with a pair of pink galoshes, then rummages around one of the other garage bays and brings out a pair of rubber hip waders that fishermen use.

"No rain shall touch us," she says.

"Let's just hope it hasn't stopped raining by the time we put this to the test."

We haul the gear to the living room, which gives us the shortest run down to the guest house, and I become quite possibly the first person in history to don rubber hip waders over a terrycloth bathrobe. My reflection in the living room door is of someone you would commit to an institution. Holly, meanwhile, looks downright adorable with her pink galoshes pulled over her blue jeans.

"No fair that you get to look normal," I tell her.

"You look like you sleep with fishes," Holly says.

"Let's hope not. You ready?"

She nods, and the two of us crawl under the car cover. Rain hisses across the glass door and windows, and it thunders against the roof. "I've got the doorknob," Holly says. "Hard to turn it through the fabric. It keeps slipping."

"I'll close it behind us when we get out," I tell her. "But we have to make sure the cover doesn't get caught."

What I don't tell her is that this is going to be an unmitigated disaster. No way we come out of this anything other than soaked and tangled in knots, but probably laughing hysterically. A gust of wind passes, and Holly yells "Now!" I hear the door open, the first of the rain spitting against the cover, popping it like a thunderstorm hitting a camping tent, and then we are outside, shuffling our feet, the wind whipping the car cover all around us.

The cover clings to our ankles, presses against our bodies. I nearly topple from the force of a gust, and it takes some fumbling and both of us working together to get the door pulled shut against the storm.

Holly is already laughing. It isn't quite pitch black under the cover now that we're outside—just a dismal, deep shade of gray. "This way," she says, full of confidence. We stay huddled together, hands fumbling through the fabric to stay in communion with the wooden rail, the cold of the wind and rain penetrating through our shroud, but so far, no moisture getting through to us. I take up a fold of fabric in front of me to keep from tripping, leaving our boots exposed to the driving rain and the wet deck.

"Steps!" Holly cries. "Twelve of them!"

Halfway down the flight of steps, buffeted by the storm, this begins to feel like a very bad idea. Our legs could get tangled; we could have a nasty fall; and suddenly I see myself driving Ness's daughter to the hospital with a broken arm, her crying hysterically in the passenger seat, me in the emergency room in hip waders and a robe trying to explain to Ness what in the hell I was thinking.

We reach the bottom of the flight of stairs, but there are two more to go. And long lengths of boardwalk between.

"Maybe we should ditch the cover and just make a run for it," I suggest, my voice muffled.

"Not a drop shall touch us!" Holly cries. She has one arm around my waist, and I have an arm draped over her shoulder. We shuffle as one, like we're running a three-legged race where our feet don't go in the same sack, our entire bodies do.

The fabric no longer whips around as angrily as before, thank goodness. The rain is soaking it and weighing it down. It trails behind us like a leaden wedding dress. We lean into the wind and stagger down the second flight of stairs, Holly seeming to know where she is going, then we tackle the last flight.

"Almost there," she tells me. And I feel like a climber who can see the crown of some inhospitable peak just a few steps away. One great push. So close—

We bang into the glass like birds. My forehead cracks against a window, and it sounds like Holly strikes her knee. The rain is no longer pelting us. We are pressed against the side of the guest house. I can't believe we made it this far. And suddenly, this is an adventure the way simple challenges with made-up rules are life-or-death scenarios for kids with their active imaginations. Suddenly, this is important. And fun.

Holly whoops when she finds the doorknob. It's a struggle to get it turned, but then the door flies inward, and we tumble along after it. The car cover finally claims us, tangling our feet, and I brace for impact, one arm around Holly and twisting her so she lands on top of me.

There's an *oomph* and a grunt from both of us. The wind is knocked out of me, and we have to fight to dig our way out from the wet fabric. Rain courses down the folds in rivulets, getting all over the floor and soaking us as we scramble for the open door.

We slam it shut. Holly is panting and giggling. I fight with Ness's robe to stay decent. The guest house is now a base camp, a temporary shelter against the storm, a small island at sea.

"I think we're stuck here," I tell Holly.

She pushes her hair off her face. We both got doused crawling out from under the car cover. She wipes her face and looks at her wet palms. "So close," she says.

"I don't think it qualifies as rain if it's indoors," I tell her. "Just tossing that out there."

"I second the motion," Holly says. And then: "Victory!" She dances around the room in her galoshes, leaving wet bootprints everywhere, while I gather the drenched cover and dump it in the bathtub.

After I change into dry clothes, and after Holly has explored the guest house—*her* house—I show her the book that was the subject of all our troubles.

"Read me a page," she says.

And so we arrange ourselves on the big bed in the middle of the downstairs loft, a pile of cushions behind us, and I start to read the adventures of Long John Silver, a sea cook turned treasure hunter, and of pirates and sea chests and treasure maps. And I don't stop reading aloud, even as Holly drifts off to sleep.

I just lower my voice and keep reading, and the storm outside does not abate, but Holly mumbles something, snuggles closer, and I have to set the book aside for a moment. It strikes me that my daughter would be nine right now if I'd carried her to term, if my body hadn't betrayed us both. She would be nine, and I would read to her like this.

I cover my mouth as the tears come hard and fast. The noise of the rain masks my sobs. Holly throws an arm across me and rests her head against my shoulder, and I fear she'll wake up and ask me what's the matter, and I'll have to make something up. Something a bright girl like her will know is a lie.

But she mumbles these words instead, a soft admission: "I don't really hate the rain," she tells me.

And then she falls back asleep, there in my arms, and I wish for her to have happy dreams.

-26-

I drift in and out. Dreams mix with the wild scene outside—
pirate ships plying the coast; men in slickers with treasure
maps digging greedily at the wet sand; thunder transmuting
into cannon-fire as my imagination melds the real and the unreal.

At one point, a man appears at the window in a yellow raincoat
and yellow rain cap. He looks nothing like a pirate. He looks like
Ness. It is much later that I realize it *was* him, that he came back
home to find the note from his ex, the house empty, and checked
on us here before deciding to leave us sleeping.

Even though I'm wide awake now, I let Holly doze with her
head on my arm. I'm struck again by how quickly she took to me,
and I hope it's a healthy thing. It could be that she's perfectly
well adjusted, that she's bright and courageous and comfortable
in her own skin. Or it could be that she is desperately seeking
something that's missing from her life. I'm no expert in child
psychology, so I have no way of knowing which is more likely.

And maybe I'm looking too far for the culprit. Maybe the one
desperate to connect is me. I push this question aside, not caring
to examine it. When Holly stirs, I wiggle my arm free and get
up to use the bathroom. She's outside the door when I get out,
rubbing her eyes and yawning. We trade places without a word
between us.

"I think your father is home," I say when she emerges. "And we napped through lunch. Should we go up to the house?"

She nods, looks out at the rain, then back to me. "Maybe we should just run for it," she says.

"Let's do it."

We squeal and laugh all the way to the house, getting soaked. We arrive at the living room to find folded towels set out for us and one on the floor just inside the door. Ness appears while we're drying our hair. "I'm going to my room to change," Holly announces. "Let me know when lunch is ready." She drops her towel in a heap and marches toward the north breezeway.

"How about a hello?" Ness asks his daughter. "Maybe a hug?"

Holly makes an exaggerated turn, like a jetliner banking through the clouds, and steers toward her dad. She gives him a perfunctory hug, rolling her eyes at me, and then pads off for her room.

"I am so sorry," Ness says. "Something came up, and I had no idea Holly would be—"

"It's okay," I tell him.

"—hate you had to babysit—"

"It was fine. We had a good time. The rain probably messed up whatever you were going to show me anyway."

"Well, not really. It's supposed to storm all day tomorrow as well, but it won't affect us. In fact, we have a series of flights to take tonight."

He glances at his watch. I've noticed that he does this constantly. It's a trait I've seen in a lot in the people I've interviewed over the years. For some, it's because they live by appointments: you're lucky to get fifteen minutes of their time. For others, it's ambition: they're in a race to get all they want accomplished. Ness is a playboy without a schedule, so he fits neither of these easy molds. Perhaps he's a third type: the schoolboy wondering when class will get out and he'll have his freedom again. Maybe he only does this around people like me, obligations he'd rather not have.

"Where are we going?" I ask. Funny, I expected to travel someplace exotic when I first got here, and now I don't want to leave.

"It's a surprise," Ness says. "Besides, if I told you the name of the place or where it was, you still wouldn't have a clue about our final destination."

"Will we be diving?"

Ness cocks his head. "In a way. Now stop asking questions—"

"I'm a reporter," I remind him. "You stop picking up shells."

"I just might," he says. And before I can press him on this, he's telling me what to pack. "One change of clothes, toothbrush, toiletries, no makeup, no perfume, no mask or fins, no wetsuit, no bathing suit."

"That's a list of what *not* to pack," I say.

"Comfortable clothes. Shorts. T-shirt. Nothing too warm."

I'm confused. Nothing warm, but no bathing suit?

Again, he glances at his watch. "We'll leave in half an hour."

"What about Holly?" I ask.

"Monique will watch her until her mother picks her up. Speaking of which, I got an earful from Vicky about who was in my bed this morning when she got here." He lifts an eyebrow in a *Care to explain that?* sorta way.

"I wasn't in your bed," I say. "I was . . . I got drenched running up here after I found your note. I went in search of a towel, found your bathroom first—"

"And my robe."

"And your robe, yes. My clothes are in the dryer. I was looking at pictures of Holly on your desk when your ex came in."

"What did you think of her?"

"I'm sorry, what?" I try to transition from being defensive to having a chat about his ex-wife. "She was . . . nice, I guess. Of course, she seemed to think we were sleeping with each other. Hard to blame her, considering. Pretty embarrassing for me."

"Wow," Ness says. "That must be awful, having people think something about you that isn't true. I can't imagine."

I start to ask him to elaborate, when I see him staring past my shoulder. I turn to find Holly standing at the end of the breezeway.

"You guys aren't in love with each other," she says.

"I'm a reporter," I tell Holly. "I told you, I'm here to do a story on your father."

Her lip quivers. I can see the joy from earlier in the day drain from her face. Without a word, she turns and runs down the hall, and I hear Ness curse under his breath. I start to follow Holly to her room, but Ness tells me I'm better off leaving her alone.

"She was bound to find out," he says. "Don't make it worse for her."

I have no idea what this means. And I don't see Holly again as I gather my things down at the guest house—using an oversized rain jacket and umbrella this time. I bring my solitary bag up to the house, and Ness leads me to the front door.

There's a helicopter outside. The pilot tells Ness that we should go before the next squall hits. And maybe it's the rain, maybe it's not getting to shell that day, maybe it's the lingering soreness from seeing Holly so upset at us, but the week has taken a turn. The joy is no longer on Ness's face. And I remember what Victoria said about that smile being his shell, that he is not a happy man, and perhaps this is my first glimpse of the true Ness Wilde. Either way, the week threatens to become one of those bright, half-buried horse conchs that you reach for only to discover that the rest of the shell is missing, that there was nothing priceless about that find after all.

-27-

I'm glad I amended Ness's packing list and brought a book. My phone doesn't work for much of the helicopter ride, and then we land at a small airport and transfer to a private jet. Once we break above the rain clouds, I can tell by the setting sun to our right that we are flying south. Ness is pensive and quiet. I attribute this to conflicts with his ex or his daughter, but it also occurs to me that he left in a hurry that morning to tend to an emergency. Perhaps it's something else entirely.

Rebelling against my reporter DNA, I decide to let it go and to lose myself in the book I brought along. *Treasure Island* was losing me, felt more like a romp a young boy might like, so I picked out *Moby Dick* instead, which I vaguely remember *not-reading* in college and instead using online notes to squeak out a B or a C on some paper. Little did I know all those years of bullshitting my way through coursework would nicely prepare me for a career in journalism. As it turns out, it pays pretty well to make up entire stories on slivers of fact.

I read for a few hours, and then the copilot comes back to serve us a meal. After the trays are taken away, I rejoin Ishmael on his whaling adventures, but I'm only half present in the book. My mind flits. The article I've written about Ness bends and sways like a tree in a shifting breeze. Somehow, two years of work now feels . . . unimportant. Trivial. I remind myself that vacation does this to priorities, and the past few days have been like a vacation. When I get back to New York—among the symphony of sirens and car alarms and shrieking subway rails—I will remember what's important. That's when the story will coalesce and take shape. It'll be easier to update my piece about Ness when he's not sitting across from me, staring at his laptop, scrolling but not typing, reading something with a frown. It'll be easier when I'm not thinking about Holly, and the way she looked at me, both in joy that morning, and in anger the last time I'm likely to ever see her.

Maybe it's meeting Holly that's made the article difficult to ponder. It's easier to demonize a man than it is a father, especially one who begs for hugs and leaves lights burning even when she isn't home to use them. Getting to know Ness as a person has been a mistake, rather than a boon for my piece. The issues I want to write about are larger than one man, larger than any of us; they concern the entire globe; they concern our environment, our politics, our collective choices. Tearing him down felt good before. Now it feels hollow. I imagine this is how Ahab might've felt if the book in my lap had turned out differently.

I drift off in my seat thinking of white whales, of ghosts who haunt us, of the destructive forces in our lives. I think how *we* are often that force, chasing what we should leave alone, what we should simply let go. But letting go is harder than destroying ourselves and those around us in a mad chase to feel . . . right with the world. Losing our child was this thing for Michael and me. We tried too hard to replace her. And when we couldn't, there was nothing left to salvage. It was that white whale or nothing. There was no in-between where we might survive. Where we might not drown.

Turbulence wakes me. I find a blanket tucked around my shoulders, my book set aside. Ness glances up from his laptop.

The cabin lights are dim, his face cast in a pale glow from the screen.

"Another couple of hours," he says softly.

"Where are we going?" I murmur.

"Middle of nowhere," Ness says. "The last place anyone thinks to look."

I try to fall back asleep, thinking on this and other puzzles. Half the time when I crack my eyes, Ness is staring at his screen. The other half of the time, he's staring at me. The darkness, the shuddering of the plane, the cabin to ourselves, my sleepy brain, a morning spent with his daughter, his pensive mood, all swim around me. An old memory returns—a collection of disjointed memories—all the impossibly long nights spent awake at summer camp, confiding to strangers in whispers for hour upon hour, never wanting to sleep, and falling for other girls my age with reckless speed, promising each other we'd be best friends forever.

"We had a daughter," I say, out of nowhere. I leave my eyes closed. The darkness is a safe place.

Ness says nothing.

"She came premature, and they couldn't save her."

I dab at my eyes with the blanket, and Ness's seat squeaks as he adjusts himself. I feel his hand on my foot. A friendly gesture. "I'm sorry," he says.

"It's just that . . . I would love to have a daughter who hates me," I say. And I find the courage to open my eyes. Tears stream down my neck. I wipe them away as quickly as they come. I'm trying to make him feel better, but I'm making us both feel worse.

"It's just a phase kids go through," Ness says. "Everyone assures me she'll grow out of it."

"You could wait for her to grow up, or you could meet her halfway," I say.

"I try." Ness closes his laptop, leaving us to the dim emergency lights. "I only get her every other weekend, and her mom often schedules camps and sports to fill those up. I've watched her grow up from the bleachers."

"Does she take to strangers easily? Because she . . ."

I don't know how to say what it felt like for her to bond with me so quickly, that it was part flattering and part sad.

"I saw the two of you napping in the guest house," Ness says. "Does she do that sort of thing a lot? Maybe not that exactly, but she does like it when I'm seeing someone. And she's always crushed when they don't stick around."

"They," I say.

"People I've dated since my wife left me."

"They don't stick around, or you don't have them back?"

Ness shrugs. "It's complicated. What's funny is that I think Holly just wants me to be happy. I think it's selfless on her part, that she wants some fairy tale for me, not for her."

"Why does she think you're not happy?" I ask.

"You're asking a lot of questions. Is this for your story?"

I consider this for a beat. He's asking me if this is on the record or off the record. Do I want to know but not be able to report what I find? Or would I rather wait and find out by other means and be able to write what I discover? It's the riddle of the non-disclosure agreement all over again.

"This is for me," I finally say. Which feels dangerous. Like I just crossed a line that shouldn't be crossed—sliding from reporter to acquaintance. Maybe even friend. But I don't see an oil magnate across from me right then; I don't see the subject of any story. Just a man, a father, someone I've spent too much time around the past few days not to empathize with.

"I'm not an easy person to live with," Ness tells me. "I try. Man, I try. I don't want to be like my father, but we are who we are." He shrugs. "I can't sit still. I have so much I want to do, and I don't feel like I have time for it all. I have a hard time delegating, an even harder time trusting people. Here's the thing: Vicky cheated on me. Another parent she met at a PTA meeting. And when she left, I gave her everything she asked for, custody, the houses she wanted, the money she demanded, because I figured the affair was my fault for not being there. My fault for being a bad father."

"Why do you think you're a bad father?"

"Because it runs in the family." Ness turns toward the window, where the moon bounces off the top of the clouds and lets in the faintest of ethereal glows. He's little more than a silhouette, but I see him wipe his cheek. "Even my grandfather, who was a good man through and through, wasn't a great father to my dad. I didn't tell you the full truth about that the other day. It's not that he was abusive, just absent. I think the same propensity to feel overwhelmed with guilt allowed him to let someone else raise his kid. Or maybe, like me, he was scared he'd screw it all up."

"What is it you're chasing?" I ask. "What're you looking for?"

"Redemption," Ness says. And the answer comes so fast, that I know he has asked himself this very question countless times. "I want to leave behind a better world than the one I was given. And like I told you the other day, I was given a world in a lot of pieces."

"Your grandfather bought up shoreline and protected it to redeem himself. How will forging shells help anyone?"

Even in the dark, I can see Ness stiffen. I hate myself for saying it. I'm more curious about him than the stupid shells in that moment, but the conversation hemmed us in like a lee shore in a storm.

"Why does this no longer feel off the record?" Ness asks.

"I'm sorry," I say. I lean forward and place a hand on his knee. "I really am. That wasn't me being a reporter . . . just me being confused."

"No, that's okay." Ness straightens himself in his seat, puts his laptop aside. I lean back in my own seat. "Of course they aren't real," he says. "The problem with those shells is that they're too perfect. Maybe that's why Arlov had to have them around. I don't know."

Before I can press him on this, Ness reminds me that we're talking off the record. And then he flashes a mischievous smile brighter than the moon. "But if you want to get back *on* the record, I've got something you can print. A scoop just for you. Something I've never told another reporter."

"What?" I ask.

"The story of my name."

I try to hide my disappointment. "I know it," I say. I can't remember where I heard it, somewhere in all the hundreds of interviews and articles I've read about him. "Your middle name is Robert. Your father thought it would be cute, since you were born around the time he tried to make the company more green. What I'd much rather hear about—"

"No, the Wilderness thing? I don't know who put that together, but it's a coincidence. My grandfather on my mother's side was named Robert. The real story is less interesting. Well, to most people, I imagine. But when my mother told me how I got my name, it led me on a trip where I discovered the single greatest thing she ever taught me about my father."

I wait. And damn him, he has me curious.

"I was named after a monster," Ness says.

"You were not," I say. "You mean the loch?"

"Yes, precisely. Loch Ness. And my mom swears it's the truth. The two of them spent their honeymoon on the Isle of Man, and they visited Scotland and the loch, and she said my father was taken with the lore of the place. But even more with the tourism. Have you ever been?"

"No."

"I went. I wanted to find out what my father saw when he came up with this name. It seemed mysterious to me. It haunted me. All I had were a few hints from my mom, where they went, some things he said. So I went there by myself hoping to find out where I came from. Where I *really* came from, you know? Not my name, really, but to get to know my dad. And it hit me on my third day there. A woman in a cafe recognized me. You know what she did?"

"Ask for your autograph? Show you a shell from her collection?"

"She spit on me," Ness says.

We fly along in silence.

"Why?" I finally ask.

"Oh, it wasn't the first time it's happened. It's all the things you have planned for your story, I'm sure. My father rolling back the green initiatives when they ended up not being as profitable. All the oil exploration the company has done under my watch. Videos of flooded homes, of major cities underwater, the expense of the levees around New York, Miami, Boston. All the breakwalls going up around the world. Pick a reason.

"What was important for me was the timing of this incident. There I was, trying to find myself on the shore of my namesake, obsessing over this question of what my father saw in his unborn son. You see, I spent those days around the loch pretending to be my father. I tried to see the town through his eyes, tried to imagine I had a new wife whom I knew to be pregnant, and a future child that I knew was going to be a boy. I thought of what the place had been like back then, what my father might've seen, the world I was going to be born into.

"My father was taken with the lore of that place, but also the tourism. This was the hint I got from my mom. He told her that the people there hate what their community has become, but that they *need* it. They hate the signs everywhere, the glass boats on the water, the subs that take gawkers out on fruitless dives, the statues and the stuffed purple sea monster toys, but they can't let go of it. They can't stop. You see?"

"No," I say. "I don't."

"*We're* the monsters," Ness says. "The Wildes. My father was a monster. His father and his grandfather were monsters. And he knew I'd become one too—"

At this, whatever holds Ness together, whatever keeps his emotions at bay, cracks. And he bends forward and weeps in his hands. Five or six shuddering sobs before he gets himself together. I am too stunned by the breakdown to react, to lean forward and put a hand on his shoulder, to offer him a shoulder to cry on. It is the most unexpected thing I've seen from a man full of surprises.

Just as suddenly, he sits up, presses at his eyes with his fists, and takes a deep breath. He doesn't apologize or seek anything from me, just continues his line of thought as if nothing had happened, as if I hadn't seen this small fissure in his otherwise perfect shell.

"Everyone needs what we provide." He swallows and composes himself further. "This plane? All the jets out there? The people who fly on them? They need us. They need the oil. It doesn't matter if we get it with greener methods these days, doesn't matter that we haven't had a major spill in forty years, that we're investing in alternate forms of energy. My great-grandfather did none of those things, because nobody cared back then. By the time his son was born, everyone had their fuzzy picture of who we were, the ugly legend. And the more they needed us, the more they hated us. It kept them from having to blame themselves.

"My dad saw that at Loch Ness. He saw people blaming a monster for all the things wrong with the world at large. He saw how we do this all the time. You want to know what the worst of it is?"

"What's that?" I ask, my voice a whisper.

"The people who live around that loch, their monster doesn't even exist. They had to *create* it."

Part IV:
A Dive Too Deep

=28=

I wake in the middle of the night to the soft bump of landing gear hitting some unknown tarmac. Ness has moved to another seat, one that faces forward, and is peering outside. My only sense of how long we've been in the air is the two meals we were served. It felt like an eight-hour flight, but it could've been four or it could've been twelve.

The air outside is humid. I imagine we're in the Caribbean, where I know Ness owns several islands. It occurs to me that I don't have my passport, which might get interesting. The mystery of our destination will soon be solved by the nationality of the jail I end up in. But we don't head for a customs building or the small airport when we deplane. Our bags are moved directly from the jet to an idling helicopter, and our trip has now taken on the air of the absurd.

It only gets crazier.

The helicopter takes us up and out to sea. I've ridden on a lot of helicopters in my line of work, and the mix of exhilaration and terror never lessens. I gaze down at the airport and then the wider land for hints about our location. The sporadic dots of lights from homes and a few moving cars reveal the outline of a small island. Tiny, in fact. I'm not great with distances, and our altitude and the dark make it even trickier, but the entire island looks to be no bigger across than Manhattan is long.

"Bermuda?" I ask. I have to raise my voice over the noisy rotor. This helicopter isn't as sturdy and well insulated as the one we took from Ness's house.

"Tristan da Cunha," Ness says, which doesn't solve the mystery of where in the hell we are.

"Never heard of it," I confess.

"It's about as far from anywhere as you can get." He leans close so we don't have to shout. "About twelve hundred miles from Saint Helena and fifteen hundred from South Africa."

"You brought me to the *Southern Hemisphere?*" I ask incredulously.

"You wanted to see what led me to those shells, right?"

I settle back in my seat. The scope of this story has shifted yet again, and not for the first time, I wonder why Ness is even taking me on this journey. He confessed as to the veracity of the shells on the plane. With the verdict no longer in doubt, that leaves only his justification. But why care what I think?

Suddenly, an answer to this last question falls into place.

The last time Ness made me keep something off the record, he gave me a glimpse of the truth in his grandfather's journal, knowing that I wouldn't be able to write my piece afterward. Perhaps he hopes he can do the same here, that he can show me some validation that would make the highly illegal seem perfectly okay. Maybe I was right to suspect that he's working on an eco-education program, some way of raising awareness of species that have gone extinct. He said he wanted redemption. This fits. It all fits, but I don't see how it will keep me from writing a piece about it. Unless he *wants* me to write that story. Unless I'm a tool for his ultimate redemption.

I hate that my mind goes to places like this, but it does, like filings to a magnet. When Ness takes an interest in something out the window, I lean across to check for myself, to get my thoughts elsewhere. Below, I see the lights of a ship. My stomach sinks as I realize we're going to *land* on it.

Rain beads on the window—the stars and the moon are obscured as we drop through the clouds—and I wonder what the chances are that we left a rainstorm, flew however many thousands of miles to the other side of the globe, and are landing in yet another shower.

Red and white flashing lights illuminate the aft deck of the large ship. I can see a giant 'H' marked out on the deck. The helicopter touches down with a jarring double-bounce and a thump. Ness steadies me as I lurch into him. Men with glowing orange cones signal one last thing to the pilot, and then the door opens, and a man in a jumpsuit holding a large umbrella helps me out of the helicopter.

"Welcome to the *Keldysh*," the man says to me. He shakes Ness's hand. "Hello, boss."

"Lieutenant Jameson, Maya Walsh of the *Times*. Maya, this is Lieutenant Jameson. First mate on this vessel."

"You can call me Jimbo, ma'am."

"Would you mind showing her to her room?" Ness asks. "I'm going to speak with the captain and check the Mir."

"Yessir."

Ness guides me away from the helicopter, which is spinning down its rotors and being strapped to the deck by a crew in rain slicks. It appears it will be staying with the ship. Perhaps belongs to it. Rain pops against the umbrella, and the deck is shiny and wet; it gleams from all the bright lights scattered across the ship. I can feel the world moving and swirling beneath my feet and am thankful that a childhood on boats has made me resistant to seasickness.

"Get a good night's sleep," Ness tells me. "I'll see you in the morning."

Before I can complain, or ask where he'll be staying, or realize that it shouldn't matter, my mind is adjusting itself to the distance between us. Staying in his guest house and knowing he is right up there on that dune was one thing; sleeping in the plane with him across from me was another; but neither of those were by any circumstance other than necessity. And once again, my summer-camp brain leaves me unprepared for this intense closeness followed by a sudden absence. As he walks away, something inside me is stretched like taffy. I look away before I feel it break.

Beside me, a stranger in a gray jumpsuit with the name "Jameson" on his chest indicates the way. I follow him numbly into the riveted hull, through cramped steel corridors, and to a bunkroom that makes my college dorm seem like some palatial resort in retrospect.

The lodgings do not matter. I'm exhausted and discombobulated. I still don't know where I am or what the hell I think I'm doing. I unpack my bag, change into sleep shorts, and fall asleep with *Moby Dick* in my hands. I don't open the book. Don't need to. It just feels good to have something solid there, to not be chasing after a great big nothing. This white whale has a name, at least.

-29-

I wake to the smell of coffee brewing and the clang of boots on steel decking outside. It takes several minutes of lying in the dark to realize where I am, to make sense of which direction the door is in relation to my bed. I'm not in my apartment in New York. I'm not in Ness's guest house. Not on a plane. I'm on a ship.

I stretch as much as the small bunk will allow, get up, and refresh myself in the tight confines of the pantry-sized bathroom. I brush my teeth and then figure out the shower, which is basically the bathroom itself. A nozzle in the wall and a drain on the floor suggest the rest of the room is just meant to get soaked. I close the door, lower the toilet lid, and take a steaming hot shower. I get dressed and then braid my hair into something utilitarian. It's the military-feeling surroundings, I think. And the fact that my hair will never fully dry in this humidity.

Donning the shorts and t-shirt Ness suggested I bring, I grab my book and follow the wafting promise of coffee down the corridor, up one deck, and to a small mess hall or break room. Conversations continue after a brief pause and curious stares. Heads track me. I'm an alien in the midst of these jumpsuited, tight-knit oil roughnecks, or shell miners, or whatever they are.

"Ms. Walsh?"

A woman my age, but more muscular and with short-cropped hair, approaches. Her accent sounds vaguely Russian. We shake hands. "Maya," I say.

"Petrona. Welcome aboard. Coffee's over there. Eggs and ham? Or do you prefer porridge?"

"Eggs and ham," I say. I make myself a cup of coffee. A heavyset man watches me and puffs on his vape. The cloud smells of mint and strawberries. "What is this ship?" I ask Petrona.

"The *Keldysh?* She's an old research vessel. Decommissioned years ago until Ocean Oil got her fit again. A floating four-star hotel and world-class laboratory." She says *laboratory* the way a Brit might, pronouncing the *bore* in the middle. "But mostly it's home to the Mirs five and six. Finest shellers on the seven seas—"

"That's enough," a voice behind us says. I turn to see Ness entering the mess hall. He smiles at Petrona and wags a finger. He has something in his other hand. "Ms. Walsh is a reporter. The less you say the better."

Someone seated at one of the tables laughs.

"How come you get coveralls, but you told me to wear shorts and a t-shirt?" I ask, studying Ness's getup.

"Because shorts are what you wear *under* your coveralls." He presents me with a neatly folded pair of coveralls of my own. I unfold them and see my name embroidered on the chest. "I was bringing them to you so you wouldn't look ridiculous around here in your skivvies. Which you do."

There's a pause.

"So stop looking ridiculous," he says.

More laughter from the peanut gallery. I go with it and put the coveralls on right there. They're a perfect fit. I don't ask how he procured them in such short order. Must've set this up days ago when I accepted his invitation. So whatever he has planned, everything is going according to it. Thus far, at least.

"Eat up," he says. "You're going to get hungry today, trust me. But go casy on the coffee."

••••

Too often, a thing stares me in the face long before I recognize it. I should have known what we were doing. Something the rain won't affect, but no swimsuit needed. A sort of diving. The next progression of shelling. But it isn't until a deckhand is cracking the hatch on the bright yellow submersible that I see what Ness is up to. It's almost too late to complain.

"How safe is this?" I ask.

"Perfectly safe," he says. "The Mir Mark Five is rated for depths this planet doesn't even possess. You could sit at the bottom of the Mariana Trench in this puppy." He slaps the hull with his hand, which rings like an empty oil barrel. A perfectly normal empty oil barrel. The kind I imagine the ocean deep would crush in its fist.

"How deep are we going, exactly?"

"A little less than twenty thousand feet."

"That sounds like a lot."

Ness laughs. "It is. We're at one the deepest points in the South Atlantic." He gestures toward the sub. "Ladies first."

"Always with the 'Ladies first,'" I say. "Why do I expect things to go really poorly when you say that?"

"Because you think I'm inviting you to your doom. And maybe I am. Now watch your head when you get in. There are pipes and sharp corners everywhere. Russians are fond of such things. And don't touch any buttons or levers."

I find myself crawling inside the oblong craft. The passenger compartment is a rough sphere right behind and above the sub's twin folded arms. There are wide portholes everywhere. I settle into the far seat despite my trepidations and watch the deck crew scramble around in the rain coiling cables, signaling to one another, and checking out various parts of the sub. There's a scraping noise above me. Through a porthole in the roof, I can see the treads of someone's boot. I watch as a thick cable is attached to a stout bar. Ness crawls in beside me.

"I take it you want to drive," he says.

"No, I don't. Switch." I make to get up and let him slide under me, but he places a hand on my arm.

"I'm just kidding. There are controls on both sides. But I will let you take the wheel for a bit. It's easy. Like playing a video game."

"Awesome. So it's exactly like something I never do."

"You'll be fine."

"I swear to God, Ness, if our lives depend upon me operating this contraption, I want the hell out right now."

"Okay. You don't have to do anything. Sorry. Just trying to lighten the—"

"You aren't lightening the mood!" I say. And I realize I'm panting. Just like the first time with the dive gear. Someone swings the hatch shut by Ness's side, but he braces it and pushes it back open.

"Just one second," he tells someone. And then he turns to me. "We don't have to go if you don't want to go. But I assure you, it's perfectly safe. People have been going this deep for nearly a century. The equipment has gotten nothing but better. You are safer in this than you were in the helicopter."

"That's supposed to make me feel better?"

Ness shrugs.

"Why didn't you just tell me yesterday that this was what we were coming here to do?"

"Because you would've worried all night. You wouldn't have slept. And you'd be even more panicked now after getting yourself worked up for hours over this."

He's right. But I don't like decisions made for me, even if they are in my best interest. *Especially* when they're in my best interest. It assumes someone else knows me better than I know myself. And so I hate that he's right.

"I just need a minute," I say.

"Take your time."

I get my breathing under control. After a moment, I nod my assent, even though I'm not quite ready, because I want to show him that I'm braver than he gives me credit for being. I *am* brave. I know this about myself. I have kicked ass in a man's world because I embrace being doubted. I embrace being underestimated.

"Okay," I say. "Let's do this."

Ness gives a thumbs-up to someone outside. The hatch swings shut with a clang.

"That's my girl," he says.

And I almost don't hate him for saying it.

-30-

My stomach turns as the submersible is hauled into the air. As soon as we leave the deck, the sub twists on its cable, and the world beyond the circular portholes of glass goes spinning.

We go up and out. I can see the rail at the edge of the ship pass beneath us, hear metal creaking, and then we begin to drop—and I find myself clutching Ness's arm, fearful of grabbing any part of the sub, any of the levers and buttons, and prematurely detaching us from the crane.

Ness has a headset on, is talking to someone, probably the crane operator. A second headset hangs from a rack on my side of the sub. I pull it on and listen to a woman's voice counting down numbers. When she gets to zero, the swell of the stormy sea thwaps the bottom of the sub, sending a rattle through it and into my bones. I hear Ness's voice in my headset and also beside me: "Touchdown."

But we aren't through descending. We've only begun. Another wave shakes the craft, foam and salt sloshing up the porthole beside me, and now I have Ness's arm wrapped in both of mine. The water rises up the portholes in front of us, bubbling and frothing, the gray overcast sky replaced with the deep blue sea. And then we're below the water. The Atlantic closes up around us. And the world is silent, peaceful, and still.

"Ready to detach," Ness says.

"Detaching."

There's a mild clank above our heads. Otherwise, nothing seems different. But I sense that we're free of the ship.

"Unless you want to drive, I'll need that arm," Ness tells me.

I realize I'm still clutching him for balance. "Oh, right."

I let go, and Ness grabs the joysticks on either side of his seat. He pushes them to one side, and I feel a sense of acceleration as we move away from the mothership. The fat hull of the research vessel recedes until it's swallowed by the black. Just before it disappears, the view reminds me of looking up at Ness's boat while diving, but on a completely different scale.

"What does that do?" I ask Ness as he adjusts some knobs.

"It controls our rate of descent. We drop at about fifty meters per minute. We should touch down in a little less than two hours."

"TWO HOURS?"

I immediately regret shouting. Every sound is amplified in the small metal sphere and the headsets. Ness raises an eyebrow.

"What happened to sixty feet, ten minutes?" I ask. "Sixty feet. Ten minutes. What happened to that?"

"We're going a lot deeper for a lot longer," Ness explains. "I promise you it's safe. I've done a hundred deep dives in this baby, and she's done thousands more without me."

"But two hours just to *get* there?" I now understand why Ness insisted I use the bathroom after breakfast and why he told me to go easy on the coffee.

"Yeah, and we run on battery power, which I need to conserve. I'm going to dim the lights for now. The heater has to stay on, or we'll freeze in here. But let me know if it gets too cold for you." He flips switches, and the banks of internal lights go off. There is enough left from the dials and indicators to see around us. Ness seems to study one readout after another, checking things. All I see is the inscrutable cockpit of a jumbo jet wrapped around us.

"There's a bag on the shelf behind you," Ness says. "A couple of apples, granola bars, some juice. Go easy on the juice, but if you have to relieve yourself, there are ways."

"Do I even want to know?"

"Probably not. Oh, and I packed your book and borrowed a reading light from one of the bosuns. It's in there as well."

"I can read about the hunt for Moby Dick at the bottom of the sea," I say in perfect monotone, so he knows just how enthused I am.

"Spoiler alert," Ness warns. "Down here is where the Pequod ends up."

"Gee, thanks."

"Yeah, well, it's how it gets there that's interesting. You should read it anyway. Great book, even if no one recognized it at the time."

"Is that what you're up to?" I ask. "Is that what this is all about? Being remembered as someone great, even if it's only after you're gone?"

Ness laughs. He turns and looks at me in the dim light of the indicators. "Really? We're going to do this here? At . . ." He checks something. "Two hundred meters and falling?"

"Why not? I've got you here for the next two hours. Interview on."

"Five hours, if we spend an hour at the bottom."

My bladder clenches. "Five hours," I say, mostly to myself. "So tell me, what did you mean by redemption on the plane last night—"

"That was off the record," Ness warns.

"Okay." I try to think of how to rephrase what I want to ask. "How about this? Why do you want to show me whatever led you to the creation of these shells? Do you expect me to rewrite my story so that it's mostly about this? Are you trying to be remembered differently than your father?"

Ness doesn't reply immediately, which makes me think he takes the question seriously, is at least introspective enough to consider this as a possibility.

"I don't care how most people remember me," he finally says.

"*Most* people?"

"That's right. But I do care what Holly thinks. And she sees me the way you do." He turns to me. Is back to his serious self. And from what Victoria told me, this is the Ness that I believe. Not the smiling and laughing man—not that he isn't capable of joy—but there's meat inside that shell; it's not all rainbows and sunshine in there. "Holly won't care about any of this now, maybe not for years, but I want her to know the truth someday. I don't care if you write that truth. In fact . . . you want to know what I think this is about for me?"

"Yes," I say. "Are you just realizing it right now?"

"Yeah," Ness says. "I am. I think this is a test—"

"You're testing me? Why do you care what I think?"

"I don't. I mean, I do. What I mean is that I'm not testing *you.* I'm testing myself. Seeing what would happen if I told people the truth."

I laugh at this.

"I'm serious. Because I could get into a lot of trouble. I could spend the rest of my life in jail. But I want to tell Holly someday. I want to explain myself, tell her why I wasn't around as much as I should've been, why I drove her mother away, why I—"

He turns to the porthole on his side of the submersible and is quiet for a while. When he speaks again, his voice breaks. "Why I tore the family apart. Because it's gonna take a lot to make that worth it. And if she thinks it was frivolous, that none of it mattered—all the hours I was gone—then she'll hate me for the rest of my life and then keep on hating me for the rest of hers. And I've felt that hate in my own heart. Felt it toward my dad. And my granddad. Which is why when my granddad passed, and his journal fell into my possession, and I saw how wrong I was—

that's when I knew I had to leave something behind for Holly. That I couldn't do everything in secret. Not forever."

"Do what in secret?" I ask.

"Soon," Ness says. "Soon."

"Look—"

"You'll know everything in a few days," he says, cutting me off. "And then you can decide what to write, if you write anything at all."

He turns to face me. Even in the dim light, I can see that his eyes are filmed over with tears. "I was familiar with your shelling pieces back in the day, and I read some of your more recent stuff before you came over that first night. I trust you. And it's even better to see that Holly trusts you. That means the world to me. She might be angry with us for a few days for not being in love, but when she reads what you have to say—if you have anything to say—and sees the truth instead of all the lies out there about me, that'll go a long way with the healing."

"That's too much to put on me, Ness. I have to be objective. You can't use her like that to make me write what you want to see. And you can't use me like this hoping I'll write something nice about you. I hate to break it to you, but I'm a resistant cuss. If I like you, I'm just as likely to rip you apart to prove I'm capable of being fair."

"No, you're right. It's too much to ask. And I don't mean any of it like that. It's just . . . I can see how this all plays out, how it *has* to play out, and I guess I'm thanking you in advance. I shouldn't do that, I know. Now I'm the one skipping to the end."

"Yeah. And you should be prepared for me to disappoint you, Ness. Because I probably will."

Ness adjusts one of the levers on his side of the sub and settles back into his seat. "I don't think that's possible," he says. "I don't think you can."

-31-

Flying commercial as often as I do, I feel trained for this journey to the bottom of the sea. The sub is far more comfortable than coach in a 797. More leg room, better snacks, and no one behind me coughing and sneezing. I read for an hour, wondering when these people are going to get to sea already and get to whaling, and I take occasional breaks to gaze out at the pitch black beyond the glass.

The only thing I see out there is the small bubbles forming on the portholes; it looks like we're in outer space but with stars that can't sit still. As we plunge down and down, the sub makes creaking sounds, which Ness tells me at least a hundred times is perfectly normal. He says the military subs do the same thing, that it's just the metal settling against the phenomenal pressure outside, that at this depth, a watermelon would instantly become the size of a grape.

From what I can tell, Ness is good at a lot of things—but reassuring people is not one of them.

"Probably a good idea to kill the book light," he tells me. He turns on an interior light, which bathes the interior of the sub in a red glow.

"Is that a bad thing?" I ask. Red is always bad. This is a bad thing. Something is wrong.

"The red light? No, that's to save our vision. We're almost to the bottom."

There seems to be a red glow *outside* the submersible as well, some kind of dim light beneath us. Ness steers the craft to the side and rotates us. I can hear the motors whirring elsewhere in the capsule.

"That's the Mid-Atlantic Ridge," Ness says, pointing through one of the portholes. "I'd guess a hundred people have laid eyes on it in person like this. Far fewer than have been in space."

This factoid gives me goose bumps. The previously surreal in my life now feels banal in comparison to where I am, what I'm doing, what I'm seeing.

"Do you want to steer?"

"Sure," I say, even though I don't really.

"I'm slowing the rate of descent." Ness adjusts a knob. "If you think of the sub as having four wheels, the stick on the left controls the driver's side wheels, and the stick on the right controls the passenger side. If you want to rotate, move them opposite each other. Try it."

I do. Hesitantly at first, but then with more force as I feel how slowly the craft responds to input. The light beneath us rotates. It's also getting brighter outside, the dull red now beating crimson.

"You can control the depth by pushing the controls toward or away from each other. And adjust your pitch by rotating them."

"I just like spinning in circles," I say, and Ness laughs.

"The cool thing is you can flip this switch, and then you're controlling the sampling arms. Usually, one person drives, and the other person operates the floodlights, the arms, and the research tools."

"Do I need to know how to do all that?" I ask.

"No. This is mostly a sightseeing tour. I just want to show you something, an idea I had one day when I was down here, so you can see where it led me. So the rift here, this is from the sea floor being torn apart. You remember from grade school how Africa and South America fit together—?"

"Plate tectonics," I say.

"Right. Well, this is the wound from those plates moving apart. That's magma down there, flowing up through the wound. It cools when it hits the water and throws off a ton of steam. There're all kinds of temperature gradients down here. It's one of the ways our oil platforms generate power. But there's something even more interesting about these vents."

Ness takes over the controls and brings us down through a cloud of black smoke. He turns the interior lights off again. The sea floor rises up. It looks like a flat expanse of sand and rock, just like the ocean floor I've seen while snorkeling in twenty feet of water. But now we're a *thousand* times deeper.

"Watch," Ness says. He flicks a switch, and floodlights bathe the area in front of us. One of the vents is just a hundred or so feet away. The water and smoke swirl there. The crust throbs red. I'm seeing inside the Earth. To me, this is as wild and inhospitable a place as the surface of Mars—

And then there's a different sort of movement. An erratic, zigzagging shadow. "There," Ness says, but I already see it. A fish. Or squid. An oblong creature with a fin and a snout, but it's gone before I make out any more detail.

"What the hell was *that?*" I ask.

"A fish. And there are tubeworms and shrimp and crab down here. And slugs. Also, it's currently sixty degrees Celsius out there. It's even warmer closer to the vent."

"Sixty Celsius—" I try to remember formulas I haven't had to use since college. "About one-forty Fahrenheit?"

"Not about," Ness says. "Exactly one-forty. Nice." He seems impressed. "That's why I had to switch from the heater to the cooler when we crossed the thermal barrier. Otherwise we'd cook in here. As it is, we can't stay long or the battery will go dead."

"What if that happens?"

"They'd have to send the other sub down with a cable to retrieve us. It's happened before. We'd be fine for a couple of hours, but it does get uncomfortable. Anyway, this is just a sideshow, one of those really cool things you have to see while you're in the neighborhood. The real magic is over here."

Ness grips the controls, and we lift from the sea floor. I watch the floodlit sand for more signs of life. I see what look to be shrimp running. "I think we had all of two days in class about these lifeforms," I say, marveling at the sight. "Exo-something organisms?"

"Two days, huh? What's amazing is that the biodiversity down here is almost as great as in a rainforest. They discovered these ecosystems back in the 1970s. It defied everything we thought we knew about life, where it could live, what it could adapt to. Now we know that life can live practically anywhere, that it even grows like lichen on the surface of the space station. I was thinking about this one day, down here, getting some samples. And it struck me both how robust and how fragile nature can be. It seems as though life can adapt to anything, but then a small change wipes out an entire species."

He's quiet for a moment. Then picks up where he left off.

"The crazy thing about these vents is that the chemistry of the sea is completely different here. There's no sunlight to get everything going. The base unit of energy is hydrogen sulfide, which is toxic to the creatures we know up top. Resemblance between these animals and the non-vent kind can fool you. But they do share ancestors.

"Here. Check out this gauge. That's our current sea temp. You can see how quickly the temp falls away as we leave the vent. If we keep going, it falls below zero. The pressure and salinity are the only reasons the water doesn't freeze."

The readout shows nineteen degrees Celsius. I think that's about seventy degrees Fahrenheit, but I'm rounding. "Right now we have something like surface sea temp," I say.

"Right. But go either direction, and you get something warmer or something cooler. The temperature gradients form rings around the vents. It got me wondering: If life exists in these extreme ranges, why did it get hammered by a few degrees rise in the rest of the ocean? Look."

He sees something I don't. Ness bursts into activity, driving the sub down to the bottom and then controlling the arms, scooping something up. A fountain of sand erupts where the arm attachment hits the sea floor.

"Gotcha," he says. It's the most excited I've seen him. He works the arms back toward the sub, then throws more switches. "Won't be sure until we get back to the surface, but that looked like a good sample."

"Of what?" I ask.

"I'll show you when we get back to the estate—"

"Jesus, Ness, enough of this. What the hell are we doing here? And yes, I'm skipping to the end of the story. I don't care anymore. None of this makes sense—"

"Breathe," Ness says. And I realize I'm panting. Hyperventilating.

"I need out of here," I say. My heart is racing. I feel trapped, first by Ness and his meaningless clues, and now by the thought of twenty thousand feet of water above us, the creaks and groans of solid steel as the sea is trying to crush us, and the realization that there's nowhere to go, not for hours, and I swear the air in that tin can is growing stale, is getting thin, is running out—

"Look at me," Ness says.

"I—can't—see—" I labor between pants for air.

Ness floods the submarine with that red light. I only see a spot of it; the rest of my vision has closed in around the edges, irising shut. I feel Ness's hands on either side of my face, supporting me. Making me look at him. He has arranged himself sideways in his seat. He is asking me to breathe in, to hold it. I try.

"Let it out," he says. "Slowly."

Puh puh puh. The best I can do is three short and rapid exhalations. And then I'm gasping for air again.

"Listen to me," Ness says. I concentrate on his voice. Part of me believes I will die here, at the bottom of the sea, and that there's something romantic about that. A good death for a rubbish life. As a staff writer, I'll get a killer obit in the *Times.*

The other part of me is certain that Ness will save me. That he won't let me die. And the resistance I feel around him, that I protect myself with—I let it go. I want him to save me. I don't want this rubbish life to end so soon.

"That's it. A deep breath. Hold it. Concentrate on me. Just look at me. Listen to my voice. Good. Now let it out."

I don't know how they got there, but my hands are on his cheeks. I feel two days of stubble rough against my palms. I see his lips moving, his eyes locked on mine, all in that red glow of lights meant to guard our vision.

I can breathe again, barely, but I don't want to let go of him. And I don't want him to let go of me. I can breathe like this. To release him would be to drown. I feel like I should warn Ness that he'll have to hold me like this, and I'll have to hold him, at least until we get to the surface. I feel like I should warn him to get away from me, warn him of what I'm about to do.

And it's hard to say who moves first. There is a lightning bolt of awareness, an electrical shock as my mind rewires itself to cope with this looming fact: We are about to kiss. And then I'm pulling him into me, and I swear I feel him pulling me as well, and lips that I have damned crash into the lips that damned them. Holding his face, like one might cup a chalice, I realize how thirsty I was for this. How badly I want him right then, in that moment. I don't care who he is, who I am, or about any story. We are at the edge of the world, in the depths of space, where the laws of biology and the rules of physics do not seem to apply.

His lips feel warm and full against mine. Through closed eyes, I see hot magma and the cool, deep blue. I feel the rush of the Atlantic as it fills the space around us, swirling, lifting us into weightlessness. Breaking free from the kiss for a moment, I manage a deep breath. A heavy sigh. Then I moan and collapse into his lips once more.

His hands feel strong on my back, on my waist. I run my hands up his arms, to his shoulders, through his hair, pulling him into me, our kiss turning into something as crushing as the depths.

"Maya—" Ness mumbles around my lips. He's about to talk sense into us both.

"Shut up," I whisper. I grab one side of my coveralls and pull the snaps apart, which go like cracked knuckles, popping staccato from neck to navel. I start to wiggle my arms out, and Ness says, "Are you sure?" And I say, "I'm hot. I need out of this."

Ness pulls away from me and reaches for a knob. "I can make it cooler," he says.

"Just help me out of this." I wiggle and contort my back, but one of my arms is stuck. Ness laughs and helps me. Kicking off my shoes, I wiggle the coveralls down my legs until I'm free of them. The air in the submersible is blessedly cool on my feverish skin. Adjusting myself on my seat, sitting on my knees, I lean over Ness and tear the chest of his coveralls apart. He gets his arms free. I pull his white t-shirt over his head and toss that aside. Kiss him again. Our tongues touch, soft and warm. Gentle. I bite his lower lip to let him know gentle is nice, but it's not everything.

"Mmm," he murmurs, pulling away. Again, I fear he's about to talk sense into the both of us. Mention Holly. Or professional codes of ethics. And I'm going to have to explain to him how what happens at the Mid-Atlantic Ridge stays at the Mid-Atlantic Ridge. But he says, "Gotta save the battery," and reaches around me, embracing me, and I laugh as he fumbles for switches behind me, a pump running somewhere for a moment, Ness cursing, the pump switching off, and then the red lights around us and the harsh white floodlights outside all going dark.

He leans back into his seat, and now it's just the constellation of indicators and dials around us, the distant red glow of lava leaking from the Earth, the shadows of animals that should not exist, and this, between us, which should not be possible.

I run my hands over his chest, that swimmer's chest. I touch the black pearl on that thin leather strap, study him for a moment, then lean in for another kiss. Ness cups my breasts through my shirt, and I arch my back with pleasure. I press myself into his hands and grab a fistful of his hair. Arching my back further, I bang my head on a pipe. We both laugh. "This thing was not built for this," I say.

"The arms go down," Ness tells me. He fumbles between the chairs, and the armrests slide down level with the seats. It makes a short bench. "I've never done this before," Ness says, seeming to read my mind. "I promise. But I have considered the various complexities."

"Show me what you've considered," I say, kissing him. In this moment, I don't care if I'm a one-night stand. I don't care if this is the last time we touch. I don't care if being in the same room together is awkward later. I want this, whatever the costs. Something about being so close to death, about this inhospitable place, makes me want to feel *alive*. And something about being trapped with Ness, about the last three days spent in each other's company, has me craving what I know I'll soon regret.

Ness places a hand on the top of my head, an odd gesture, but when he lifts me up, I realize it's to keep me from banging into anything. I hold his arms, can feel his muscles flex. To be lifted and moved so easily feels exhilarating. My desire to be in control of every situation is gone. I am floating. Bobbing on the sea. Ness lays me down on my back. He pushes my shirt up, slowly, as if asking permission. I lift my arms up over my head in assent. Starting at my neck, he kisses his way across the smooth hollow of my collarbone, sending trills of electricity through me, then works down to my breasts, kissing them, cupping them with his hands, and I place mine on top of his and make him squeeze harder. My nipples ache with pleasure. I pull my bra down and guide Ness's head. His tongue circles my nipple before taking me between his lips.

Ness slowly kisses his way up my chest, up my neck, finds my lips again. He brushes loose strands of hair from my face. The frenetic energy is gone, replaced by a comfortable caressing, a writhing embrace, a pleasurable squirming. I wrap my arms around him and squeeze. I kiss his neck.

"Maya," Ness whispers in my ear. If there is more, it is lost as he buries his head in my shoulder. The steel shell around us groans. We are the torus inside. There is no space nor time. No concept of being. Just a floating feeling, a sense of escape and flying, another Icarus kiss, completely free, the empty cosmos around us, exploring each other there at the bottom of the sea.

Part V:
Surfacing for Air

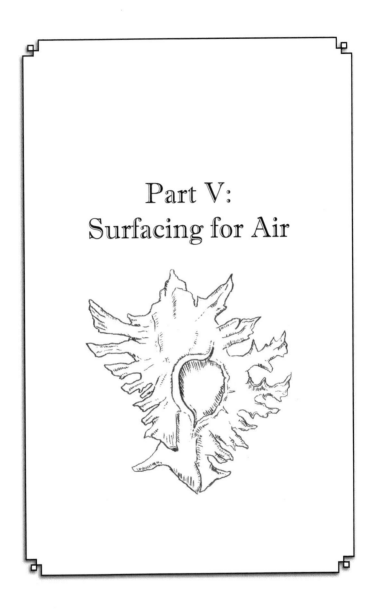

-32-

"Shit, I think the mics were on," Ness says. He finds one of the headsets and places it back on its rack. I'm pretty sure I knocked it off trying to get my arm out of my coveralls. "The operators on the ship must've heard everything."

"Tell me you're joking," I say.

Ness hesitates.

"I'm joking," he says.

"Come lie back down," I tell him. "And by lie back down, I mean curl up in an awkward ball on top of me while the edge of this armrest gouges into my spine."

"I have to get us surfacing," he says. "We've almost stayed down as long as we can."

I groan in complaint. I'm as scared to leave this place as I was to come here. I don't want to go back to the old rules. I like the Mid-Atlantic Ridge rules. "Have them send the other sub," I say.

Ness laughs. "It's a two-hour ride back to the top if we start now. You'll be sick of me by the time we get there."

"I doubt that," I tell him.

The sub rocks slightly as it leaves the sea floor. A small motor whirs somewhere behind us. Ness checks one more gauge, then asks me to get up. He arranges himself on the small bench and motions for me to get on top of him. I curl up across his chest and lap, my head on his shoulder, my lips brushing his neck, and he smooths my hair, which has largely come loose from my braid.

"That was amazing," I say. I feel like a teenager, where kissing and fondling are as extreme and satisfying as sex. More satisfying. It's like we both knew to dance along that last line, not wanting to cross it, not wanting to mess up the moment.

Ness kisses my forehead. "I forgot to ask if this was going to be off the record or not."

"Definitely off the record," I say, laughing. "And look, I won't make this hard for you—"

"Don't," he tells me. "Please don't break up with me at the bottom of the ocean. It'll make the next two hours really awkward."

I laugh.

"Besides," he says, "I like you. I have since the moment you stormed out of my house and called me a sociopath. So you're the one who's gonna have to decide what comes next, not me."

"The story," I say. "My job." I think of all the complications that would've been ridiculous to ponder an hour ago but which now swirl all around me, the myriad reasons this is a dumb idea. I think of the five-hour drive back and forth, how much a pain in the ass dating would be, how everyone in the office will think the wrong things but will be partly correct. How they'll say the wrong things, which will be partly true. What my sister will say if I tell her I'm dating Ness Wilde. What Henry will do. His mustache will spin if I tell him about this. Agent Cooper will flip. I think about the rest of my story and my responsibility to our readers, and how hard it'll be to write that last piece. All this and more haunts me in the space of a heartbeat.

"Stop stressing," Ness says. He runs a finger across the worried furrow in my brow. "Let's take it one day at a time, see if we can even get through this week."

"Is that how long this usually lasts?" I ask him.

Ness kisses my temple and doesn't respond. I choose not to press him, not to mess this up. Instead, I nestle into his arms and tell my worrying brain to take a vacation, to think on these things later. I allow myself to enjoy this moment, me and Ness in a sphere of twinkling lights, the black world outside fading to a dull crimson, and then a deep, rich blue, as we rise toward the surface and I fall in and out of sleep.

••••

Ness wakes me and says we're fifteen minutes away. So begins the strangest search-for-clothes-after-making-out that I've ever encountered. I get my bra arranged and my shirt back on, then wiggle into my coveralls, trying not to hit any switches with my elbows. As Ness puts on his headset and takes over control of the sub, I comb out my hair with my fingers and then put in a new braid.

"Okay," Ness says into the mic. "I've got you now. Not sure what that was all about. Comms acting glitchy. No—no, I don't think we need to tear anything apart to sort it out. Everything else is online. Yup. See you in five."

He smiles at me. I push his microphone out of the way and kiss him quietly. I want to see if the rules of the deep still apply this close to the surface, and they seem to.

"Holly will be so proud of us," I say.

Ness laughs. He covers the mic with his hand. "I've got her next weekend if we want to plan something. I'm sure she'd love to see you."

"I'd like that," I say. I feel a shiver from having crossed some new line, some thermal barrier.

"Maybe together, the two of you can explain how the cover to my Shelby ended up in the guest house bathtub."

"Is a Shelby a car?" I ask.

Ness shakes his head. "You were so much sexier fifteen thousand feet ago."

"Thanks. How do I look? Is it obvious we made out? It's obvious, isn't it."

"No. You look like you had a claustrophobic fit."

"Excellent."

"And then somehow ripped off your jumpsuit and put it back on with the buttons snapped all wrong."

I look down and see that the top snaps don't line up, that all of the snaps are off by one. I start redoing them. "You better have that mic off," I say.

"Whoops," Ness says, but I can tell he's joking. I'm beginning to be able to read him. He takes a bit more getting used to than even Melville.

Outside, the water brightens, like the sun is rising. But we're the ones coming up. We're in a golden sphere, approaching the horizon. Ness takes the controls again and guides us toward the underbelly of the ship. Along with the great hull of the craft, and its massive propellers, I see the fins of a diver treading water. We break the surface just a few feet from him; the diver gives a thumbs-up through a porthole, has a cable in his hand. Ness arranges the arms of the sub to provide a ladder to the top. There's the clanging of metal on metal, and then the slap of a hand on the hull.

"Locked in," Ness says into his headset. And up we go, softly spinning again, water sheeting across the portholes, the sea falling away beneath us until the railing of the great ship swings below our feet once more.

We touch down with a clang, and Ness pops the hatch, water dripping down in a veil. As I crawl out of the sub, I feel like I'm in possession of some incredible secret. Like a kid sneaking kisses behind my parents' backs. All the questions the deck crew has for Ness are about the sub, not about what happened between us. I marvel that no one suspects anything, that such an incredible moment—making out with someone for the first time at the bottom of the sea—could be contained by the two people involved. Part of me is dying to get on my phone and tell someone; the other part wants to keep this selfishly for myself and never tell another living soul.

The next hour is a blur, my head still swimming, my hormones coursing and adrenaline raging. I barely have time for a shower and a quick lunch before Ness is saying we need to leave. After I grab my bag from my room, I track down Ness's room with the help of a crew member. He startles when I walk in, was just in the act of stuffing the last of his things into his bag. As we navigate the tight corridors of the ship together, I brush his hand with mine. He turns as he ducks through a doorway and is grinning from ear to ear.

The helicopter ride back to the island is smoother this time, the rain having slowed to a trickle, the sky clearing. We land on that small island about as far from civilization as one can be, and get back on the plane. I look forward to the flight. The time to think. To relax. Ness stows our bags and then walks to the rear of the plane, past the eight leather recliners, beyond the bathroom, and to the door at the very back.

He opens it and waves me toward him. The flight crew folds the steps behind me and shuts the door, and the jet engines whine as they power up. "Ladies first," Ness says, in what has become a little mantra of sorts, a private joke between us.

"What's in there?" I ask.

"A bed." And when he sees the look on my face, he quickly adds: "I'm not suggesting anything. Just thought you'd be more comfortable. If you wanted to get some rest. That's all."

I squeeze past him and into an opulent bedroom. Rich cherry veneer, a queen size bed, a lounging area, a closet, a pile of pillows. It reminds me of the master stateroom in a yacht I toured once for a shelling piece I wrote.

"Is this the same plane we flew in on?" I ask.

"Yeah," Ness says.

"You mean you let me sleep in that chair on the way here instead of telling me about the bed?"

Ness bites his lip. He looks guilty. "I . . . didn't want you out of my sight. And it's not like I could've stayed in here with you. Not then. So yeah, it didn't occur to me to send you back here."

"You're just saying that now to be sweet," I say, a hand on his chest. "You didn't think that at the time. Not yesterday."

"I did. I thought it all day when I had to leave you on Wednesday, when I had to put that note in your door. If it hadn't been an emergency, I wouldn't have left you. I didn't want to go."

"I'm so confused." I place a hand on my forehead. "Why is this happening?"

"Get some rest," Ness says. "If you want, I can stay out here—"

"No, I want you in here with me. I'm not confused about that. Just about . . . life."

The room sways as the plane begins to taxi. I lose my balance, but Ness steadies me and steers us both so that we collapse into the bed.

"Should we be buckled up?" I ask, scooting so that my head is on the pillows.

"Probably," Ness says, but neither of us gets up. We just slide back in the silk sheets as the jet accelerates, clinging to one another and laughing, and I feel young, dangerously young, like new love feels when you have no idea where it might lead.

We are entwined and kissing before the plane leaves the tarmac. At one point, I have to pull away and pinch my nose and blow to relieve the pressure in my ears. "Only you could be cute doing that," Ness says. I crawl on top of him and stretch out, so our bodies are pressed together from head to toe. There's no pressure for us to get naked, to move too fast, even though we both must know our time is limited, that there's no way this can work, that it's too ludicrous to contemplate.

And maybe this is what dooms his relationships. Maybe his fame and wealth and reputation never recede enough for two people to simply be a couple. Perhaps I'm the one who's Icarus, destined to get burned.

Ness rolls me over and kisses my neck, my shoulder, my cheek, the crook of my arm. I try to imagine what this is like for him. I'm so caught up in the absurdity of making out with him that it doesn't occur to me that he might be feeling the opposite. That I'm overly normal. And then I see everything in a new light, and I feel sorry for Ness. Whoever he's ever been with, there's the pressure he must feel to just be himself, not the CEO of anything, not the son of someone, not the great-grandson of someone, but just a man. Maybe he's looking for normalcy. Maybe he's trying to forget that he was named after a monster.

-33-

Not long after the plane levels off, Ness gets up and says he'll be right back. I take the opportunity to use the en suite and freshen up. I have to dig my toiletry kit out of my bag. Ness's bag is beside mine, and I feel a twinge of reporter curiosity that I have to wrestle away. I feel guilty for even thinking it.

Ness returns with a tray. There are two glasses of fizzing champagne and a bowl of strawberries and blackberries. He sets the tray on the bed, and I ask him about the tattoo on his shoulder. I noticed it on the dive trip and again in the sub. He lets me lift his sleeve to study it.

"It's the Crux," Ness says. "Also known as the Southern Cross."

The tattoo is simply four stars arranged in a crooked pattern.

"It's the closest thing this hemisphere has to a North Star. It isn't over the South Pole really, but it points to it."

"What's the significance?" I ask. "Have you spent a lot of time down here?"

"I have, but that's not why I got it. Well, not really." He hands me a glass of champagne.

I take a sip and grab a strawberry from the bowl. "This is going to sound snobby," I say, "but I was totally meant to live like this."

Ness laughs. "You would've made a fine Egyptian princess."

"And died when I was twenty from an infected tooth and then had my brains slurped out my nose." I feed him a blackberry. "So why'd you get the tattoo, then?"

"Because . . ." Ness takes a deep breath. And then a sip of champagne. "I guess I spent a long time searching for myself before I finally realized I was looking in all the wrong places. College, marriage, work, meetings. When I got into shelling, I realized there was half a world I wasn't seeing. Like the other side of a coin. Options I never knew I had. It hit me in Australia, off the Barrier Reef. I think it was there that I realized what kind of process my grandfather went through."

"You mean from reading his journal?"

Ness nods. I take a sip of champagne and enjoy the light airy fizz against my tongue.

"So what's your background?" Ness asks. He's rubbing my arm and studying it.

"Are you asking me what kind of breed I am?" I pull my arm away from his touch.

"No . . . God, no. Not that. I love your skin. Your complexion is amazing. I mean—of course I want to know where your parents are from. I want to know everything about you. What I meant was, what was your childhood like?"

"Yeah, sorry," I say. "Didn't mean to snap at you like that. That's just usually what people mean when they ask that, so I get testy about it. My childhood was basically me and my sister sticking up for one another, people picking on us, black kids and white kids. Meanness is just as immune to color as kindness, as it turns out."

"I'm sorry to hear that. Must've been tough."

"We got through."

"What does your sister do?"

"She's an investment banker. She would tell you she stares at charts all morning and PowerPoint slides all afternoon. She thinks I live this amazing life, of course."

Ness smiles and makes a show of sweeping his arm at our surroundings.

"Touché."

He laughs. "Okay, so now that all that's out of the way, exactly what kind of mongrel are you?"

I grab a pillow from the bed and swing it at him, and Ness has to block it with one hand and save his champagne with the other. "If I spill this on my pants, they'll have to come off," he warns me, laughing.

"If you really must know, my mom was from Antigua and my dad was from Boston. They're both . . . they passed away when I was younger. I mean, I was an adult, but it was years ago. So I'm able to talk about them without turning into goo."

"Can I ask how they met?"

"Yeah, well, it's almost as good as how your parents met. Just a bigger spot in the sea than an oil rig. My dad went to Antigua for a destination wedding. It was for one of his frat brothers, who got hitched right out of college. My mom was a server at the place where they had the reception dinner. One of the other frat guys had too much to drink and came on to my mom, and my dad rescued her. Or as he used to tell it, he stole her away and was only able to do so because of the favorable comparison he made to his drunk friend."

"So you've got island blood in you," Ness says.

"Yeah, and Boston is a sea town if ever there was one. I think that's why I feel lost when I'm away from the water."

Ness nods and smiles. "That explains so much."

"Yeah? Glad it was that easy for you to know the entirety of me."

"Not the entirety, but what drives you. Most of us have simple passions at the core of who we are. Those passions might change over time, but at any one moment, I feel like there's a striving inside us that frames our decisions. The shame is that most people never ask themselves what their passions are, much less look deep into others. They just do whatever feels right at any one moment, bouncing from thing to thing."

"So is redemption your passion? You mentioned that in the sub."

"Maybe," Ness says. "I have a lot of passions. Too many, perhaps."

"Well, just so you know, I understand trying to atone for a father's sins. I totally get that. My dad wasn't perfect either."

"Yeah? How so?" Ness brushes the hair off my face, then rests his hand on my shoulder. I see worry in his furrowed brow.

"Oh, he wasn't bad to me," I say, reassuring him. "Nothing like that. My dad and I were real close. He just had . . . he did some things that I later learned weren't very good."

I eat a strawberry and take another sip of champagne, feeling dangerously honest.

"What did your dad do?" Ness asks. "I mean for a living. You don't have to tell me any of that other stuff if you don't want."

"It's hard to tease those two apart, actually. I thought my dad was a spy when I was really young, some kind of superhero private investigator. But he mostly followed people around and took pictures of them without their crutches, or with other women, and then handed that info off to lawyers so they could rain hell down on people."

"Sounds like they were the kind of people who deserved what they got," Ness says. He pulls the comforter over my bare legs when he sees me rubbing the goose bumps away.

"Yeah, that part of his job I understood. I mean, I do now. But I used to sit with him in his car when he had me for the weekend, just like you have Holly sometimes—"

"So your parents were divorced?"

"It's . . . complicated. They split up, but they stayed married. My dad moved back in with my mom when she got diagnosed with cancer. Anyway, when I was young, they lived apart, and my dad would take me on these jobs with him. Side jobs. He would have me sit in the passenger seat and run the laptop while he took pictures of people with this great big lens." I shake my head, remembering.

"Jeez, now you *have* to tell me."

"You have to promise not to tell."

"I get confused," Ness says. "Was that a teaser or a cliffhanger?" He laughs, but when he sees I'm dead serious, he raises one hand. "Off the record. I swear."

I readjust myself on the bed, holding my champagne flute so it doesn't spill. "Okay, so keep in mind that this was back when facial recognition software first got really good but before people *knew* it was getting good. You know what I mean? Well, Dad was one of the first in his trade to see the potential. So he would park outside brothels, strip clubs, seedy massage parlors, places like that, and shoot everyone who came out. I mean *everyone*. Then he'd run the pictures through the DMV database, which a friend on the force got him access to. That was my job, running the laptop and switching out the memory cards. I was better at it than he was. We'd get a name from the DMV, do a Google search, and see if anyone had a high profile, if they were worth anything—"

"Blackmail," Ness whispers.

"Yeah. Basically, instead of waiting for someone to get suspicious and hire him, Dad started sampling the crowd to drum up more business for himself."

I feel like shit admitting my role in it all. It took me years to come clean with Michael. I have no idea why I'm telling Ness.

"That's fucked up," he says.

"I know. It's not something I'm proud of."

Ness's face lights up. "You know, I've heard about scams like this. There was a senator from Connecticut who got ruined by something like that. Claimed he thought it was a regular massage parlor—"

"Senator Hutchins," I say. And then, sheepishly: "I was with Dad that weekend."

Ness leans back to study me. "No. You're kidding, right? That was your dad?"

I feel a flush of heat on my neck, remembering the weeks after the incident. "I thought I was going to go to jail or something. I was too sick to attend school, couldn't even tell my mom. It was the first time in my life that I started reading the paper— the physical thing. Which probably led me down the path I took, career-wise. Not just from reading the paper, but seeing the difference between telling the truth in print and all the sneaking around my father did for a living."

"You took down a United States senator," Ness says. "Hell, I wish I could do that to a few of them." He shakes his head. "You were more powerful in third grade than I am now."

"And I don't even know how many other people I helped ruin like that. For me, it was just a game. It felt like the kind of video game my sister liked to play on her computer. Maybe that's why I don't have the stomach for them."

"You know, what you did is right up there with destroying the world's oceans and wrecking a billion miles of shoreline," Ness says.

I know he's joking, but neither of us laugh.

"I don't know why, but it feels good to tell someone without building up to it for years and years, without dreading the conversation. I haven't told many people. Not sure why it feels safe to tell you. Maybe because you've shared things with me that I have to keep to myself. Like mutually assured destruction."

Ness runs his hand down my arm. "I like you, Maya Walsh. I like that you challenge me, make me think. I like that you're complex. I even like that you don't like me."

"You're one of those guys who falls in love easily, aren't you?" I ask. I don't mean it to sound harsh, but as an honest question.

"Maybe," he says. "Is that a bad thing?"

"It depends. Do you fall out of love just as quickly?"

Ness considers this. Looks sad for a moment. "I don't think so. I love my work. I have a lot of passions in life. The people who've left me recently, they haven't wanted to share me with those things."

"As long as it's not someone else, I can share. I get lost in my work as well. Michael used to have to stand in front of me and shout my name to pull me from whatever article I was working on. It drove him nuts. He couldn't understand my ability to disappear like that."

"No one disappears like I do," Ness warns me.

"Challenge accepted," I say, offering my hand.

Ness takes my hand, but he uses it to pull me into him, nearly spilling my champagne. "Close your eyes," he commands. And I do. Ness kisses me and tells me I'm beautiful, and then he says, "Close them tighter."

I squint until not a sliver of light comes in.

"I win," Ness says.

=34=

When we land, I can tell that we're not back in Maine. The flight didn't feel long enough, and the temperature and the humidity are too high. I feel both before we get to the front of the plane. I glance back at Ness, who is smiling guiltily.

"Detour," he says.

"Where are we?" I ask.

"The nearest thing I have to a home."

Outside, the midday sun has heat waves shimmering up from the tarmac. It's stuffy, but the faintest of breezes wafts through, bringing relief. I look around for an airport. There are no other planes. A single hangar and a small cluster of structures the size of outhouses, a few silver tanks streaked with rust that I assume hold fuel. Or used to. The pilot hands Ness our two bags, which he throws on the back of a nearby golf cart. There's another cart nearby. Two islanders help the flight crew with their bags.

"Get in," Ness says. "You drive."

I jump behind the wheel of the golf cart. When I hit the accelerator, the silent whine of a strong electric motor rockets us forward. Ness clutches the oh-shit handle and laughs. "I took the governors out," he tells me.

"Of course you did," I say.

"Take a right past those bushes."

We cruise along white sandstone-paved roads, seeing nothing and no one. The golf cart's windshield is down, and the breeze feels nice. Now and then, we pass twin ruts of sand that jut off into the scrub brush, trails only golf carts and feet have been down. Ness is gripping the cart with one hand, has the other on my thigh, and is watching the world zip by. He doesn't tell me to turn, and I don't ask.

Ahead, I see the road bend to the left. Scanning the low island that direction, I spot a structure beyond a stand of palm trees. The palms here remind me of the ones along Ness's driveway in Maine. He said this place feels like home to him. I wonder if that's why he has the trees transplanted, if the cost is justified by the longing he feels.

Supporting this theory is the fact that this house looks a lot like the one in Maine. Wood siding, the same bright Caribbean colors, open doors with flowing white linens. Small and cozy. The central part of his Maine estate without all the wings and additions.

"Pull around the back," Ness says.

I swing around the end of the house, and the view on the other side causes my foot to slip off the accelerator. I find the brake pedal and bring us to a jarring stop. Ahead of us, a tiered patio steps down toward a pristine white powder beach. I barely see the cabanas and the pool and the amenities. It's the water beyond the titanium sand that draws me in. Not blue, not even the bright green of a clear lagoon, something more like sea foam. A green so bright it has a tint of yellow. The color of clarity. Of shallow water over white sand.

"If you don't start breathing, I'm going to have to kiss you again," Ness says.

I tear my eyes away and lean over to kiss him. "Where is this?" I ask.

"The Bahamas. Tara Cay. And yeah, the water here is unbeatable. I've been to more beaches than I can count, and when I saw this one, I never wanted to leave."

"Why *do* you leave? Why would you ever leave?"

"Work," he says. And I'm reminded that he leaves a lot of beautiful things behind for his work. "Let's put your stuff away and see if anything's washed up."

"There are shells here?"

"Not on this beach. Too shallow. But we'll take the boat out and hit the ocean side. I haven't been here in a few weeks, and there's been a good storm since then, so we might get lucky."

"I feel lucky just to see this. Is this one of the islands your dad bought for you?"

"No. Those are down in the Caribbean. I gave them back to the countries that owned them, and they put them in a preserve. And yes, the tax benefits were enormous. Make sure you put that in your article."

I'd forgotten about my article. I'd forgotten that I'm a reporter. I'd forgotten about the fact that the FBI is looking closely into Ness and those shells. Right then, I'm not sure I could find my apartment if I were dropped a block away from it.

The rest of the day is just that sort of discombobulated blur. I try not to dwell on all the nagging doubts and fears, choosing instead to just enjoy where I am. Ness lets me pilot his center console around the back of the island. It's a big thirty-foot Contender, nicer than the one at his other house, but sun-beaten and salt-worn. Well used. Amid the rocks on the Atlantic side of the island, we find fighting conchs, sozon's cones, and a horse conch. My life feels complete when I turn up a scotch bonnet in a tidal pool, the shell in very good or excellent condition, and Ness has to assure me ten times that it wasn't planted there. That it is a real find. I don't even dare put it in the shelling bag I borrowed from the house. For the rest of our expedition, I carry it with me in my palm. I know even then that it will be the one shell I walk away from this experience treasuring. I have this, even if everything else is taken from me.

Back at the house, we take turns showering. With towels wrapped around us, there's a feeling of familiar intimacy but danger as well. We haven't yet been completely naked in front of each other. He must expect it as much as I do, the inevitability, but not knowing when it might come is like holding a grenade with the pin pulled. We both dance around it as we get dressed while the other isn't looking.

Dinner is on the patio. A fire in a raised metal pit crackles. We watch the sun go down as dinner arrives. I meet Gladys, the chef, and her husband, Nick. Ness introduces them like they're family. When he tells Gladys that my mother was from Antigua, she shrieks and cups my face in both her hands, like an island hundreds of miles away is somehow next door. For the rest of the night, any time I catch her looking at me she bursts into a wide smile.

"I wish I had my laptop," I say after dinner, while enjoying a glass of wine.

"Party foul," Ness proclaims.

"To write," I say. "I feel inspired to write some fiction. Make something up. Something less impossible than this, so people would buy it."

Ness sips his wine. "Ever written a novel before?"

"Started a few. Meandered. I vacillated between feeling silly and feeling pretentious. Like some parts weren't serious enough and other parts I was trying too hard to be profound."

"Sounds like me learning to play the guitar. I would go back and forth between teaching myself chords and trying to learn complex tunes one contorted note at a time. I think that, with a lot of art, you just have to be bad at it a long time before the magic happens. And I suck at being bad at things."

I laugh at the play on words. "Me too," I say. "I mean, I'm really good at being bad at things, but I hate it. So I avoid it."

"Dangerous habit," Ness says. "Life is too short. And you're lucky you don't have your laptop."

"Why is that?"

"Because if you pulled it out, I'd toss it into the sea."

I laugh at him.

"I'm not kidding," Ness says, even though he laughs with me. "Speaking of the sea," he continues, "it's warm enough to go for a dip. You wanna?"

"I would, but someone told me a whole bunch of things *not* to pack, and one was my bathing suit."

Ness lifts his hands in defense. "I didn't know you were going to jump me in the sub and that I'd be bringing you here!"

"I totally didn't jump you. You took advantage of me in a weakened state."

"Whatever. I'm going for a swim. If you wanna come, it's dark enough that I won't see anything. Not that I'd be looking anyway. And not that I haven't already seen your breasts."

"The lights were out. You didn't see anything."

But Ness is already up and out of his chair. I refuse to move, electing to enjoy my wine, the stars, the sound of the gently lapping water before me, the crack and pop of the fire, and the distant hiss of waves crashing on the other side of the island.

Ness sheds his shirt before he gets to the sand. I study his silhouette as he drops his shorts and then heads out into the water. Gladys appears beside me, gathering the dessert dishes.

"You a mad woman," she says.

"Oh, we were just playing," I tell her.

"No, you crazy not being out there with that man. He insane for you."

"He barely knows me," I tell her.

"All right then, tell me why he never bring no woman here. I say you mad."

She laughs on her way back to the house, and I hear her talking with Nick, realize the two of them are probably gossiping about this last-minute arrival and this mysterious woman with half an island in her.

"Fuck it," I say. I leave my wine and head down the tiered patio. At the sand's edge, I pull off my shirt, take off my bra, drop my shorts and then my underwear. "No regrets," I say. And by the time I get to the water, I'm running and laughing. I'm remembering what it feels like to be free again.

-35-

The best kisses in the world take place at night, in the ocean, with two naked bodies coiled around one another, only the stars to keep them company. Weight disappears, and our bodies with it. Ness stands on his toes, me clinging to him, my arms wrapped around his neck and my legs around his waist, our lips tasting the salt on each other.

The water is warm enough that I barely feel it, heightening the sense of my loss of self. And when we move, microscopic sea life blooms green and gives off an ethereal glow. Above us, a path of dense light reminds me where the Milky Way got its name. The stars are intense. Like the sky is as alive and excited as every cell in my body.

We stay in the water until I can barely feel anything with my fingers, they're so pruned. Our bodies hardly ever came apart the entire time, so that when the water flows between us, it chills my breasts and stomach, which have been against Ness for what feels like half an hour. I think I stayed pinned to him to avoid access to other parts of our bodies, and so he couldn't see me in the bright starlight. As we exit the water, there's no avoiding it. I can feel his eyes on me. Holding my hand, he leads me down the beach where a blanket has been laid out.

"Did you plan this?" I ask.

"No," he says. "Gladys did, I guess. I saw her out here arranging something."

"So you were kissing with your eyes open," I admonish him.

"Guilty."

There are towels on the blanket. Ness and I dry off. He wraps his towel around me and rubs my arms. The breeze is soft, but it chills my skin where it's still wet. We lie down on the blanket, huddle under one of the towels, and Ness runs his hand over my hair as we watch the sea slide toward us and then away, over and over.

"You shouldn't be shy," Ness says. "You're gorgeous. Women half your age must loathe you."

"Everyone in New York is gorgeous," I say, deflecting his praise.

"I'm serious. Inside and out, you are intoxicating. And you were right, I was coming on to you that first night. It wasn't just the wine, either. I was excited that you agreed to come out and talk to me. Made me think you weren't out to get me, you know? That you were interested in my story, interested in hearing the truth. It makes it easy to open up to you."

I think about why I really went up to interview Ness, and my heart aches for him. But I bite my lip and don't say anything.

"A lot of shooting stars tonight."

I scan the sky. I haven't seen one yet. We rub our feet together to keep them warm. I see a flash of light overhead and squeeze Ness's hand. He squeezes back. "Make a wish," he says.

"That would be greedy," I tell him. "I'll let someone else have it."

And then, maybe because I'm fighting so many dark secrets about why I wrote my articles and why I went to see Ness, and maybe because I'm terrified to share something that will drive him away from me, but I'm terrified that if I don't say anything he'll know I'm keeping something from him, I decide to give him a dark secret that I've never given anyone before.

"I've got to confess something," I tell Ness. I wiggle away from him and prop myself up on my elbow. He studies me intensely, brushes the hair off my face.

"You used to be a man," he guesses. "I'm totally cool with that."

I laugh. "I'm serious," I say. "I'm about to tell you something I've never told another living soul."

His hand falls still for a moment, and then he seeks out my hand. He waits.

"There was a time when I didn't care about shells. Not one bit."

Ness doesn't laugh at how insignificant this sounds. And it does sound insignificant to me, saying it, but only because I'm not sure how to tell the rest of the story.

"My sister and I had a rough time in school. I guess the things society tolerates come and go, and so we had friends with two moms or two dads, but there weren't any other mixed-race girls in our elementary school. Parents came in color-coded couplets. Except ours.

"Our parents talked about moving us to another school, but they didn't. I think we stopped telling them how bad it was because we worried it was all our fault. And you know, looking back, it wasn't like the school was against us. It was probably five or six kids. Everyone else was nice to us or ignored us. But at that age, you just remember the ones who are after you."

Ness squeezes my hand.

"So anyway, I hated my skin. When I was six or seven, I would alternate between covering up and staying out of the sun, hoping I'd turn white, or I'd lay out in the back yard with no clothes on trying to get darker. Neither of which worked like I hoped. All I wanted was different skin. I would have killed to have different skin. I even used to have these dreams when I was a kid where I could step into a skin suit and zip it up and no one would know it wasn't mine."

I wipe a tear off my cheek. I feel bad for ruining the moment, but what started as an urge to share something, anything, wells up into a desire to really have this off my chest.

"So the reason I got into shelling—it has a dark history behind it. I'm almost ashamed of it. Which is difficult, because it's become the thing I most love doing in the world. But it all started when I was nine. Like I said, for a few years there, I didn't care about shells. I liked them when I was real young, because my parents and my sister did, but then I became consumed with this self-loathing, which is a crazy thing for a little kid to feel, and that's all I thought about.

"Then one day, we were on a hike on the bluffs up from my childhood beach, and we came across this writhing ball of hermit crabs. Like two dozen of them. They were crawling all over each other. You could hear them crinkle as their little legs tapped on each other's shells."

"They were swapping," Ness says.

"That's right. I sat with my mom and watched crabs crawl out of one shell and into another. Some shells were empty. It was all this furious activity, hermit crabs leaving one home and jumping into another."

"And you wished you could, too."

I bob my head, my vision swimming with tears. My voice cracks as I try to get it out. "I told my mom— told her 'I wish that was me,' and she said—" Ness gives me a corner of the towel, and I dab my cheeks with it. "She said, 'Why would you want to leave our house?' and I said, 'I want to leave *me*.' And I don't think she ever got it. But I was mesmerized with this idea. I never saw shells as anything other than rocks that came in pretty shapes. Didn't realize what they were. But after that day, I wanted to find all of them. I thought there might be one out there shaped like me that I could just crawl into."

I'm bawling by the time I finish. Ness grabs me and pulls me against him, letting me sob into the crook of his neck. He kisses my cheek, smooths my hair, and holds me. I cry so hard that I shudder, letting out this thing that I've contained all on my own for far too long, this dark secret to my passion, this ignoble reason for what I do and who I am.

"I think you're perfect," Ness says. "You are perfect just like you are. With every chip and ding. With the polish rubbed off. There's nothing wrong with you in the world."

I control my sobbing so I can hear him. And then I'm not crying anymore. I'm kissing him. And this time the kissing grows into something frantic, a rawness from having exposed myself, from becoming more than merely naked. Throwing the towel off, hot now, I straddle Ness and sit up in the breeze. I let him see me in the cast of starlight. His hands are on my hips. They trace up my waist, cup my breasts.

"I want you," I tell him. "Right now."

I feel his hands stop. Something flashes across his face. "I can't be an escape for you," he says. "Not some temporary home."

"I don't want temporary," I tell him.

With this, his hands move again. He rolls me over and lowers me to the blanket. As he kisses my neck, and then down my body, I keep my eyes open. A field of stars glitters above us, the sea lapping nearby, streaks of light as foreign bodies strike the Earth's atmosphere, exploding and burning upon entry. Ness's mouth is against me, and now I can't tell if all the stars I'm seeing are real. My vision bursts with them. I have to close my eyes; our hands interlock; I arch my back and moan with pleasure.

When I can't take it anymore, I pull him up so I can kiss him. So our chests are together. So he can enter me. And for the first time, I forget who this man is outside of any context beyond the last few days together. I let go of his past. My past. There is nothing behind us, nothing before us, just a promise of now. The world is not flooding. All the tides are slack. Waiting. Pausing. Nature catching her breath. While the two of us lose ourselves in each other.

-36-

The next morning, I wake up before Ness. I watch him sleep for a long while. I notice that the crease in his forehead is gone. Like the worry that seems to plague him during the day is giving him respite in his sleep.

When I can't hold it anymore, I get up to pee. I grab my phone on the way to the bathroom to check the time, and marvel that I have signal. It's just wi-fi, though. I wonder how this works with Ness's "no laptop" rule, but I use it to check my email and my messages while I'm on the toilet. I have a depressing metric ton of both. I scan for important names, see my sister asking me how things are going, that she assumes the silence is a good thing, reminds me to let Ness know she's single. I stifle a laugh at this. What in the world am I going to tell her?

There are tons of messages from Henry. I have a workaholic breakthrough by opening none of them. Just one day of not caring what the emergency is. A way of honoring Ness's laptop rule. Leaving the bathroom, I worry my flushing might've woken Ness, but he's still sound asleep. I decide to venture out for coffee. As I'm passing the bed, I see inside Ness's bag, which is open. It's the bright orange plastic case that catches my eye.

I freeze, glance back at the bed, see that he isn't moving, then crouch down beside his bag. I pull the case out. It's identical to the murex case Agent Cooper gave me. In fact, I fully expect to see a lace murex inside as I work the latch. Instead, some water sloshes out, and I have to tilt the case in a hurry to get it level and keep from making more of a mess. I lift the lid slowly. Inside is something that looks like a cross between an auger and a cerith. Not quite as smooth as the former or as bumpy as the latter. When it moves, I realize where it came from. And why the water inside feels so warm. And why these cases have rubber seals.

I close the lid, secure the latch, and put the case back in Ness's bag. My mind is racing, but it's going around in circles. These clues seem important, but they aren't spelling out the big picture. When I stand, I turn to find Ness stretching in the bed. He looks over at me.

"Morning, gorgeous."

I feel terrifyingly naked. I don't know how much is my usual shyness and how much is my swimming thoughts.

"C'mere," Ness says.

I crawl into bed and kiss his neck. "My breath is awful," I say.

"Is that your polite way of saying that it's my breath that's bad?"

"No, but I assume it isn't hunky dory either. I'm going to make coffee. You want some?"

"Yeah, because that'll fix our problems."

I laugh and push him back against the pillow when he tries to sit up. "Stay here," I say. "I'll get it. And can I borrow a robe?"

"I like that look," he tells me.

"It's chilly," I say.

Ness waves toward the closet. I find a robe hanging on the back of the door.

"Oh, and do you have a landline?"

"Why?" he asks.

"I need to call my sister. She was expecting me to check in today. I didn't know we'd be in the Bahamas."

"Sure. Make sure you use the country code."

"Okay. Back with your coffee in a bit."

I grab my cell phone on my way out. While I'm sorting out the coffee and filter and putting water in the coffee maker, I pull up Agent Cooper's phone number in my directory. I also find an alarm radio on the kitchen counter and figure out how to pair it up with my phone. I choose a beach playlist. Ness yells his approval, and I crank up the volume. I find the house phone, remove it from its cradle, and take it outside while the coffee is percolating.

There's static atop the dial tone as I head out onto the patio. Too far, and the phone won't work. I balance between distance for privacy but not so much that I lose reception. Agent Cooper picks up on the third ring.

"Hello?"

"Cooper. It's Maya Walsh. Listen, I don't have a lot of time. Just wanted to fill you in on something."

"You can call me—"

"Stan. Whatever. Just listen. That case you found? It's a research sample case. Insulated. It's watertight to keep water *in*, not out. Ness is taking live mollusks from the deep sea. That's where he's getting his shells."

"Hydrothermals? Maya, nothing like the lace murex lives down there."

"I know. The laces aren't the thing, don't you see? Ness reacted to seeing the *case*, not the shells. The shells are blinding us. You. Us. Whatever. The point is, I think he's after those shells maybe to breed them. Or something. He wants them alive. This isn't about forging shells at all."

"Breeding shells isn't illegal," Cooper says. "We give out permits for that."

"To anyone? He said something about senators, doesn't trust them. I don't have it all figured out yet, but I know for a fact he's doing something illegal. He admitted that. And he's keeping these samples hidden from me. I think he's growing shells, and maybe it's the scale of his operation that's an issue. I mean, he's got entire islands where he could be breeding these things. Maybe selling the shells as if found. Or using what he breeds to move into cast fakes, like you suggested. I don't know."

"Maya, I want you to come in and debrief with me. I want you out of there."

"I can't. Not now."

"You're in too deep. I'm telling you. If you were my agent, I'd be ordering you to get out of there."

"Good thing I'm not, then. Anyway, I've gotta go."

"Wait. I wanted to talk to you about the article."

"Can't. I'll call you later."

I hang up. My palms are sweaty. A mix of thoughts rush through my head. The first is that the FBI just recorded me, and that Cooper is probably already listening to our conversation again to make sure he got everything. The next is a feeling like I'm betraying Ness, which stings deep, because I'm pretty sure I'm falling for him. The last thought is of my own wound, because it's obvious that he hasn't been telling me the whole truth, which sucks because of the aforementioned falling-for-him bit. But it's also a salve for my guilt. Maybe we're betraying each other. A little.

Back in the house, I find the coffee pot full. Crosby, Stills, Nash, and Young are singing about eighty feet of waterline, nicely making way. Ness is sitting up in bed on a throne of pillows as I deliver his coffee.

"Your sister convinced I haven't murdered you and dumped your body at sea?" Ness asks.

"Not exactly. She says she wants a photo of me with today's paper to be sure I'm okay. I told her we don't get the *Times* where we are. Thank goodness."

"That's what I love about this place," Ness says. He cradles his coffee with both hands, takes a deep breath through his nose, and arches his shoulders back as he stretches. Letting it all out, he smiles at me. "No stress. No work. And the sea in every direction."

"Yeah," I say. "It's perfect here. But I'm guessing we have to get back."

I try not to make it sound like a question, like I'm eager to leave. I wish I could be more like Ness. Or maybe I'm too much like Ness. But this vacation has become work all of a sudden. I remember why I'm out here, what I'm hoping to uncover. And the lack of computer and cell coverage has me feeling isolated. Cut off. Something's going on, and I won't get any closer to it by staying here. And I hate myself for feeling this way.

=37=

The following day, I wake up in Ness's bed back in Maine. The memory of Tara Cay is a memory as perfect as it is small. Like a beaded periwinkle, or any shell that requires a magnifying glass to fully appreciate. It was paradise crammed into a fistful of hours, the sort of moment you can lose if you're not careful.

The view from Ness's bed is almost as glorious. The storm has passed. Dawn is just breaking, the disk of the sun rising above the Atlantic and throwing the sky into pinks and reds. I watch the colors bloom and fade; sunrises like this are over in a blink. The sky changes from second to second. It reminds me of my week with Ness, which came and went too fast, every breath full of something new and strange and wonderful.

I reach for my phone on the bedside table. The flight home was a blur. I only remember passing out in bed, falling asleep curled up against Ness, eager for the answers he promised I would get today. I want this journey behind us so I can see where the next one will go.

My phone tells me it's Saturday, which is almost impossible to believe. There are dozens of missed calls and even more texts, but all that will have to wait until I have coffee in my veins. Is it really Saturday? I think back: Monday, we shelled on the beach,

Tuesday diving—God, that feels like a lifetime ago—and on Wednesday morning it rained, but that afternoon we flew halfway around the world, spent Thursday at one of the deepest parts of the Atlantic Ocean, Friday on Tara Cay, and now it's Saturday.

Hours earlier, I woke up to Ness getting quietly dressed. Sweatpants and sneakers. I asked him where he was going, and he said for a run. When I asked where, he said, "To the end of the driveway and back. To get the mail."

I've not yet gotten out of bed when I hear him coming down the breezeway. The sunrise has nearly lost its hues, is now just a single yellow orb. Ness has a triangle of sweat from his neck to his navel. It occurs to me that he may have run the entire length of that long shell-covered driveway to the outer guard gate. My thirty minutes on the treadmill after work and occasional Pilates feels inadequate.

"What's for breakfast?" I ask, stretching.

He strides into the bedroom, hair matted with sweat, a blank look on his face. He throws a newspaper onto the bed. "Betrayal," he says. "More than I can stomach."

He storms into the bathroom while I gather my senses. A different man returned from the one who left the house. What does he mean by "betrayal"? I gather the paper, which flew apart from being thrown onto the bed. I check the Arts & Culture section, an old habit, and see nothing. And then I find the front page. And my heart sinks. I scan the familiar article, making sure it doesn't have anything about the FBI in there.

"I didn't know about this," I yell at him. "I swear."

I grab my phone. Ness's grandfather stares accusingly at me. His image takes up half the front page of the *Times*, practically everything above the fold. The headline says: "Part 2: The Grandfather." I check the byline, and there's my name. It's the piece, word for word, nothing changed. The very piece I told Henry he couldn't run. I find him on my speed dial. Henry picks up after the second ring.

"Where the hell have you been?" he asks.

"What is this?" I shout at him. "You promised me."

"I've been trying to call you for two days."

I think of the flights, being in the sub, the island, all the emails from him.

"You promised me," I say. "I'm working on the story of a lifetime, Henry, and you've just fucked it up."

"It wasn't me," he insists.

"You run the paper!"

"I don't *own* it. Jesus, Maya, have you been following this? Your piece has gone nuts. The board's been all over me wondering why the second story hadn't run yet. I've been trying to buy you time—"

"Why not run the one on his father, then? How did they even *get* this one? How did they know about it?"

I hear Henry take a deep breath. I get out of bed and walk through the closet, try the door to the bathroom. It's locked. I can hear the shower running. I go back to the bedroom as Henry explains.

"We sent the files off to the printer last week, remember? The story was running when you went home that night, which was when I got a call from Wilde's agent and then you-know-who. So the story was in our system. Someone in the office must've tipped someone on the board to let them know it was here, that we already had it. I swear to you, Maya, I did everything I could. This was going to run yesterday. I stalled as long as possible. They were going to fire me and run it themselves if I refused."

I cradle the phone with my shoulder while he's talking and pull my shorts on. I don't want Ness to see me naked. Whatever I thought I was doing with him, whatever the last two days were, it's obviously over. I'll be another picture on the wall. I wonder, idly, if maybe some of those women hurt him instead of the other way around, if I didn't have that completely backwards as well.

"Maya, you're not going to like this—"

"Jesus, Henry, what?"

"They're making me run his father's piece tomorrow, and the piece on Ness for the Monday edition."

My thoughts go immediately to Holly. Those stories will always be out there. Forever. And I can tell from Henry's voice that there's no stopping them. It's a done deal.

"What if I quit?" I ask. "Can they legally run them if I'm no longer at the *Times*?"

"Yes," Henry says. It's the first time he hasn't doubted that I'd do it. "I'm guessing this puts a dent in whatever you're working on up there?"

"Yeah, that's toast." I put him on speaker and pull my shirt on. I look at the rumpled bed. Was I even the one who slept in it? Was that me in a goddamn submarine? On a private jet? On an island? Nothing makes sense. A voice from New York has dragged me back into the real, and out of wherever I've been. I pick up the phone and take it off speaker just as the shower door slams shut in the bathroom. "Listen, Henry, I've got to go. I've gotta see if I can make this right."

"One last thing," Henry tells me. Ness steps out of the bathroom and gets dressed in the closet, doesn't glance at me. I'm torn on whether I should run to him, throw myself on my knees, explain what happened, tell him it wasn't my fault—or if I should let him cool off.

"Whatever this did to your current story," Henry says, "you should know that this series is a big deal right now. I've got a dozen requests from major media who want to interview you, and book publishers want the rights to this. We have a few Hollywood studios talking to our legal department right now. You've got the book rights, but we might move ahead with the film stuff, while the iron is hot."

"Please, Henry. Don't do anything until I get back to the office."

Ness looks at me as I say this. He's pulling his running shoes back on, is wearing blue jeans and a button-up.

"It's out of my hands," Henry says.

I hang up in disgust. Ness strides from the closet and through the bedroom, into the breezeway.

"Let me explain," I tell him.

He whirls around, points a finger at me, and tries to form the words; I can see in his eyes, in the twitch of his cheeks, in his furrowed brow, that he has legions to say. But all that comes out is: "You promised me."

He heads toward the front door. I follow him, explaining anyway. "I told my boss not to run it, that I would quit if he did. The board pressured him." How to explain all the politics of a multimedia conglomerate owned by a company that started out selling dish soap? "They already had the story, Ness. They were going to fire my boss, the editor in chief of the goddamn *Times*, and run it anyway. There was no stopping this."

"Then why make the promise?" Ness asks. He hesitates at the top of the stairs, and I think for a moment that we'll be able to talk through this. Then I hear him say, "I thought you were real."

He opens the front door, leaves, and slams it behind him. I run up the stairs, fumble with the latch, and hurry out onto the porch. Ness is already around the low wall toward the garage; I hear the rapid *crunch crunch crunch* of shells from him running. By the time I get around the corner, the garage door is opening, and a bright red convertible with a white stripe down the middle is growling out in reverse. He doesn't look my way as he roars by.

This is where I let him go, where I lose him, where I slink home to New York and never see him again, where our tryst is a memory, and whatever story I could write from this wreck of a week is left unfinished, with no resolution, with no way of piecing together his scattered clues.

But I say, "Fuck that." I say it out loud. I turn to my car. And then I remember my keys are down in the guest house.

I take the boardwalks at a dangerous pace. I'm still barefoot. No bra on. My thoughts whirl. Surely he'll understand. Once the adrenaline wears off. Once the sting of betrayal cools. I'll write a retraction. An even bigger piece. When word gets out about how the *Times* ran this story, there'll be mud on their faces.

Get real, Maya, I think to myself. When was the last time a retraction ran anywhere but in a small inset on page twelve? The untruths go on the front page. Corrections are buried.

I'll write the piece anyway. I'll make it a book. I can fix this.

Fetching my keys, I run back up to the house, out the front door, and jump in my car. I speed across broken shells. I want to catch Ness, don't want to sit at the house and wait for him to return. He might stay away until I have to leave, might have Monique or his guards throw me out. Approaching the first guard gate, I lay on my horn, and the gate comes up. A new guard comes out with his hand held up. I blow right by him, kicking up a cloud of dust.

I don't see a trail from Ness's car. Too far ahead of me. I get my car up to sixty on that gravel road, reach over my shoulder and grab my seat belt, click it in. Tall trees whiz past, trees that don't belong here. I feel a kinship with them. These trees understand.

The second guard gate eventually comes into view. Ness has already passed through. A paved highway waits for me on the other side. This time, the gate doesn't open. A guard steps out, hands raised, asking me to stop. The other guard probably called ahead. This one doesn't look too happy. I roll down my window as I crunch to a stop.

"Hey, hey," the guard says. "Take it easy. What the hell is going on?"

"Which way did he go?" I ask.

The guard scrunches up his face. "Who?"

"Ness. Mr. Wilde. Your boss. Which way did he turn? Where would he be going?"

The guard glances up the driveway and deep into the estate. "I haven't seen him since an hour ago when he came to get the mail. Is everything okay?"

"That doesn't make sense—" I say. But then it does. I throw the car into reverse and back into the empty parking space beside the guard gate, making a quick three-point turn.

"I'm going to ask you to wait here," the guard says.

But I'm already gone, peppering the shack with bits of ground shells as I spin out.

I know where Ness went. I have no idea where it leads, but I know how I missed him.

-38-

Finding the turnoff isn't easy. I remember about how far down the driveway I was, but I have to creep along with my window down and peer between the trees for the gate. I also look for tire treads veering to the side, or grass flattened on the shoulder. I'm feeling more and more certain that I've passed the spot, that I need to turn back and look for it again, when I see the gap between the trees and the black gate in the woods. I pull into the gap, hoping it'll open automatically. Then I remember the keypad. I get out to study it.

There's a small LCD screen. I punch in four numbers. The cursor is still blinking. I add two more numbers, and a red light flashes twice. A six-digit code. One of the only relevant numbers I know to try is Ness's birthday. I try it twice, once with the day before the month and once the other way around. I get red lights both times. The guards are probably on their way. I listen for their jeeps. The hidden road seems to run through the woods to the south. Forgetting the car, and not knowing how far the drive goes or where it leads, I decide to go ahead on foot.

This is where shoes would've been a good idea. I stick to the sparse grass where I can, and I stay out of the deep tire treads full of rainwater. The trees only go a few hundred yards, and soon I can see the open field beyond: tall grass, a road cutting through it, the shoulders maintained. To my left, due east, the field runs a long distance before it becomes scrub brush and dunes that must slide down to the sea. Ahead of me, I can see where the road itself leads: to the lighthouse, with its white and black stripes. Maybe a mile away, out on a jut of coast. I start walking.

The hike gives me time to reflect, time to compose what I'll say to Ness, what I'll write in my piece, what I might be able to say to Henry to keep the rest of the story from running. I dream of storming into a board meeting and telling them what shortsighted and stupid idiots they are, that this is so much bigger than the tawdry gossip I've been compiling, that the last week might have had far greater implications than the last two *years* of my work.

The sun beats down. The ground is still soggy from the heavy rain the day before. My feet are covered in mud; it cakes up between my toes.

What will I tell my sister? When all this is over, and I have nothing but a destroyed family behind me and two days of perfect shelling and two days of perfect bliss, what will I say happened?

Henry's news of book offers and film deals haunts me. I can see one way this turns out: with my wealth and notoriety increased, with the publication deals that have always eluded me, with the big-screen dramatizations my long-form colleagues at magazines often get, all at the expense of ruining what might in fact be a decent man.

The parallels to that future and Ness and his family are eerie. I think of how it must feel with all his wealth coming on the back of a broken and flooded world. Maybe he hates himself like I used to hate him, like everyone I know hates him. I may have the same life ahead of me, especially if our affair leaks out. There will be lights flashing, people asking me to sign my book for them, and the pain in my gut like I've been punched. Because of what made it all possible. Who I had to hurt. What I had to destroy.

I feel closer to Ness in this moment than I did in bed or on the beach. I feel so close to understanding him perfectly, to knowing his demons. That's who you interview to get at a man: not his family, his friends, his coworkers, his competitors. You interview his skeletons and his demons. I feel like I've finally met them. I think of how he got his name, how we all need monsters to blame, but how those monsters are our own construction. I did that. I helped torture him. Because it made me feel better.

I damn myself as I reach the lighthouse. I think of all I will say to him. How I will pour my heart out. This is how it always works in the movies, right? Two people fall in love, there's a massive misunderstanding, but it all works out in the end. I tell myself this: that it'll all work out in the end. It has to. It can't end with everyone broken. Who does that?

Beside the lighthouse are a number of vehicles: Ness's red sports car, two sedans, a panel van, and a pickup truck, all splattered with mud from the drive out. Shielding my eyes, I gaze up at the top of the lighthouse. No sign of activity there. No other building attached. Just a tall black-and-white-banded tower of stone.

Trying the door, I find it unlocked. I let myself in and call for Ness. No answer. Off the small entry hall, there's a set of spiral stairs running up. I take them two at a time and feel winded by the time I get to the top. There's no one there, just a spectacular view. I didn't pass any doors along the way, didn't see or hear a single soul. I wonder if maybe there's a trail that leads down to the beach, if there's another building. I work my way back down and look for any door or passage I may have missed on the way up.

Nothing.

Back in the foyer, I poke around fruitlessly. A cardboard box with some light bulbs. An empty coat rack. A small table and chair. A scattering of tools.

I leave the lighthouse and walk around the building. Bingo. On the other side, there's a set of stairs leading down. The door at the bottom of the stairs is locked. There's a keypad by the door;

it looks newer than anything else around the lighthouse. I bang my fist against the cool steel and shout Ness's name, wait for an answer.

No one comes.

I could sit down and wait, see if the guards get to me first or if Ness comes out. Now that I have a pause to think, I wonder about all those cars, what they're doing here, why the lighthouse is empty. My fight with Ness fades for a moment as I realize something fishy is going on, as the reporter in me resurfaces from beneath the damaged lover.

What code would he use? I try his birthday every way I can think of. And then I realize who will know. But I've got no way to get in touch with her. I pull out my phone. One measly bar. And the battery is low from getting in late last night. I leave the sunken stairwell and walk around the lighthouse until I have two bars and the data light comes on.

I search my email inbox until I find Henry's instructions for driving up here. There's a number for the guard gate and one for Ness's house in case I'm running late. I try the house number. It rings eight times before I get voicemail. I hang up, count to ten, and try back.

This time, someone answers after the third ring. A man. "Vincent?" I ask.

"Speaking," he says.

"This is Maya Walsh. We met down by the boathouse the other day. I'm a . . . friend of Ness's." It feels painful to say, for this is both an understatement and a lie. "I need a huge favor. I need to get in touch with Victoria Carter, Ness's ex. Can you help?"

"Sure. I don't have her number on me, but I can track it down for you. Is this a good number to call you back?"

"How long will it take?" I ask.

"Ten minutes. I'm down at the boathouse now. Monique might have the number if you want to try her."

"Yes. Give me her number."

I wait while he pulls it up. I watch the woods, where I expect the guards to emerge at any moment. Vincent gives me the number, and I hang up and call Monique. She answers on the first ring.

"Monique? This is Maya Walsh, Ness's friend, the one staying in the guest house. I need to get in touch with Victoria, Holly's mom. Do you have her number?"

"Yes," she says, "but I don't think she'll pick up. I always have to leave a message. She's a very busy woman."

I clench my fist in frustration. "Okay, give it to me anyway. Or can you think of some way I might get in touch with Holly?"

"Why? What's going on?"

A jeep emerges from the woods, one of the white security vehicles. A man on foot follows soon after.

"Nothing much," I say, my heart racing. "She left something down at the guest house, and I think she needs it. What's Holly's number?"

I put her on speaker. Monique tells me the number, and I key it into my phone.

"Oh, Ms. Walsh? You might want to text her first. You'll freak her out if you just call."

"Of course," I say, but I'm glad of the reminder.

I open up my messenger.

`Holly? It's Maya. Can I give you a quick call?`

I hit send and back around the edge of the lighthouse. The guard on foot has jumped in the jeep, which bounces down the muddy road toward me.

I watch my messages. After an eternity, my phone vibrates in my hand.

`Sure.`

I call. Holly picks up and says, "Headquarters of the No-Rain Society." Which is better than a greeting or an apology or an explanation for how we left things.

"Reporting bright and sunny conditions here," I tell her. The jeep is halfway to the lighthouse. There's no place for me to hide. "Hey," I say, trying to keep my voice calm. "There's totally nothing to do here. I was going to get the cable going, but the customer service people won't talk to me."

"Yeah, they suck," Holly says. "Gimme a minute. I'll call and have it up and running in no time. That book was boring, right?"

"No, that's okay," I say, a bit desperately. "I don't mind calling them. I was just hoping maybe you knew your dad's security PIN. That's what they're asking for. But if not, no big deal. I can get back into that book."

I duck my head back, thinking one of the guards in the jeep saw me. I hear the engine rev. Only my pulse is racing faster.

"Oh, no worries," Holly says. "That's easy. It's my birthday."

"Of course," I say. I hurry around the lighthouse and down the steps toward the door. Holly says something, and then she's cut off. I look at my phone. No bars. I hurry back up, wave the phone at the fickle gods of cellular communication, and get a single bar. I start to call back, can hear the guards talking on the other side of the lighthouse, one saying to go inside, the other saying he'll check the back. As soon as I call Holly, they'll hear me. When— bless her—my phone vibrates with a text.

`Dropped you. 09-22-28. 18r`

Back down the steps, I figure I've got one chance. I punch in the code, expecting more damn red lights.

But there's a clunk, a green light, and I push my way inside.

-39-

wo pair of muddy boots greet me inside the door. Beside them are Ness's running shoes, as well as two pairs of ladies' shoes. A rack is nailed to the wall, several jackets hanging from it. An umbrella leans to the side in a beat-up plastic trashcan.

The room is lit by bare bulbs screwed into outlets along the wall, metal cages around them for protection. Voices can be heard below me, leaking up a narrow staircase. I hear the guard outside clomp down the stairs. I hold my breath, waiting for him to come barging through the door. We seem to be standing there, listening for each other. After an eternity, I hear him march up the stairs. Either he doesn't have the code or doesn't expect that I would.

Barefoot, I steal across the room and try to pick out the conversations below. I wouldn't think a lighthouse would have a basement. I wonder why Ness would come here. I reach the rail and peer down the stairs. Someone in a white lab coat walks past. A woman. I sneak around the railing and lower my head to get a better view, watch her stop at a table and talk to someone. The acoustics below—the distant clatters and the way voices are swallowed—make it sound like a much bigger room than this one.

I decide to creep down the stairs. There's no sense of danger, not from Ness, not from whatever this is. It isn't until I see the massive room that I feel afraid. It looks like a warehouse. Racks of shelves cover the far walls, and the shelves are stuffed with what look like aquariums. Long tables run the length of a room the size of a large grocery store. There are industrial machines and what looks like laboratory equipment everywhere. Microscopes. Vials. Twisting tubes of glass. Expensive centrifuges. Reminds me of my marine biology labs from undergrad, but on steroids.

The scope of the place is breathtaking. All cut out beneath a lighthouse. This facility must be newer than the run-down structure that stands above it, though. Added here. Is this where he breeds his hydrothermal shells? Was what I told Agent Cooper spot-on? I watch the man and woman as they huddle together, studying an object in the woman's hands. There's a plastic sample case on the table near them. It looks identical to the other two I've seen. I wonder if this is that cross between an auger and a cerith from Tara Cay, from our underwater expedition.

The stairs go down to another floor, deeper still. No one sees me creeping behind the rail. I sneak down, make the turn, and continue to the next floor without being spotted. Here, another large open area takes up half the space. A hallway leads off in the other direction, lined with doors—offices, or maybe small labs or storage rooms. All the doors are closed save one. There's a light inside. I listen for voices but don't hear any.

The rest of the space looks similar to what's above, but with no workers. And rather than the long work surfaces, here there are lines of aquariums, water gurgling noisily, pumps and circulation fans whirring. Most of the aquariums are lit. Pipes and electrical wires form a maze across the ceiling, dipping down here and there to service the tanks. I creep over and peer inside the one nearest me. What look like white and orange nutmeg seashells litter the bottom of the tank.

I look around to make sure I'm alone, and then spot a familiar sight in the tank behind me: creamy white lace murexes with their jagged, decorative shells. An entire tank of them. But Cooper said there was no such thing. I reach in to grab one of them, the water warm up to my elbow, and bring it out.

The shell isn't empty. There's a slug inside. A gastropod. Was Cooper right all along? Is Ness taking some other species of slug and moving it into cast shells, creating the perfect fake? Maybe something in that process coats the shell enough to fool a testing machine. Or he makes the shells out of calcium carbonate from crushed-up species that are more common. Ness's driveway is a clue to all that he has access to. Probably dredges the shells up from his private beaches and islands. Then the shells are formed here, injected into some mold, and finally non-extinct species are moved in to make them look real.

My story has an ending, I realize. Here it is. Closure. For the piece, and for me and Ness. I came here to explain myself, to apologize, but all that guilt vanishes in an instant. The story that ran in the *Times* this morning wasn't my doing anyway. I was apologizing for something that wasn't my fault. But Ness . . . he lied to me from the beginning, was leading me on a wild chase, flying me to the Southern Hemisphere when the murexes were sitting in a tank a short walk from his house all along.

I hear a door shut down the hall behind me, turn and see a man in a white lab coat, his face illuminated by the tablet in his hand. He looks up before I have a chance to duck and hide. His eyes widen. I bolt for the stairs. I hear him shout for me to stop.

I race up two flights. The man yells for someone to grab me. I have the murex in my hand; I close my fist around it. I see Ness as I pass through the floor above. He looks up from a workbench, from a microscope; his face was hidden before. I freeze for a moment. As I take off again, Ness lurches up and knocks his stool over. He gives chase as well. Several people are shouting at me, shouting at each other to grab me. I don't pause to sort it out—I just run.

The cold metallic taste of adrenaline fills my mouth, my body dumping that storehouse of energy. I make it to the top of the stairs and yank open the door to the outside. Before I shut it, I get an idea, hurry back inside, grab the umbrella. Ness is up the stairs, yelling for me to wait. I get outside before he reaches me, slam the door shut just in time, and slide the umbrella through the handle so it catches the jamb.

The door pulls inward, but the umbrella holds. I don't wait to see how long. I run.

Racing around the lighthouse, I see the jeep with the two guards in the distance. They appear to be driving up and down the tree line, still looking for me. My car is out there, beyond the woods. Ness and the others will be out of that buried laboratory in no time.

I just need to get to safety, and then I can call Cooper, call the cops, get someone to pick me up, blow the lid off this place. My mind races. I consider hiding in the tall grasses, but they'd find me eventually. I consider trying all the cars, seeing if the keys are in any of them, and then driving one of them back to the gate and to my car on the other side.

But the jeep blocks my way into the woods. They'd get me there as well.

Only a few heartbeats pass as I consider all these options. The umbrella rattles, holding Ness at bay. I need to get to the house. There are a handful of possibilities there, all of them insane. I could grab the boat and make my way up the coast to the next dock or bay. I could hide and call Henry or Agent Cooper, either of whom will send someone to help me. I just have to get to Ness's house.

The edge of the tall bluff is just paces away. I run to the edge and gaze down at the beach. The dunes are steep here. But I can slide. I can make it to the beach and follow the coast.

I hear the door fly open behind me. I have to decide before they get up the stairs and see me, so I jump from the edge and into the steep face of sand. I stay on my back, arms wide, legs locked in front of me, and glissade down the sand in an avalanche.

Coming to a stop on a grassy ledge, I scoot to the edge and jump again. This time my feet catch, and I go end over end. I try to protect my head, to arrest my fall, and end up in a spread-eagle sprawl at the next lip of dune, my hair full of sand.

The murex is gone, my hand empty. I don't have a hope of finding it, don't even think of looking for it, but then I see it right along the ledge. It feels important somehow. Evidence. To replace the ones I lost. To make it up to Cooper. I grab the shell and lower myself off the next ledge, another avalanche of sand rushing along with me as I slide the last hundred or so feet to the beach.

I catch my breath at the base of the bluff. Looking up behind me, I see Ness peering down. He doesn't hesitate for long; he jumps and begins sliding down the cliff face. I take off, running north, knowing I'll never outpace him. He runs for exercise. My only hope is that he's tired from his jog this morning, that he'll cramp up, that he'll let me go. Silly hopes.

I aim for the hard pack by the ocean where the running is easier. Looking over my shoulder, I see Ness is already a third of the way down the bluff. I concentrate on pumping my legs but check his progress now and then. I have a few hundred meters on him by the time he reaches the beach and takes off after me.

Palpable fear chokes me. I don't know why—maybe it's the anger I saw on his face when he slammed the newspaper down— maybe it's the stakes of this dangerous game—maybe it's the size of the counterfeiting operation they're running—maybe it's from watching too many movies, or from running from the guard at the gate, or from breaking into the lighthouse, or from all the secrecy, but I fear that Ness might kill me if he reaches me. I can't explain the terror, but it's real. Like the panic in the submersible. The surety that my life is in jeopardy.

I pull out my phone while I run, need someone to know what happened to me. No signal. The battery alert is flashing. I put it away, can't run while operating it anyway. Ness is gaining, and my lungs are burning. There's the inexorable tug of him reeling me in; his house is too distant, and I know there's no hope, nothing I can do, that I should just stop and give up, but I run and run until he is right behind me, until I can hear him panting, can hear his feet slapping the sand, so close that I dare not turn and look, until he is right upon me, until he tackles me.

His arms wrap around me, and he twists so he takes the brunt of the fall. The air goes out of me anyway. I make the decision to fight, to not let him take me without a struggle, but I can barely breathe, can barely move, and Ness has me pinned on my back, straddles me, is breathing hard himself, and I kick and try to throw my knees into his back.

"What's gotten into you?" Ness pants.

"You're hurting me!" I scream. I twist my head to see if anyone will come for me, if Vincent or Monique might be able to hear me from the house.

"Stop fighting and I'll let you go," he says.

"If you would have let me go from the beginning—" Deep breaths. "—I wouldn't *have* to fight you."

I bring my arms close to my face, dragging his hands with me, and sink my teeth into his wrist.

Ness curses and lets go of me. I try to kick away from him. He pins me down again.

"I'm the one mad at *you*, remember? What the hell are *you* upset about?"

"You're a phony," I spit at him. "Everything about you is fake." I take deep breaths. "Your smile, your damn shells, the trees, everything!"

I get a hand free and swing the murex at his face. The sharp crenelations open a gash. Ness covers his cheek, and I wiggle away. I stagger a handful of steps, wait for him to tackle me again, but he just sits there. I head for the house. My legs are jelly. I can barely stand, but I resolve to get there, to get help. Looking back, I can see that Ness hasn't moved, is just holding his wound, watching me.

I take advantage of this and pause to collect my breath. I rest my hands on my knees and eye him like a wounded mouse might eye a hawk.

"What did you think I was going to do, write you into some kind of hero?" I ask.

He stares at me.

"And then you dump your shells on the market, right? Or have you been doing that already? How many of your celebrated finds happened right up there in that lab?"

I stagger toward the house. Checking my phone, I see the battery is dead. I don't care. I feel dead, too. Emotionless. Betrayed to the core.

"This is not a fake!" Ness roars behind me. I turn to see him holding the shell in one hand, his cheek in the other. He gets to his feet, and I steel myself to run again.

"You still don't get it, do you?" He raises his voice above the crashing sea and the wind. "Skipped right to the end, and you still don't understand."

"Stay away from me," I tell him.

"I'm not going to hurt you," Ness says. "Not like you've hurt me."

I don't know if he means the story that ran that morning or the gash on his cheek. I no longer have the right to say it wasn't my fault. Both wounds were. I know that. I made a promise I couldn't keep.

"Let me off your property," I plead. "I don't know what's going on up there, but I know it isn't legal. Let me go."

"You think I would *hurt* you? Goddamnit, Maya, I think I'm in love with you."

"Shut up!" I scream at him. "Don't say that. You don't get to say that." I cover my ears and jog toward the house. When I look back, Ness is running after me. It's no use. My legs give out, and I tumble to the sand. Ness circles in front of me and falls to his knees. Tears are streaming down his face, blood down his cheek.

"Listen to me," he begs. "Just listen."

I bow my head, stay on my hands and knees, try to fill my lungs.

"No, it's not legal what we're doing. We're trying to clear some hurdles, make it legal, but it hasn't been easy."

"You're going to crash the market for shells," I tell him.

"Yes, we are. I aim to. Because we're going to bring them back. Don't you see?" He shows me the murex. Its white shell is pink with his blood. Ness peers inside, touches the slug, and I see the creature move. Ness turns and hurls the shell into the sea. He sits back on his heels, wipes the blood from his cheek.

"I used to shell beaches as a little boy with my grandfather, and he told me once that we collect dead things. That the shells are worthless, but we collect them because they're beautiful." Looking up, he smiles at me, even though his eyes are still crying. "Another metaphor for your collection," he says. "How shelling is like love. Collecting empty, pretty things."

I don't say anything. I conserve my energy.

"After he told me this, I started looking at the living creatures inside. I followed the shells with snorkels and then dive tanks. Grew up. Never forgot what he said. And one day, I went down in a Mir to oversee a geothermal installation, and I started thinking about the vents, where the water is toxic and warm. Acidic, like we've made the sea. But there was *life* there. Trapped. It couldn't populate the rest of the sea because of the cold all around it. The animals there were boxed in, fit for a different world, for a world not of sunlight but of harsh chemistry. I wondered if we could bring them out, give nature a nudge, find something in their DNA that might help."

"No," I said. "I don't believe you."

"We started with the trees because they were simple and we could grow them quickly. I hired the absolute best. From what we learned with the trees, we were able to get two dozen species of gastropods living in existing sea conditions. And more on the way. The FDA thinks we're working on algae for biotic oil production, that our proposed bills to relax some regulations have to do with that. There are politicians on our side, but others who will shut us down if they find out, who will think we're playing God, creating little Frankenstein fish, that we'll cause more damage than we'll repair. But we're only doing what nature does best. She just needs our help. Because we took her by surprise."

I don't want to believe him. I don't care how it all fits, how this makes more sense than the monster I made up in my mind. I want to believe in the monster. I *need* to believe in the monster. It's simpler. I can wrap my head around that. It's more difficult to think that Ness is out to save the world. It's more difficult to think that he sees anything in me.

"The feds are onto you," I say. I want him to know he won't get away with this, that it's too late.

Ness nods. "I know. I think they suspect. They don't want this either. If the market for shells crashes, entire departments will get shuttered overnight. It'll be like the end of prohibition. No more jobs for the people who track down crooks. No more retail. No sales tax. All gone overnight. No one wants this, don't you see? It'd be like turning the loch back over to the monster. The circus would have to pack up and go home."

I shake my head. Ness reaches out to me, and I flinch. I can see that this reaction hurts him worse than the blow I struck. He is only holding out his hand, hoping I'll take it.

"Come with me," Ness says. "Come with me, Maya, and I'll show you." He turns and looks back to the lighthouse. A handful of figures can be seen up there, little dots on the ridge. "This is where the story ends. Right up there. Where it always ended. I was going to take you today—it was the plan all along. I was going to show you the sample we took from the Mir, you and me. I was going to show you the progress we've made."

He frowns. His cheek is bleeding badly. "And then I saw the story this morning, with your name on it, and I thought I was an idiot to fall for you, that you were running that piece all along, that you were probably going to write about what happened on the sub, on the island, that I was setting myself up for all that again. While I was running back to the house, all I could think was that I made a mistake taking you to my most special place, my true home, that you—"

"I'm sorry I hit you," I say. "I'm sorry about the piece that ran today. But I . . . I don't believe what you're telling me—"

"Why not? I'm willing to believe *you*. Right now. I believe that you had nothing to do with that story. I believe that you'll set it all straight if you have the chance. I believe this, even though I have a long history of watching people betray my trust. A long history. But I believe you, Maya. Now I really need you to believe me."

"I'm sorry," I say. "Ness, this is just too much."

"Is it? You've seen the shells. You've seen inside them. You know they're real. I need you to look past everything you know about me and the years of mistakes I made. Stop judging me by my father and his grandfather. Judge me by this week. By our time together. If that's all you had to go on, what would you believe?"

I rest my face in my palms. My shoulders quake as I let out a sob, an exhausted cry. I expect Ness to reach out and comfort me, but he seems to know not to. I can't believe any of this is happening, that my life somehow got caught up in the nexus of whatever it is Ness is trying to do and whatever it is the feds are investigating. All for running that damn story, for wanting to get back at the man I blamed for taking my childhood away.

"What do you think of me, Maya? From this week. From yesterday. From the guy at the bottom of the sea. From the beach. Tell me this is just a shell. Say it. Say you don't believe me."

"I can't," I sob. I shake my head, try to compose myself. I no longer feel in danger of Ness harming me. The danger I feel is far graver than that.

"I need you," Ness says.

"To write your story?"

"No. Screw the story. Someone else will write it. They'll get the facts wrong, but I don't care anymore. It's the shells. The shells are going to come back. That's all that matters. We're so damn close, and I want you to be there when it happens. I want you by my side."

"Why?" I ask.

"You know why."

I look him in the eyes. I see him through a veil of tears. But I'll know if he's lying. I've seen this enough times to know. I've heard the words from those who didn't mean it, who didn't really mean it.

"Say it," I say. "Say it, and make me believe it, damn you."

Ness smiles. Blood trickles down his jawline. The sea crashes and roars beside us.

"Ladies first," he says.

-40-

But I can't say the words. This is how relationships are most like the things I collect: We build these hard exteriors. We pull ourselves inside, block off the only way in, don't let anyone see our true selves. Ness waits for me to tell him that I love him, but I'm still scared. I still doubt. Nothing feels real. Because I won't crawl out and feel the world for myself.

"Show me," I tell him. "Prove what you're saying is true, and then I'll decide how I feel. I want to see what you're doing up there. Make me believe you're doing something good."

This is the most I can give him, this opening, my willingness to have been wrong about him one last time. For the moment, with him wounded and bleeding and me untouched, I believe that I'm not in danger, that he isn't out to hurt me. Not only is he the one bleeding, the anger is now mine alone. My own sins have been forgiven.

Whether Ness really meant to show me what lies beneath the lighthouse or not, the secret I've uncovered there puts all the rest into perspective. And I realize the truth of what he hinted at once, that the story he wants to tell will make a mockery of my pieces. Maybe the story that ran today, the one that will hurt Holly and perhaps no one else, enraged him because of my betrayal, not because of his desire for self-preservation. I allow myself to believe this as I follow him in the direction of the estate and toward a flight of stairs that winds up the bluff. I allow myself to consider that he was angry in the shower not for the damage I caused his family's reputation, but because he feared I felt nothing for him, that I had been using him all along.

I nearly press him on this, but I choose to walk in silence.

We tread up creaking and salt-air-worn steps, palms on rough splinter-toothed rails, Ness climbing ahead of me. I remember following him into his house what seems like several years ago. A lifetime ago. I came here to write about the world he wanted to destroy, to hoard for himself, to spirit away—and now he says it's a world he wishes to save, to protect. I feel a tug in every direction on the deepest parts of my soul, this compound wish to be with a man both dangerous and protective. A man who could wreck vengeance on my behalf, but never upon me.

My mother pointed this out to me on a shelling walk, before I went off to college. "You'll love most the ones who can hurt you," she warned me. It was a version of my father's more pithy: "Men are pricks." However stated, it's a lesson that must tragically be learned, not told.

"You okay?" Ness asks as we reach the top of the stairs.

I nod, out of breath. He's the one with twin trails of blood curving down his neck. He's the one whose family name is besmirched in today's paper. And he wants to know if a flight of stairs has wronged me. And in that question, and that steely gaze, I don't doubt for a minute that he would burn the stairs into the sea if I hinted at any offense.

"I'm fine," I say.

We follow the ridge toward the lighthouse. There's a winding dirt path worn into the grasses right at the edge, and I realize that Ness must walk from the estate to his secret lair sometimes. Perhaps every day. This is where he's been the last four years, watching the sun rise over the glittering sea to his left, then watching the sky redden and the planets and stars come out as he winds his way back home at dusk. All for what? I want to see. I want to meet the people in the white cloaks, these people who moments ago I feared. I see two of them far ahead, by the lighthouse. I see the jeep and the guards as well. They watch with hands shielding their eyes as we approach.

Fifty meters away, and the men get in the jeep as if to come out to us, but Ness waves them off. I see them hesitate for a moment, but then they drive sullenly away, disappointed perhaps at this tease of danger, this thrill of excitement, of actually being needed.

"Do you want to call someone and let them know where you are?" Ness asks.

I consider this. It surprises me. Not that he is aware of my trepidation, but that he considers I might want some way to allay those fears, some way to let my boss or my family or the authorities know where I am. "My phone is dead," I tell him.

"You can use mine." He offers it. I consider the wisdom of calling Agent Cooper, filling him in, but I wave the phone away. The gesture is enough. To actually make that call would do more harm than striking him, I sense. Trust must be met with trust. Ness puts the phone away.

"This is my lead scientist," he tells me, indicating one of the women I saw in the laboratory beneath the lighthouse. She's standing with her hands in her smock, looking worriedly at Ness's wound, then suspiciously at me. "Ryan, this is Maya Walsh. Maya, Ryan."

We shake hands. She has a firm grip; she does not smile at me.

"And this is Stewart, my chief geneticist."

Stewart is smoking an old-fashioned cigarette. I wonder if this is a habit he picked up from Vincent or vice versa. He exhales a cloud of smoke, then shakes my hand. "The reporter, eh?"

"Not today," Ness says. "Today she is only a friend. I want you to show her around."

I follow Ryan and Stewart down the stairs to the back entrance, through the locked door held fast by Holly's birthday. Ness follows. Inside, the others kick off their shoes and don white booties. I take a pair from the cardboard box and pull them on too, realizing that only Ness and I are barefoot, that he must've kicked off his booties in pursuit. Twice I catch Ryan shooting Ness an *Are you sure about this?* look. And I catch him nodding almost imperceptibly. There is great risk in bringing me here, I realize. And it's a risk he had planned on taking a week ago. With or without me, he has decided to blow the lid off his work here.

"We do most of our research on this floor," Ryan says as we head down to the vast space I ran through earlier. "Genetic sequencing takes place over there. We examine samples from the vents, looking for base pairs that confer temperature and acidic advantages—"

"So they're real," I say. "These shells grow themselves. They're not, like, transplanted in."

It occurs to me that this might've been where Dimitri Arlov worked. Maybe he took the murexes home because he was proud of them, or simply because they were beautiful, or as a memento.

"Yes, they . . . grow themselves," Ryan says, hesitating as though she's reluctant to say more.

Ness interrupts. "Maya knows enough of the science to understand how this works," he says. "Just explain it."

Ryan shrugs at Ness and then turns to me. "They're real, but we designed them. We have complete DNA samples of hundreds of extinct species. We use their nearest living ancestor to breed the first generation. And then we create enough genetic diversity for the species to become self-sustaining. Technically, it's a new species, never seen before. But it looks the same. And it should fill the same niche. Should give us the biodiversity we've lost, which may trickle up the food chain."

"Show her the murex," Ness says.

Stewart nods and leads us down the next flight of stairs.

"What makes you think these animals will survive in the wild?" I ask.

"We have tanks on the lower level with live rock and water samples taken from various offshore locations," Stewart explains.

"What about—?"

"Predators included," Ness says behind me. He then pardons himself. He's dying to talk, I can tell, but seems to want all this to come from someone else. He's trying to be an observer, and I can tell that's hard for him. While Stewart takes me toward the rows of tanks, I watch Ryan inspect Ness's gashed cheek.

"I've seen the murexes," I tell Stewart. I spot some knobby whelks in a tank a few rows down. Large shells. "What about those?"

"The whelks," Stewart says. I follow him to the tank. He reaches inside and pulls one out. I watch the slug's foot retract and swell to plug its home. "These were the fourth species we revived. They can already handle acidity levels plus eighty."

"Plus eighty?"

"Eighty years out," he explains. "Where we project the levels to be eighty years from now, anyway. It should give them plenty of time to adjust on their own. But if not, we can help them along again. Our command of this is only getting better."

He passes me the shell. I touch the slug's foot, feel it react to the stimulus, stiffen under my finger. I place the shell back in the water, lowering it to the bed of sand rather than dropping it. There are several tanks of this species. The digital thermometers against the glass show different temperatures, and notes are written in black wax right on the glass. I turn to ask Ness something and see Ryan dabbing Ness's cheek with a rag, cleaning the wound I made. A pang of guilt laced with a twinge of jealousy courses through me.

"Why me?" I ask. And I realize that this is the question that has haunted me all week, from the guest house to the helicopter to the depths of the ocean floor to the beach. *Why me?* I wipe my wet hand on my shorts and close the distance between Ness and myself. "Why not show this to the scientific community? Publish a paper? Do a TV special on Discovery? Why would you show *me?*"

"We need to win public support before any legal campaigns start," Ness says. "We need the whole world on our side."

"Who would be against this?"

I know as soon as I ask. Ness answers anyway.

"The same people who were against me before," he says. "The same people who burned one of my father's oil platforms. The ones who see any tampering with nature as bad, who have given up, who won't be happy until *we're* the ones who go extinct. And they'll have people they normally hate on their side, the people who don't believe in playing God. And of course, there are those who love shell collecting for the money and not the shells. They won't support this either. Neither will those who get paid to crack down on operations like this."

He's right, of course. He's absolutely right. About all of it. It's just what he told me on the beach an hour ago.

"So who *will* support this?" I ask. "Politicians?"

All three of them laugh, and I hear how ridiculous this sounds. The lobbying will be fierce. And when did reason ever stand a chance in that game?

"The people who love the sea are our only hope," Ness says. "And they tend to love quietly. They love in the middle of the night with their flashlights. They keep their love from others. But we need them to be loud. We need to win this all at once or we don't stand a chance."

I shake my head. Making my way to the stairs, I lower myself to the treads and sit down. "No," I tell him. "No."

Ness sits beside me. I can sense his desire to put a hand on my knee, realize that somehow this sort of gesture has become natural between us, but he resists the urge.

"You never stood a chance," I say. "Not with me. Oh, Ness, what did you think I'd be able to do? Work a miracle for you? Get people to agree on this? Help get policies written by force of will, by some lyrical appeal to nature and love and life?"

The way he's looking at me, I can tell that he did believe this. And the way Stewart and Ryan look piteously upon this man I think I love, I can tell that they told him so, that this was a fool's errand from the start, the errand of a hopeful, romantic fool.

"That's your grandfather," I say. "Your grandfather had the right words, and he lived in the right time. He could have convinced his generation to undo what they'd done—"

"The science wasn't ready," Ness says.

"Well the people of our time won't be ready. You'll have the majority of hearts, Ness, but you won't have much else."

"Write the story," he tells me. "Write the truth, and the rest will come."

"It won't," I promise him. "Ness, listen to them." I indicate Stewart and Ryan. "They're right. They aren't hopeless romantics like us. They deal in the concrete, in the knowable—"

Ness leaps up and takes two angry steps away from me. His body is rigid, his fists clenched. I think for a moment that he's angry with me, but consider that he might just be angry at the world. He must know that I'm right. Without realizing it, I'm behind him, one hand on his shoulder, the other lacing between his knuckles, coaxing that angry fist into an open and then interlocked hand. My mind is whirring, with ways to soothe him, with ways to take the bubbling vats of wonder in that room and bring my childhood to life once more—with ways to heal what I've wounded, what all of us have wounded.

"There is another way," I whisper, even as it comes to me, even as I realize what we have to do. I don't want anyone but him to hear, so I say it with a whisper. "Ness, there is another way."

-41-

The bow of the boat undulates with the sea, rising and falling, rising and falling, a hiss of foam forming along the fiberglass sides and then sighing back into the ocean with the rhythmic and hypnotic grace of a swell rolling toward the beach. I watch the spray, enjoying the small rainbows that materialize and disappear like a mirage, and consider this illegal cruise of ours.

My father used to take me on boat rides like this. Late in the day, after pinky-swearing that we would not be skunked, after snorkeling every shell-hole we knew and casting lead sinkers and plastic lures until our arms were tired, we would race off with the setting sun on our starboard side to shell from the rich.

Just south of our home inlet, past the private beaches, there was a resort with hundreds of blue lounge chairs and umbrellas, a place where you were chased off if you didn't have on the right colored wristband, where the towels and foot showers and the very sand itself were only for the well-to-do. My father and I would anchor beyond the swim buoys after the sun had set and snorkel ashore to steal a shell or two that had been carefully set out by the night staff for the early risers to discover.

We didn't keep these shells. Nor did we take them for any reason other than to *not-be-skunked*. We simply took those shells because they didn't belong there. Because they were paid for, as much a part of the resort package as the slices of fruit on the buffet table, carefully parceled out at all times of the day so every guest got their allotment, but so that every guest secretly felt that maybe, due to their industriousness or skill, they got just a *little more* than their share.

Some were perhaps even clever enough to fool themselves into thinking the shells they discovered had washed up of their own accord.

Father and I would secret these shells away, disappearing into the foam, and kick and laugh and swim back to our anchored boat. The shells would be deposited on the public beach across the narrow strip of road from our boat ramp, for someone else to chance upon.

An illegal boat ride on the edge of day and into deep water. I wonder if my father would be proud of what I'm doing this morning, all these many years later. It's a different sort of law I'm breaking, but the moral code feels the same. Only this time, the shells that could get me into trouble are already in the boat.

Ness kills the motor and lets the boat glide along, the last of the wake fizzing and becoming part of the rising and sinking Atlantic. I open one of the great plastic tubs that line the bow of the boat. The shells inside writhe and crinkle. The shells are *alive*.

I feel Ness's hand against the small of my back. We rock together, knees bent, studying his work. I turn to Ness and wrap a hand around the back of his neck, pull him close for a moment, breathe in the sunscreen and sweat and salt sea. He kisses me on the top of my head. "You sure?" he asks.

"I'm sure," I say.

We each grab a side of the first bin, which has dozens of species in it, and hoist it to the top of the gunnel. A pause, a moment to reflect, and then we tip it over. The shells tumble out by the thousands. They plop and hiss and throw up bubbles on their way down, like little exhalations of freedom and joy. Ryan guessed that four out of every ten will end up food for something else. The rest will survive. And breed. And die. And one day be discovered on a beach.

Someone will pick up the pretty dead things, and see the worth there, but Ness and I will know the truth.

We grab another bin. And I've never felt more alive.

Acknowledgments

Hey. The story isn't over yet. Keep reading.

But first, I want to thank my mom, Gay, and my late grandmother, Cutie, both of whom got me hooked on shelling. It was at Figure Eight Island in North Carolina that I decided olives were my favorite shells and where I spent my summers hunting for sand dollars. To this day, I remain on the lookout. And while I hunt, I think of my family, and all the ways that shelling is like relationships.

I'd also like to thank the amazing group of authors who took pity on my Y chromosome and offered me their friendship and their wisdom: Barbara, Bella, Candice, CJ, Jasinda (both of you), Liliana, Stephanie, and Tina. You all inspire me and have taught me so much. Thank you from the bottom of my heart.

Finally, the readers. Thank you for your time, your emails, your tweets, your reviews, your friendship, and your feedback. And thank you for being as brave in reading outside your comfort zone as I'm trying to be in writing there. See you at the next wild place we find ourselves. Because you know this isn't over yet. There's always another page to turn in order to discover a little more . . .

The Beach:
One Year Later

"We are tied to the ocean. And when we go
back to the sea, whether it is to sail or to watch
– we are going back from whence we came..."

– John F. Kennedy

-42-

The best memories I own—the ones I choose to travel back to when I'm at my desk and should be working on my next article—are the beach trips my parents took me on as a kid. I travel back to the days when both of them were young, alive, and in love. Back to when my sister was my best friend in the world, my playmate, my fellow sandcastle architect. We would play a game in the car, seeing who could spot the ocean first. It was a parent's ploy to keep us quiet, to keep us staring intently down the road ahead. And then someone would spot a glint of the summer sun on that wide blue, and all of us would erupt at once, fingers pointing, a family laughing.

My mother loved seashells, my grandmother as well. My father was into sharks' teeth, and he had a knack for finding them. Some were fossilized and millions of years old. Those teeth will continue to wash up long after all of us are gone. They are glimpses of another time, when the sea was full of life.

I used to think my happy memories lay in the past because I'd never be happy like that again. Young and carefree. Surrounded by people I love. Still shells to uncover here or there that careless others overlooked. I thought we were destined to get old like the Earth does, for all that lives is bound to decline.

But that's not right. Life is what we make of it.

When Michael and I lost our child, I thought there was something wrong with me, that I was dead inside, that Michael was right to call me an empty shell. But some of the beautiful things in life are grown and others are discovered. Some are made and some wash up and tumble into our lives. Entire generations of people have forgotten that we have a choice. Ness has shown the world what it means to grow beautiful things. Someone else showed me that a life can be found just as well as made.

"I saw it first!" Holly yells, leaning between us and pointing through the windshield.

"Seat belt," I tell her. "I want to hear it click."

"But we're practically there!"

"And you practically have the ice cream I'm practically going to buy you once we get to the boardwalk."

"Okay, okay."

I glance at Ness and see him smiling as Holly buckles up. "Clickety click," she says for emphasis from the back seat.

We find a parking space near one of the beach accesses. A wooden flight of stairs arches over the grassy dunes. Holly races ahead, flip-flops in one hand and snorkel mask in the other, while Ness and I carry the cooler between us.

"All the beaches I own," he tells me, once Holly is out of earshot, "and this is where you want to spend our holiday."

"This is where I used to come as a child," I tell him. "Besides, how can we see if we're winning the war unless we visit the front lines?"

He grumbles his disagreement. I think he's worried someone might recognize him. But the last time that happened, he only had to pose for a selfie. No one spit on him. He's still not used to that.

We stake out a space on the crowded beach. Holly has already—and unsurprisingly—made friends. She asks if she can go in the water. I make sure the lifeguards are watching the waves and not flirting with tourists, and I give her a thumbs-up. Ness and I lay out the blanket. He puts sunscreen on my shoulders, and I return the favor.

I had hoped to see shells washing up, being discovered, a sign that our illicit wildlife preserve just north of here was beginning to have some distant impact. Beyond the breakers, snorkelers dive deep, their fins kicking in the air, disappearing, and then their heads bobbing back to the surface with whale-like plumes of water spraying from their snorkels.

A good sign. Something down there worth diving for. But it's the kid Holly's age who comes running to his parents with an object in his fist that gives me hope. I watch as the father checks the boy's shell and goes from being proud to horrified. "It's still alive, son," he says, and makes his boy rush as fast as he can to put it back in the water.

The parents look at each other in silence, eyes wide, while I squeeze Ness's hand.

"This is why I wanted to come," I tell him.

"If you love it so much, maybe we'll come back for our honeymoon," he says.

I nearly call his bluff and accept, but decide to tease him further. "I've got a better idea. There's this great lake I've heard about in Scotland—"

Ness wrestles me down on the blanket and kisses me. "I don't think so," he says, rubbing his stubble against my neck. When he sits up, peering down at me, I reach out and run my thumb along the scar on his cheek.

"Stop it," he says. And I know he means to stop thinking what I'm thinking, to stop blaming myself, not to stop touching him.

"I love you," I say. It's rare that I get to say it first. And while Ness gets mad when I apologize, he never seems to notice when I say I'm sorry in some other way.

"So what's the plan tomorrow?" he asks. "Want to rent a boat?"

"It might rain tomorrow," I tell him.

"The Society won't be happy about that."

I smile.

"Hey," he says, "I can always take Holly to the arcade if you want some quiet time to work on your article."

"I think we have to stop calling it an article," I tell him. "It's gone way past that. I'm pretty sure it's going to be a book."

"Even better. I can't wait to read it."

I prop myself on my elbow and watch the boy reluctantly release his catch back into the sea. The ocean still has something to give, it seems. It just takes us giving a little back.

"You'll be the first one," I promise him. And this is how the book will end, I decide. How it *should* end. The story of the great shell collector will close with the death of his hobby. And the start of something else.

www.hughhowey.com

18820000R00167

Printed in Poland
by Amazon Fulfillment
Poland Sp. z o.o., Wrocław